T0193235

CHRONICLES OF
RHYDIN

CHRONICLES OF

STARS AND SHADOWS

AARON GOODING JR

CHRONICLES OF RHYDIN
STARS AND SHADOWS

iUniverse books may be ordered through booksellers or by contacting:

iUniverse
1663 Liberty Drive
Bloomington, IN 47403
www.iuniverse.com
1-800-Authors (1-800-288-4677)

ISBN: 978-1-5320-8470-6 (sc)
ISBN: 978-1-5320-9575-7 (hc)
ISBN: 978-1-5320-8471-3 (e)

Library of Congress Control Number: 2019915254

Print information available on the last page.

iUniverse rev. date: 02/18/2020

Beginning of a New World

Beginning of a New World

THIRTEEN YEARS HAD PASSED SINCE the destruction of the Dark Lord's Empire. Sekmet's reign of darkness was ended by Zidane, the Elf Ruler of the Western Province of Rhydin. Alongside Zidane were his wife, Maia, and the Vampire Prince of the Southeast Coven, Kulla. Zidane's father, Draco, was found worthy to become the King of Men and wielder of the Sword of Ages and fought alongside his son. It was by the combined powers of the Bracelet of Ra, the Necklace of Isis, the Scepter of Osiris, and the Sword of Ages that Sekmet was defeated.

The Alliance of Elves, Men, Lycans, Shinobi, Dragons, and Dragon Knights held strong that night to ward off and defeat the army of Sekmet. It was on that night the Krystal Kingdom was born. The races within this alliance held true to their vow for the past thirteen years. After the fall of Sekmet's Empire, each race of the Krystal Kingdom began the reconstruction of Rhydin. Each civilization grew and thrived without the fear of Sekmet's eyes watching them. Fear did not fill the hearts of any creature that lived on Rhydin and Earth.

After Sekmet's defeat, the Orcs, Abominations, and Winged Demons that served under Sekmet's reign scattered to the various regions of Rhydin and Earth. They hid from the eyes of the Krystal Kingdom for fear of being eradicated. The former soldiers of Sekmet established small encampments in various, hidden regions on Rhydin and even on Earth. The Orcs and their comrades could only leave their camps when the shadow of night hid them. Yet, it was still a necessity to be cautious with the eyes of the Lycans and Vampires being on the watch for their movements. Not only did they have to be cautious when they left their encampments but they also had to be watchful when they were with their comrades in the scattered camps. Word spread from encampment to encampment that they were being stalked and that encampments were being eradicated by mysterious cloaked figures in the dead of night. Very few of Sekmet's surviving troops had escaped those raids. Anxiety and caution were in the hearts of the surviving soldiers of Sekmet's army.

On a pitch black night, a hunting party of Orcs and Abominations was passing through the northern region of the Woodland Realm. They wore no armor for fear of it weighing down on them. They carried only bows, arrows, and swords. Each wore a dark cloak to cover their bodies and faces as not to be recognized by any agents of the Krystal Kingdom. They were on their way back to their encampment with rabbit, deer, and other meat for the rest of the camp. At the encampment, Orcs and other Abominations were sitting outside of their tents fashioned out of deer hide and fallen trees and limbs. There were several small fires in which other Orcs and Abominations sat warming themselves. Those within the encampment rose when they saw their hunting party return from what seemed to be a successful hunt.

"Were you followed?" an Abomination of immense stature approached them. "I don't think so," an Orc within the hunting party gave a shake of his head. At that moment, an arrow cut through the air and embedded itself in the forehead of the Abomination. The Abomination fell face first to the ground with a dull *thud* that shook the ground. The rest of the camp scrambled to retrieve their weapons. Soon a flurry of arrows cut through the air killing many of the Orcs and Abominations. Only a handful were left among the fallen bodies. They huddled back to back watchful of their assailants. Their dense muscles were tense, their large hands gripped their swords and axes tightly, and their dark eyes frantically searched the thick forest for the attackers.

"Where are they?!" an Orc exclaimed as his eyes and head darted from bush to bush. At that moment, a cloaked figure leapt from the trees above and landed in their midst. With two blades drawn, it severed the heads of two Orcs from their shoulders. The remaining Orcs and Abominations turned and violently attacked the cloaked figure. Each of their attacks were swiftly dodged and deflected with ease and finesse by the cloaked assailant. The cloaked figure leapt backwards onto a boulder and then sheathed its blades. An imitation of a cawing raven was heard coming from underneath the hood. In response to this call, another caw was heard from the bushes surrounding them. The Abominations and Orcs ceased their attack on the cloaked figure to watch their surroundings. An orb of sparking energy surged from a tree top and exploded amongst a group of five Orcs setting them ablaze and scattering them. Another cloaked figure leapt from the trees. This one carried a Scepter in one hand and broad sword in the other. A barrage of energy orbs was thrown from another side of the encampment causing explosions sending Orcs and Abominations in to trees and nearby boulders. Yet two more cloaked figures emerged from the bushes. One figure carried a long broad sword in one hand and in the other it was gathering immense energy. The other carried two short swords with energy seeping from them. The remaining soldiers of Sekmet were surrounded by these four cloaked strangers. The largest of the Orcs beat his chest and raised his battle axe facing the cloaked figure standing on the boulder.

"I would not advise you attacking me. It will cost you dearly," the figure's voice was calm despite the hostility shown by the largest of the Orcs. The Orc did not heed the warning and charged at full force followed by the rest of his comrades.

"Wrong move you bastard," the figure growled as it unleashed an immense beam of energy from a golden bracelet on its right wrist. The charging Orcs and Abominations were reduced to dust and a long trench was left from the intense beam of energy that lit the forest like the Sun itself. The figure's eyes flashed silver as it surveyed the encampment, "Is that all of them?".

"I believe so," answered the one carrying the Scepter.

3

"Good," it said as it removed the hood from its head. Underneath was an elf male with ebony skin and long dreadlocks. It was Zidane, the Ruler of the Western Province, along with Paige the Elf Ruler of the Woodland Realm, Aero the Elf Ruler of the Eastern Province, and Kulla the Vampire Prince of the Southeast Coven. Paige pursed her lips together then whistled signaling ten other cloaked elves to emerge from the trees and bushes who were carrying bows and quivers of arrows including elven captains Aldar and Demus.

"This was a sizable encampment," said Paige as she walked amongst the bodies of their slain enemies that littered the ground.

"The encampment we hunted down a month ago was considerably larger than this one," Aero looked to his sister.

"This was a successful hunt, Zidane," Kulla said to Zidane as he poked at an Abomination corpse with the butt of the Scepter.

"Indeed it was, but there are many more out there," said Zidane's silver eyes looked over the many bodies of Orc and Abominations they had been fighting for over a decade.

"I have a feeling it is far from over," Aero's voice held a grim tone, as if something sinister was approaching.

"What is it that you feel?" Zidane approached his brother. Zidane could sense something troubled him.

"It feels as if there is a shadow waiting to swallow this land," Aero's dark brown eyes showed his concern.

"I pray that it is just a feeling and not a reality," Zidane patted Aero on the shoulder and then looked off in to the woods.

It was very early in the morning when Zidane returned to the palace in the Western Province. The Sun was just appearing over the trees of the Woodland Realm and shone against the stone spires and walls of the Western Palace. The morning mist was slowly dissipating from the blades of grass Sundancer trod. It was peaceful and it had been so for thirteen years. Zidane remembered the battle that was fought in front of these very walls, but no blood had been spilled on these grounds in over a decade. The palace gates opened upon seeing him. Zidane guided Sundancer in to the stable where he dismounted and led him in to his pen.

"We have been through many trials, old friend," Zidane muttered as he ran his fingers through Sundancer's coarse mane. Sundancer seemed to nod his head then neighed. Zidane smiled and fed a carrot to his trusty steed. "Rest and regain your strength, old friend," Zidane said as he left the stables.

After leaving the stables, Zidane entered the palace and walked through the maze of red carpeted hallways, then up a spiral staircase on his way to his bedchambers. He quietly opened the wooden door so that he would not wake Maia up. Maia was peacefully asleep buried under the quilt of their bed. The sun shone through the window and upon her, gently kissing the tan skin of her soft face. It warmed his heart to see his love peacefully asleep, not worrying about any impending battles. He smiled and closed the door. He walked only a few feet down the hall to another door and carefully opened it. He peered into the room to find his children sleeping peacefully. Both were of the age of thirteen. It was several months after Sekmet's defeat that Maia discovered she was pregnant. She was pregnant with not just one child, but twins. A boy and a girl named Tritan and Carline. Tritan and Carline had been nothing but a blessing to Maia and Zidane. They were quite intelligent beyond their age, articulate when speaking to others, and somewhat mischievous, but what child was not. Their beds were on opposite sides of the room with their wardrobes against the walls at the foot of their beds. They were sleeping soundly with the sun shining upon their light brown skin and golden brown dreadlocks.

"Poppa," he heard a voice call to him as he was about to close the door.

"Yes, dear?" he responded. It was Carline who stirred and awoke. Zidane entered the room and sat on the edge of her bed.

"I am glad you are back," she pushed back the quilt and curled into her father's arms to hug him.

"I am glad as well," a smile came upon his face. His fingers ran through her thin dreadlocks and then across her cheek. On both of her cheeks, as well as Tritan's, there was a single dark stripe that ran from her jaw up to her cheek bone. Carline soon fell back to sleep in his arms. Zidane picked her up and put her back to bed tucking her under the quilt. He kissed her forehead and then went over to Tritan's bed. He kissed his son's forehead. Tritan's eyes slightly opened to find his father standing at his bedside.

"Good morning, Father," he said in a quiet voice.

"Good morning, Son," Zidane responded as he placed his hand on Tritan's head and rubbed it.

"How did... the hunt go?" a yawn escaped Tritan's mouth.

"It was successful. Now go back to sleep," Zidane kissed his forehead. Tritan closed his eyes as Zidane left the room. Zidane walked back to his bedchamber. He again cautiously opened the door to find Maia still peacefully asleep. He walked over to an empty rack and placed his long hooded coat and Dragon Blades on it. His ears twitched slightly and turned. In an instant, Zidane found himself on his back looking up at razor sharp fangs. His eyes widened but then found that Maia had shifted to her panther form and pounced on him. She slowly shifted back to her human form still pinning Zidane on his back. His silver eyes gleamed in her amber eyes as she licked her upper lip and panther-like teeth. She leaned in and gave a tender kiss.

"Welcome home," she slowly rose to her feet and sauntered over to the bed.

"Thank you," Zidane said as he continued to lie on his back. He should have known an attack of affection was looming. He experienced many of them after he returned from a 'Cleansing Mission'. It was her way of showing that he was missed and that she was glad that he was home.

"Am I to assume the hunt was successful?" she sat on the edge of their bed crossing her long, toned legs.

"Yes, it was," he said rising to his feet.

"You, Kulla, Aero, and Paige have been tracking down these

encampments for a few years now. How many are left?" she slightly tilted her head to the side.

"I do not know. None of us know where these encampments are until we hear a call for help from a village. It can take months to track down a single encampment. I do not know when, or if, we will be rid of the Orcs," he sat beside Maia. She sighed and leaned her head against his chest. Zidane wrapped his arm around her and kissed the top of her head.

It was mid-afternoon the following day when Zidane and Maia were looking out to the Western Mountains. Maia was in Zidane's arms, enjoying his warmth and had her head turned so that she could feel the beating of his heart. There was a warm breeze that blew about. Zidane's dreadlocks blew with the wind and the Sun shone in his silver eyes making them gleam.

"You think they are ready?" a mother's concern was in Maia's voice.

"Yes, I believe so. They have shown a considerable amount of ability during their training sessions with me. They are also very intelligent," Zidane kissed her on the top of the head.

"I do agree, but are they too young to be that far away from home," she looked back in to his eyes.

"It would seem your motherly instincts are getting the best of you," he teased. She gave a light laugh, then turned to face him.

"Do you truly think they are ready for it?" she looked in to his eyes while running her fingers through his hair. She had to admit to herself that her worry for her children was becoming prevalent in her mind. The Twins had never been away from home for as long as Zidane and Maia discussed. She also knew she would miss them terribly.

"Do not trouble yourself with the thought. They will be in good hands. I can attest to it," Zidane said attempting to reassure her. Moments later, a horn was heard bellowing from the east, and a knock was heard at their door. Zidane walked back inside to answer the door. A guard waited for him standing at attention, "Yes?".

"Sir, Lady Paige has arrived, she awaits you and Lady Maia," the guard answered.

"Thank you. Please inform her that we will be down shortly," the guard bowed at Zidane's request, then took his leave.

"Who is it?" Maia had made her way inside.

"Paige is here and wishes to see us," Zidane responded. She nodded her head and followed him down the hall and down the steps toward the foyer. Paige was standing in the middle of the red carpeted foyer, wearing a long hooded cloak with her two short swords strapped to her hip and a satchel slung over her shoulder. Her dirty blonde hair hung freely to her shoulders with two braids hanging on either side of her face.

"I trust you rested well after our hunt?" Paige gave a grin when she saw her half brother and sister in-law.

"Yes, I did," Zidane responded giving a warm embrace to her.

"And how are you, Maia?" she asked giving an embrace to her.

"I am well," Maia returned the embrace.

"How are my niece and nephew?" Paige looked around for them.

"They are doing well. They are at the school house with M' Kara. They should be returning shortly," Zidane looked to Paige as if sensing something from her.

"What's wrong?" Maia's hand touched the Necklace as it was faintly glowing. From the way that Maia looked into her eyes, Paige could tell that Maia knew there was something weighing on her mind.

"I must leave," Paige gave a sigh.

"And go where?" Zidane furrowed his eyebrows in confusion. Paige knew this was a sudden turn of events for her family, but it could not be helped.

"I must go to the island of Tryphia," she looked to them both.

"Why?" Maia tilted her head to the side.

"I cannot discuss it any further. It is a matter of secrecy," Paige looked in to both of their eyes as if pleading with them to not pry any further. A few moments of silence passed and then Zidane took a few steps toward Paige.

"If you must go, then go," he looked in to her eyes.

"Please tell the little ones that I will be gone and that I love them," she forced a smile for them.

"I will not have to," Zidane looked past her. Paige turned to find Tritan, Carline, and M' Kara standing in the doorway.

"Aunt Paige!" Carline and Tritan exclaimed dropping their books and running toward her. Paige held her arms open to hug them both. They charged into her almost knocking her on to her back. M' Kara slowly made her way into the foyer and stood a few feet away. She then bowed to Paige when she regained her balance. M' Kara was the daughter of Rosey and Kulla. Kulla and Rosey married shortly after Zidane and Maia were wed. M' Kara was also thirteen years old. She was the tallest of herself, Carline, and Tritan. Her hair was the color of mahogany, her skin was of a similar tone as the twins, her eyes were as blue as the morning sky, and when she smiled she showed her father's Vampire trait. She was somewhat shy and quiet. She also wore the midnight blue crystal of the Vampires around her neck.

"Where are you…," Carline started to say, "going, Aunt Paige?" Tritan finished. The Twins developed the habit of starting and finishing each other's sentences and thinking the same thoughts.

"And how do you know that I am leaving?" Paige folded her arms in front of her chest.

"Well, you are wearing….," Tritan started, "your favorite long coat," Carline finished.

"You have a satchel…," Tritan continued, "slung over your shoulder," Carline finished.

"And when we returned from the schoolhouse …," Tritan further said, "we saw a bag of food and a few canteens of water on your horse…," Carline furthermore said, "as if you are going on a long journey," Tritan finished.

"Well you two are observant. Well I am going on a journey," Paige chuckled.

"Where are…," Carline started, "you going?" Tritan finished.

"I am going to Tryphia," Paige could not hide the fact she was leaving, nor could she lie to them.

"Where...," Tritan started, "is that?" Carline finished with both of their heads tilted to the side in confusion.

"It is an island to the east," M' Kara interjected. Everyone looked to her in shock. She did not speak much when many were around. Her shyness would overcome her and she would not say much.

"I have studied my father's maps," she gave a shrug. Everyone gave a light laugh.

"When will you return?" Zidane asked.

"I do not know," a look of uncertainty was on Paige's face.

"However long you are away, I pray the Heavens will watch over you," Zidane gave a hug to her.

"We both do," Maia added.

"I thank you," Paige nodded. She then turned to Carline, Tritan, and M' Kara who stood side by side in front of her.

"What was our last lesson?" Paige asked them almost in a militant tone.

"Respect the person to your left and to your right and that same respect will be returned," all three recited in unison.

"Very good, young ones. The last lesson you shall learn before I leave is this, 'Even the smallest of Lights in the youngest of children will always stay lit in the darkest of places'. Do you understand?" all three nodded their heads. "Good," Paige smiled at her family.

"Goodbye...," Tritan started, "Aunt Paige," Carline finished. Both gave her a hug with tears welling in their eyes.

"Goodbye, Lady Paige," M' Kara bowed.

"M' Kara, you need not call me 'Lady Paige' or bow to me. You are as much a member of this family as Tritan and Carline," Paige grinned at her formality. M' Kara's sky blue eyes brightened and she gave a big smile showing her vampire fangs. She then gave a firm hug to Paige.

"Have you been taking hugging lessons from Carline and Tritan?" she laughed, then turned her head to get one last look of Zidane and

Maia before walking out of the foyer of the Western Palace and off to her journey.

"Were you able to sense what the urgency was?" Maia did not use the power of the Necklace feeling that it would have been too intrusive.

"No, her mind is too strong. She blocked me out." Zidane shook his head.

"Do you think she will be alright?" Maia looked to him.

"I did sense there will be good surrounding her," Zidane nodded and gave a breath of relief at that feeling. Tritan, Carline, and M' Kara retrieved the books they dropped and gave a hug to Maia and Zidane. They all began to walk down the halls of the palace toward the kitchen.

"How were your lessons today?" Zidane held Carline close to him.

"They went…," Carline started, "very well," Tritan finished.

"What did you learn today?" Maia ran her fingers through her son's hair.

"We learned the history of the Elven Kingdom and a few of the Rulers. Next we study the history of the Vampire Covens of Rhydin," M' Kara responded with her eyes brightening.

"M' Kara loves history," the Twins said in unison. Their voices conveyed their boredom with the subject.

"History is a very good subject," Maia pinched at Tritan's cheek.

"That is right. If you do not know your past then you are doomed to repeat the mistakes from that past," Zidane said.

"We understand," the three young ones nodded.

"Where's Momma?" M' Kara asked.

"She went to the marketplace. She will be back soon," Maia replied.

"And Poppa?" she asked.

"He should arrive tonight. He had some business to take care of back in the Coven," Zidane responded.

"Ok," M' Kara nodded.

"Tritan, Carline, your father and I have something to tell you both." Maia said after a deep breath.

"Yes?" they both said.

"We think that it is time for you two to train under a Master," Zidane looked to them both.

"You are...," Carline started, "sending us away?" Tritan finished the question.

"Yes. We will be sending you to one of the best teachers on Earth. He goes by the name of Chen Shun. I was sent to him when I was of the age to train. He and his brother are excellent. His brother, Raoko Shun, trained your mother, M' Kara," Zidane looked to the vampire girl.

"You cannot continue...," Tritan started, "with our training here?" Carline finished.

"I have trained you both in the basics. Now you must find your own craft and learn to master it," Zidane responded.

"You will be in good hands," Maia smiled.

"Alright," both Tritan and Carline sighed.

Once they entered the kitchen they found that Rosey had returned and was preparing small plates of food for Tritan, Carline, and M' Kara. Her scarlet red hair was braided into a long ponytail while her emerald eyes were focused on the task at hand.

"Momma!" M' Kara ran over to her and gave a big hug to her mother. Rosey turned to find her daughter running toward her. She opened her arms wide to return the hug and kissed her daughter on the top of the head.

"When did you return, Rosey?" Maia asked.

"A short while ago, Little Kitty," Rosey replied as she set the table for the children to sit.

"Have you heard any word from Kulla?" Zidane asked.

"I have not, m' lord," Rosey shook her head.

"Very well. I will make my rounds and visit the villages. I will return tonight," Zidane kissed Carline and Tritan on the top of the head.

"I will go with you," Maia said.

"Alright," Zidane nodded.

"Can we come too?" the Twins had hope in their voices.

"Not this time. You need to attend to your studies," Zidane pointed to the books that were piled on the table.

"Behave yourselves while we are away. Listen to Rosey," Maia's tone was more serious reminding them to be on their best behavior.

"We will," the Twins were disappointed they were not able to shirk their nightly studies. Zidane and Maia kissed and hugged Carline and Tritan, then left.

"Now let's see what studies you have," Rosey said as the children sat at the table with their books open and a small plate of food in front of them.

Voices of Shadow

THE DAY SLOWLY TURNED TO night with a cool breeze blowing. It was a clear night and the stars shone bright. There was something different about this night. It seemed to be darker and quieter than any other night. Zidane and Maia returned from their rounds of the surrounding villages. Zidane put Sundancer back in his pen and they both entered the palace through the stables. They walked through the halls and up the stairs to Tritan and Carline's room. They found them both, along with M' Kara, on the balcony sitting with their legs crossed looking out toward the starry sky. All three of them had a piece of parchment and a writing charcoal in hand.

"Why are you all still awake?" Zidane looked to them with his arms crossed and a raised eyebrow.

"We wanted to wait…," Tritan started to say, "until you returned home," Carline finished.

"You two are sweethearts," Maia walked to them and gave a hug and a kiss on the cheek.

"Did they convince you to staying awake?" Zidane turned his eyes to M' Kara.

"They always do," M' Kara gave a sheepish grin.

"What are you all doing?" Maia sat on her haunches in between Tritan and Carline.

"We are drawing…," Carline started, "the constellations," Tritan finished as all three showed Maia and Zidane their parchments.

On the parchments, the three drew dots and lines representing the constellations in the night sky above. Altogether they drew seven.

"Do you know their names?" M' Kara asked Maia.

"I do not," Maia shook her head then looked to Zidane.

"Do you...," Tritan started. "Poppa?" Carline finished the question. Zidane took a moment while looking at one of their parchments.

"Orion the Hunter, Aquarius the Water Bearer, Libra the Scales, Draco the Dragon, Delphinius the Dolphin, the Gemini Twins, and Ursa Major the Great Bear," Zidane pointed to each one.

M' Kara, Carline, and Tritan sat in awe looking from their parchments and then to the dark night sky to the groupings of stars.

"And what is that big bright one?" M' Kara pointed to it. In the middle of the northern night sky, a star larger and brighter than all of the others shone in the blanket of night.

"That is the North Star," Maia responded looking up to it. The stars' bright lights reflected in her amber eyes as she gazed up to it.

"Why is it...," Tritan started, "bigger and brighter...," Carline continued, "than the others?" they both finished in unison.

"It is the star that leads travelers to where they are going," Maia looked to them.

"How?" M' Kara tilted her head.

"There is a story of three wise Kings who were looking for a child. For this child was very special to the salvation of mankind. They called upon this Star and it led these wise Kings straight to the newborn child," Zidane recalled this story that his Aunt told him when he was a child. Carline, Tritan, and M' Kara smiled and looked back to the North Star. Their eyes gleamed as the North Star reflected in their eyes. The moment was interrupted by a knock at the door. Zidane went to answer it. When he opened the door, he found that Kulla had returned from his business with his Coven.

"I assume all is well with your Coven," Zidane smiled.

"It is my friend," Kulla returned the smile as he entered the bedroom of the Twins. M' Kara turned when she heard the voice of her father. She leapt up and ran into the awaiting arms of Kulla.

"How is my Little Lady?" Kulla asked her as he held her close.

"I'm well, Poppa," she answered with a big smile across her face.

"And your studies?" Kulla asked in a more serious tone.

"Good," she responded with a nod.

"Good girl," Kulla gave a nod of approval. He then walked over to Zidane and said, "Word has reached my ears of an Orc encampment in one of the caves at the foot of the Western Mountains".

"Do you know how large the encampment is?" Zidane crossed his arms in front of his chest.

"We do not know. Our spies spotted a raiding party of twenty attacking a village to the North. They were last seen heading West across the foot of the Northern Mountains. I am assuming this is a larger encampment than the others we have encountered. We are going to need as many of the Rulers and Generals as possible," Kulla gave a sigh knowing a larger fight was looming.

"And what makes you think this is a large encampment?" skepticism in Maia's voice.

"This raiding party collected a lot of food and other supplies. More than the other raiding or hunting parties we have tracked," Kulla responded.

"Very well then. Send word to Aero, Aldar, and Demus. Tell them to meet with us at Eagle Eye Lake," Zidane said.

"What of Paige?" Kulla raised an eyebrow.

"She left to take care of an urgent matter on Tryphia," Zidane responded.

"I am coming with you also," Maia interjected.

"Who will look after Tritan and Carline?" Zidane turned to her.

"Rosey will be here. You need all the help you can get if Kulla's information is correct," Maia responded. "Also, you will not have Paige to aid you. I will simply take her place".

"Very well. Let Rosey know what our plans are," Zidane said to Kulla who nodded and left the room with M' Kara arm in arm.

"Alright. Let's say good night to our children," Maia and Zidane walked with Tritan and Carline to their bedroom. Both gave a kiss on the forehead to the Twins saying goodnight and sweet dreams. After putting the twins to bed, Maia and Zidane were in their bed chamber strapping on their weapons and light armor. Both took dark, long coats from the rack, then made their way to the stables. While walking down the halls, an overbearing feeling of unrest overcame Zidane. His eyes faintly glowed silver, his muscles tensed as if bracing himself for an attack causing him to halt in his walk. Maia stopped beside Zidane as the same feeling overcame her with the Necklace of Isis faintly glowing.

"What is that?" Maia was taking in heavy breaths.

"It feels familiar. Much like the feeling that overcame me when I fought Sekmet, but this is much darker and more sinister," Zidane too took in deep breaths attempting to calm his body.

"What should we do?" Maia looked to him with concern in her eyes.

"We cannot do anything. We do not know what it is, if anything at all," he looked up and down the hall, "Rosey will be here and I will post additional guards in the halls near the twins and M' Kara," Maia nodded and both continued to walk to the stables.

Kulla waited in the stables on the back of his horse alongside Sundancer who already had been saddled. Zidane hoisted Maia on to Sundancer's back and then he swung himself behind her.

"What is wrong? You both look as if the courage in your hearts has been taken," Kulla looked in to both of their eyes.

"You do not look much better," Maia said under her breath. Zidane sharply nudged her for the snarky comment.

"Nothing is wrong, Kulla. We are just uneasy about leaving the children," Zidane responded.

"Don't worry. Rosey is more than capable of watching those three," Kulla gave a chuckle. The three then rode from the stables to Eagle Eye Lake to meet with Aero, Demus, and Aldar along with other Elf troops.

The next day, Rosey walked the Twins and M' Kara from the schoolhouse back to the Western Palace. Their conversation was lively as they spoke of what happened that day with their other friends and the lessons they learned. Rosey had a never ending smile on her face when she was with the children. Their liveliness, youth, and excitement always brightened her day. She saw it as a blessing to spend time with them every day after school.

Crossing the threshold of the foyer, Rosey felt a sudden dark presence. Although it was faint, her heart sank, her stomach twisted in a knot, and her eyes widened. Her reaction to this presence lasted only a moment. She looked to M' Kara and there was an expression of concern on her daughter's face. M' Kara was clutching her heart and looked to all of the shadowy corners of the Palace. The Twins were oblivious to this odd presence.

"Odd," Rosey said underneath her breath. Although it was not an overly strong presence, Rosey kept her eyes and senses more vigilant as she walked with the children through the Palace. She did not know why she felt the odd, yet dark, sensation.

As the evening went on, Rosey thought she heard faint chatter coming from the darkest of the Palace corners as she walked down one of the Palace's halls, but no one was there. Was it fatigue that was making her imagine these things? As the night went on, she continued to feel like there was another presence in the hall behind her. She would turn to find no one or just another one of the Elf Guards patrolling the halls. Each time she felt this faint, dark presence, her heart would quicken within her chest and her breathing became a bit more heavy. She even found herself reaching for her kunai. That was when she heard the scream of her daughter.

"M' Kara!" she vanished into a cloud of shadow down the hall. She continuously vanished in and out of shadows on her way to the room where M' Kara was sleeping. Upon opening the door, she found the Twins had gone to her room and were sitting on the side of M' Kara's bed. Her eyes were wide and wild with tears streaming down her cheeks.

"Momma!" M' Kara cried when she saw Rosey enter the room. There were Elf Guards who rushed in to the room as well.

"What happened?!" Rosey rushed to her daughter and held her close.

"It looks like....," Tritan started to say, "she had a nightmare," Carline finished.

"Is that what happened, Love?" Rosey looked down and wiped the tears from M' Kara's soft cheeks. M' Kara was so distraught that she was unable to speak. All she could do was nod to Rosey's questions. Rosey turned her head to the Elf Guards who had rushed to their aid and nodded to them saying that everything was alright.

"What happened in this nightmare?" Rosey turned back to M' Kara who was still sobbing.

"S-shadows....," her body tensed when she thought of the nightmare. "A-and many chattering voices...... They were calling to me," she began to cry once more. 'Shadows and chattering voices', Rosey repeated in her mind. Was this nightmare related to the dark presence they felt earlier in the day?

"It'll be alright, Love. I'll stay with her tonight," she said. The Twins returned to their room and beds while Rosey crawled in to bed with M' Kara.

When the sun rose the next day, Rosey no longer felt the dark pressure that was present the evening before. "Did it leave?" Rosey asked herself when she rose from her sleep and looked down the hall. She breathed a sigh of relief when she saw, nor felt, that heavy presence. However, she feared its return. It also troubled her that she didn't know what it was, but it felt vaguely familiar. Like it was of the shadows.

Throughout the day it was peaceful within the Western Palace. Rosey did not feel or hear any intruders of a dark nature, nor did any of the Palace Guards. Although the presence was gone, it still lingered within Rosey's mind. Was it a trick of the mind? The feeling did leave when she woke from their night's sleep. She would remain on her guard throughout the day.

After returning from bringing the children back from the schoolhouse, Rosey felt the dark presence once more, except it was stronger than the previous night. Her knees weakened when the dark presence struck her. It was as if she were in the clutches of a cyclops. M' Kara felt it as well and struggled to breathe. The Twins turned to find Rosey and M' Kara in distress.

"Help!" both of the Twins cried out. Elf Guards from different halls rushed to help.

"What is the matter?" one guard looked from the Twins to the mother and daughter.

"We do not know," the Twins responded with a shake of their heads.

"I'll be fine," Rosey said with deep, controlled breaths. "Breathe deeply, Love," she looked to M' Kara to make sure she was doing so. M' Kara did as her mother told her and both began to calm their bodies.

"Ma'am, are you alright?" an Elf Guard stepped to her.

"Yes. A bout of vertigo," Rosey straightened up and forced a smile. The Guards looked to her and then to M' Kara who followed her mother's example of smiling.

"Inform us if you are in any need of help," the Guard said as they all returned to their posts.

"Come, Little Ones. Off to the kitchen we go," Rosey said as she guided them.

Throughout the evening, the chatter from the shadows was at its strongest and the pressure of darkness weighed even more heavily on Rosey and M' Kara. Why was it that Rosey and M' Kara were the only ones affected by it? One would think the Elves would be able to hear this chatter because of their uncanny sense of hearing, but they did not. There were instances where she asked a passing Elf Guard if they heard the chatter, but they did not. It troubled her that such a presence was within the Palace walls and she could do nothing about it at the moment. In the meantime, all she could do was remain vigilant and guarded, especially for the sake of the children.

Late into that night, Rosey was in the kitchen cleaning the tables and putting away the rest of the food when she heard several sets of footsteps. They were quick and light. She put the last of the dishes in a cupboard and slowly began to search the halls. She had a hand on one of her kunai that were strapped to her lower back. She came across two of the Elf guards who were patrolling the halls.

"Did any of you hear any footsteps in the halls?" she looked to them both.

"No ma'am," one guard responded with a shake of his head.

"When did you hear these footsteps?" the other asked.

"Just moments ago," Rosey's eyes looked past the guards down the hall and even behind her.

"Are you sure they were not ours?" the first guard asked.

"I am certain. These footsteps were quick and light," her gaze returned to them.

"We will search the halls for any intruders," the second guard said.

"And tell the others on guard to watch for anything that is out of place," the first guard added.

"I'm goin' with you," Rosey's tone was firm. The guards nodded, then they began to search the palace halls.

The halls seemed darker and quieter than any other night. The guards were patrolling the halls more attentively. Rosey, with kunai in hands, was accompanied by two more guards in addition to the two she first approached. Their eyes were watchful of the darker corners of the palace. The slightest noise out of the corners made them tense. They came to the hall where the Twins and M' Kara slept and they heard a shriek come from M' Kara's room. Rosey and the guards rushed and crashed through the door. They found several shadowy figures standing over M' Kara's bed. Two of the creatures whipped around and hissed at Rosey and the guards.

"What in the Heavens are they?!" Rosey exclaimed with a tone of fear in her voice. These shadow figures had no definite shape. Rosey and the guards could only make out what seemed to be arms and legs.

At the end of what seemed to be hands of the creatures were claws emitting a dark energy. Their bodies were long and lanky. They had no face but did have yellow lidless eyes

"Momma!" M' Kara screamed and reached out to Rosey. These shadow creatures stood between Rosey and her child. Rosey conjured the courage and charged toward the group of shadow creatures threatening her daughter. One of the creatures stepped forward and swung its arm at Rosey. In mid-swing, the creatures arm shifted in to the shape of a blade. At the last moment, Rosey avoided the attack by vanishing into a cloud of shadow and then reappeared behind the creatures next to M' Kara. One of the Elf guards charged forward and thrust his spear into the chest of a shadow creature. The creature looked at the spear that was embedded in its chest then back to the guard. The eyes of the creature glowed brightly with anger and then thrust its arm as it changed into the shape of a blade into the chest of the guard. M' Kara, with tears in her eyes, clung to the waist of Rosey. Rosey faced three other shadow creatures as the Elf guards faced off against two others.

"Stay in the corner, M' Kara," Rosey lowered herself into a defensive stance. M' Kara ran to the corner and crouched down. The arms of the three creatures turned into blades as they readied to attack Rosey. All three of the creatures slashed at Rosey with their blade arms. Rosey avoided each slash and stab whilst disappearing and reappearing into clouds of shadows. After reappearing from these clouds of shadows, Rosey slashed and stabbed with her kunai, but her attacks seemed to have no effect on the creatures. The attacks of the Elf guards on the other two creatures had no effect either. Rosey then disappeared in a cloud of shadows and reappeared behind one of the creatures and sliced its throat. What seemed to be shadow energy began to seep from the slash wound on its throat. The creature grabbed at the wound and stumbled into the wall and into the other creatures.

"The creatures are weak at the neck!" Rosey yelled to the other guards. The creatures sunk into the ground and moved across the floor like the shadows of trees as the sun moved across the sky. They moved across the stone floor and then swiftly under the door into the hall leaving the one wounded creature.

"They're goin' after the Twins! You keep an eye on this one and M' Kara! The rest of you come with me!" Rosey ordered as she rushed in to the hall and toward the room of Tritan and Carline. As soon as Rosey and the guards entered the hallway, they heard screams come from the Twins' bedroom.

"The Little Ones!" Rosey yelled as she burst into the room kicking the door open. Rosey and the guards found two of the shadow creatures hoisting Carline and Tritan out of their beds and over their shoulders. The two others stood in front of Rosey and the guards. Anger swelled in Rosey's eyes. She charged at them and then vanished into a cloud of shadows. She reappeared next to the creature that was holding Tritan and slashed at its throat. The creature dropped Tritan and grabbed its neck. Shadow energy seeped out of the wound. The other creature dropped Carline and thrust its hand into the side of Rosey. Rosey dropped her kunai as she felt this sharp pain course through her body as if a spear and been thrust into her. The hand of the shadow creature began to seep into and merge with Rosey's body and slowly take over. The shadow energy from the creature began to run through the veins of Rosey like the poison from a serpent. One of the guards threw his spear at the creature's arm. The creature quickly withdrew its hand from Rosey. The creatures grabbed Tritan and Carline and disappeared through a dark hole that materialized at the window. Three of the original five creatures left through the dark portal carrying Tritan and Carline leaving the two wounded creatures and Rosey wounded on the floor.

LOST STARS

IT WAS THE NEXT MORNING that Zidane, Maia, Kulla, Aero, Aldar and Demus returned to the Western Palace after their hunt of the Orc encampment. Once they all put their horses in the stables, a feeling of a dark, overcast shadow was within the palace. Maia looked down to the Necklace of Isis. It was vibrantly glow, warning her of danger.

"I have a bad feeling, Zidane," Maia grasped the Necklace.

"As do I," Zidane's eyes conveyed his concern.

"We'd better check on the children. I fear something has happened," Kulla looked to them.

"Agreed," Aero nodded. Aldar and Demus stayed in the foyer while the others rushed upstairs. At the top of the stairs, they were met by one of the guards that was with Rosey the previous night. A grim look was upon his face. His head was slightly lowered and his eyes averted from those of Zidane and Maia.

"Guard, what has happened?" Zidane asked with urgency in his voice trying to make eye contact with him. The guard hesitated in responding to Zidane.

"What happened last night?!" Maia took the guard by the collar of his armor to force his eyes to make contact with hers.

"There was an invasion of the palace, m' lady," the guard finally responded.

"By who?" confusion, fear, and worry were all in Zidane's voice.

"C-creatures of the s-shadow. They had no definite form. T-their reach was long, they had no faces, but did have yellow, lidless eyes," the guard's voice trembled when he spoke of the intruders.

"These creatures sound like the fabled shadow demons of the Shadow Realm," Aero said.

"They are no mere fables any more, Brother," Zidane's voice turned to that of anger.

"Where is Rosey?" Kulla looked all around for her. He thought that she would have been among the first to greet them upon their return.

"She...," the guard started to explain, but then averted his eyes.

"What?" Kulla stepped toward the guard forcing him to make contact.

"She is severely injured. We do not know what is wrong. It was as if the demon poisoned her somehow," Kulla's eyes widened with the guard's response.

"Where are the children?" Maia's voice trembled for fear of what the response was. With Rosey injured, she feared the worst. The guard remained silent as if attempting to find a way to tell them of what transpired the night before.

"Soldier, you will answer," Zidane ordered.

"The creatures came here to kidnap the Twins. They succeeded. Three of the creatures took them through a dark portal," the guard's head lowered in shame as he responded. Maia dropped to her knees as fear overcame her and anguish filled her heart, "I knew we shouldn't have left them! Why did we leave them!?". Her pain and anguish was heard and felt throughout the halls. Zidane knelt by Maia's side and held her close to him. Tears streamed down both of their cheeks. Aero walked beside them and placed his hands on their shoulders.

"Where is M' Kara?" tears were welling in Kulla's eyes from fear of what may have happened to his daughter.

"She is sitting beside Lady Rosey in the Twins' room," the guard responded. Kulla rushed past the guard to the room.

"How did this happen?" Zidane asked the guard with anger in his voice and his eyes flaring with flame.

"While we were warding off the creatures we found they were able to travel across the ground like shadows. They were able to sink to the ground and move across it with great speed. We think that is how they bypassed our guard," the guard felt a lump in his throat.

"How many were there?" Aero looked to the guard.

"There were five altogether. We severely wounded two in the fight and the remaining three escaped through a dark portal," the guard promptly replied.

"Where are the wounded creatures?" Zidane's teeth were clenched.

"We have put them in M' Kara's room and cornered them there. We wanted to wait for you to see what you wanted to do with them," the guard responded.

"Take us to them," anger and contempt for the creatures were in Maia's voice. Zidane helped her to her feet and they, along with Aero, followed the guard to M' Kara's room.

When they entered the room, they found several armed guards with their shields in front of them and spears pointed at the wounded creatures whose shadow energy was slowly seeping out. They walked past the guards and stood over the creatures. The muscles throughout Zidane's and Maia's body were tense, their fists were clenched and trembling. Zidane's eyes continued to flare with fire out of anger and Maia clenched her teeth. Zidane knelt to one of the creatures and looked deep in to the yellow lidless eyes of the shadow demon.

"What are you?" a deep growl was in Zidane's voice.

"The curse... has fallen... upon you... and your house," the creature hissed continuing to hold the wound on its throat.

"What is this curse you speak of?" Zidane raised the Bracelet of Ra to the creature. The Bracelet glowed brightly with raw energy. The creature hissed and writhed in pain from the energy being emitted from the Bracelet.

"Who placed this curse on us?" Maia bore her panther-like teeth at the creature.

"The Ruler... of all... Shadows," the other creature responded.

"And who would that be?" Aero stepped closer to the creature with his fist clenched. Neither creature answered.

"You will answer!" Zidane demanded as he pointed the Bracelet of Ra at the creatures. It glowed more brightly and vibrantly with the Sun's power. The creatures writhed in pain.

"You will... discover the identity... of the Ruler of the Shadows... very soon... Red Dragon," one of the creatures responded with its eyes glowing yellow. They both then slowly faded into the ground and disappeared. The guards in the bedchamber lowered their shields and spears as the creatures dissipated. Zidane lowered his head, his eyes glowed and the anger within him swelled. Zidane raised his clenched fist and thrust it into the stone floor, cracking it. His eyes glowed with a raging wildfire in anger as he rose to his feet.

"You must retain your composure, Brother. The Enemy wants us to make clouded decisions through anger. We will discover the identity of the ones who have kidnapped your children," Aero placed his hand on Zidane's shoulder.

"You are right, Aero," Zidane took in a breath to regain his composure. His eyes returned to their original hue and his muscles relaxed. He looked to Maia who had tears streaming down her cheeks. Zidane walked over to her and placed his arms around her.

"Let us go see Rosey," Zidane said to her in a gentle voice. She nodded and they walked out of the room to the Twins' room.

They walked in to the Twins' room to find Kulla and M' Kara sitting next to the bed where Rosey laid. Aero motioned for the guards to stay in the hall. Her face was pale as if all of the color and life had been stolen from her. Sweat poured from her forehead. Her eyes were dull and glossy, breathing was a difficult task. The veins in her face were more visible and darkened. She was under a quilt and a cold, wet cloth had been placed on her forehead to bring down her fever. They stood in the doorway and looked upon the grief in the eyes of Kulla and M' Kara.

"How is she?" Maia asked in a hushed tone.

"Her condition gets worse as time passes. She has been poisoned by a shadow demon. If her condition goes untreated for too long, then she will succumb to the shadows and become a shadow demon herself," Kulla's voice was grim. His voice trembled and tears welled in his eyes. M' Kara buried her face in Kulla's chest crying. Zidane walked to him and placed his hand on his shoulder, "We will find a way to reverse the poison and bring her back along with finding Tritan and Carline".

"I pray that we do," Kulla looked up to Zidane.

"What is your plan?" Aero looked to his brother.

"My reasoning is, if we find this Lord of the Shadows or where his stronghold is then we will find the cure to Rosey's affliction," Zidane looked to his family and allies.

"I agree," Kulla nodded.

"I suggest that we summon the aid of the rest of the Krystal Kingdom. We will need to search all corners of Rhydin and Earth," Aero added.

"Guards," Zidane called to them. Two of the guards walked in to the bedchamber.

"Yes sir?" one guard responded as they both stood at attention.

"Tell Captains Demus and Aldar to spread the word throughout the Krystal Kingdom of Rosey's affliction and the abduction of Carline and Tritan. We are in search of the Lord of the Shadows and his stronghold," Zidane's tone was urgent and commanding.

"Understood sir," the other guard responded. The guards immediately took their leave.

"Where should M' Kara go?" Kulla asked.

"She can stay in the Eastern palace with my son, Troy. I will send word with Captain Demus to post extra guards in the palace," Aero offered that comfort

"Very well. M' Kara you will leave immediately with Captain Demus and you will spend time in the Eastern Palace while we handle this," Kulla looked in to M' Kara's eyes.

"But I want to stay here with Momma," she said with a trembling voice and tears in her eyes.

"I know you do, but it is too dangerous for you to be here. There will be more guards in the Eastern Palace. I will be here to take care of your mother," Kulla attempted to reassure her. With a sniffle, she nodded and then wrapped her arms around Kulla and let out the tears that welled in her eyes. Aero, Zidane, and Maia left them by the bedside of Rosey.

SEARCH FOR THE LOST STARS

WORD SPREAD THROUGHOUT THE KRYSTAL Kingdom of the abduction of Carline and Tritan, better known as the Gemini Twins. The Elves, Vampires, Shinobi, and the Lycans of Rhydin searched every region and Province. Using the Horn of Summoning Dragon, Zidane summoned the aid of Tufar and the Dragon Knights to search for the stronghold of the unknown Lord of Shadows. King Draco, Zidane's father and the leader of the Four Armies of Earth, received word of the abduction of the Gemini Twins and immediately began their search of every corner of Earth for his grandchildren. Every cave was explored, every mountaintop was scoured, every lake and river was searched, and each person of every village was questioned about the whereabouts of the Gemini Twins, but no one had seen them pass through.

Nearly a week passed since the Twins were abducted and there was still no sign of them. The hopes of the Krystal Kingdom dwindled and it seemed that they would never be found. Each night Maia would stand out on the balcony of her bed chamber and look out toward the rolling valleys and the Western Mountains as if searching for her children. Zidane searched every corner of Rhydin relentlessly sometimes on the back of Sundancer and then other times through the air on the back of Tufar.

As the days passed, Rosey's condition continued to deteriorate. The poison of the shadow demon slowly spread more throughout her body. The color in her eyes faded, her body would periodically shake and tremble as the poison flowed through her veins and ravaged her insides. Day and night Kulla sat by her side, praying the poison would not totally assimilate her body and that her being a Shadow Shinobi would offer some resistance to the shadow poison.

Zidane returned to the Western Palace on the back of Sundancer with several Elf soldiers behind him. He slowly made his way into the Palace and up the stairs to his bedchambers. During this walk, which seemed to be an eternity, his eyes were dulled; they had lost the life that was once there. His posture was slumped, he no longer walked with the pride that a Ruler should. His head was lowered and his eyes never left the floor. He felt like he had failed everyone for not being able to find his own children nor was able to find a way to heal Rosey. All of the hope seemed to have been drained from his being. As he walked into his bedchamber, he found Maia standing out on to the balcony looking out toward the starry night sky. There were many stars in the sky, but they did not flicker and glow like they had the past nights. Even the brightest one of them all, the North Star, was dim and barely shone in the night sky. Zidane went to her and wrapped his arms around Maia to bring her close to him.

"I am so afraid," her body trembled with the fear she would not be seeing her children ever again.

"I am too," Zidane said in a hushed voice.

"I want to go look for them with you. I cannot stay in the Palace and wait while the whole Kingdom is out searching for them," she turned to face Zidane. She was looking into his eyes as if pleading with him.

"Alright," Zidane let out a sigh.

"We will have to tell Kulla," Maia said.

"Yes we will. He will be in command while we are away," both then walked out of the room and down the hall toward the Twins' bedchamber. They entered and stood in the doorway. They found Kulla kneeling by the bed with his head bowed muttering a prayer while holding Rosey's blackening hand. The shadow poison was creeping further and further into the fibers of her being.

"He has been on his knees praying for three nights straight," Maia whispered to Zidane. Zidane's heart sunk. He put himself in the position of Kulla. What if it were Maia in this position? Would Maia have succumbed to this fate if she was to stay that night the Twins were abducted? How would he be able to handle this ordeal? Zidane walked to Kulla's side with Maia close behind him.

"Kulla, Maia and I are leaving at dawn tomorrow to continue the search," Kulla did not respond to Zidane's hushed voice. All he did was continue to mutter his prayer.

"Zidane is leaving you in charge of the Palace while we are gone," Maia stepped from behind Zidane. Again, Kulla did not respond. Zidane and Maia looked to each other and sighed. They left Kulla at Rosey's bedside on both knees holding on to her with the Scepter of Osiris next to him leaning against the bed.

It was early the next morning, before the sun rose in the east, that Zidane and Maia set out on Sundancer. They rode south with a platoon of Elf soldiers.

They searched every small cave and each village looking for Tritan and Carline. They began to approach the southwest province of the Mainland where Sekmet established his stronghold and ravaged the lands of Rhydin. Now with the evil vanquished from the lands, the land was flourishing with grass and trees growing from under the ash and rocks. While riding further south, the Necklace of Isis glowed vibrantly. "Zidane, something is coming," Maia whispered to Zidane.

"What is coming?" Zidane's ears perked up as if listening to his surroundings.

"I do not know. All I see is darkness. I believe that we should send the guards east and we should take care of this unknown threat," Zidane nodded at her suggestion. He brought Sundancer to a halt, then turned him to face the soldiers.

"I want all of you to ride east and leave no stone unturned!" he announced.

"Understood sir!" the soldiers said in unison, then rode off toward the east. Once the soldiers were out of sight they dismounted from Sundancer and searched their surroundings for any sign of danger.

"What is that?" Maia asked pointing in the direction of a small grouping of trees. A dark shroud seemed to surround this grove.

"I do not know. We had best be prepared for anything," Zidane drew both of his Dragon Blades. Maia readied her bow and drew an arrow. As they drew closer to the grouping of trees, the area around them seemed to grow darker and grimmer. Sundancer was following them until they drew within twenty yards of the trees, then he stopped in his tracks. He reared up to his hind legs and neighed, stomping his hooves to the ground.

"You do not have to come in with us if you do not feel it is safe," Zidane went back to Sundancer to try to calm him down. Sundancer settled down and began to back away from the trees.

"Should we go in since Sundancer is so skittish?" Maia's nerves were visibly getting the best of her. Her breathing grew heavier and her hands trembled while holding the arrow in place.

"This shroud of darkness may be the key to finding our children and the cure for the shadow poison Rosey is suffering from," Zidane's tone was urging her to not hesitate. Maia nodded, then they both walked closer toward the trees. Once they entered the grove, they saw that the trees were perfectly aligned with one another. Barely any light shone through the thin canopy as if a sheet of shadow was veiling the grove from the Sun.

"This is very peculiar," Zidane said as he and Maia ventured further in to the grove.

"Wasn't this the spot where Sekmet built his fortress?" Maia looked all around them.

"Yes. I, along with the Dragons and Dragon Knights tore down the walls and fortress and planted trees and grass," Zidane remained on alert as their surroundings grew dimmer.

"Did you plant these trees in perfect rows like this," Maia pointed out as they ventured to the center of the grove.

"I do not recall doing so," Zidane gave a shake of his head. At that moment, their surroundings appeared to get darker and quieter. Zidane's ears twitched and the Necklace of Isis glowed vibrantly.

Zidane looked to the branches above them and saw several dark daggers raining down upon them. Maia quickly stepped forward and used the power of the Necklace to place an energy barrier between them and the daggers. The daggers deflected off of the barrier and were hurled into the tree trunks. Zidane fused the hilts of his swords and conjured an aura of flame around the blades. Maia readied her bow with an arrow ready. They stood back to back as to be careful not to be attacked from behind. A dead silence was around them. The shroud of shadows around them grew darker allowing very little light from the Sun into the grove.

"Can you see anything Maia?" Zidane tightened his grip on the fused Dragon Blade.

"I cannot," she replied aiming her arrow in the darkest corners of the grove. They then heard an ominous laugh echo around them. They could not tell from which direction the laugh came from.

"Show yourself!" Zidane demanded.

"You thought you were rid of me didn't you?" the voice seemed to move from shadow to shadow.

"Who are you?!" Maia's eyes frantically darted from shadow to shadow trying to pinpoint the origin of the voice.

"Over a decade ago you thought I was caught in that surge of raw energy from the Great Relics and the Sword of Ages," the voice echoed even more.

"We have no time for your games, coward!" Zidane yelled with his eyes flaring with fire.

"I have been patiently waiting for this moment for over a decade. I would think that you can give me a little of your time," a shadowy figure emerged from the darkest corner of the grove.

"Show your face!" Maia shouted aiming an arrow at the shadowy figure. The light that was being let in through the shroud of shadow slowly began to reveal their adversary.

"It cannot be," Zidane's eyes widened.

"Oh my," Maia lowered her bow. The figure was revealed by the dim light from the Sun. Half of his face was covered with a dark porcelain mask; he had dark skin like Zidane, white shoulder length dreadlocks, and dark abyss-like eyes. Strapped on to his waist were two swords and on his right wrist, a silver Bracelet.

"S-Stratos?" Zidane uttered as if he did not believe what he was seeing.

"You look as if you have seen a ghost, Red Dragon," a smirk was on the face of the Black Dragon Essence Bearer. He then began to gather shadow energy into his palm. Maia quickly released an arrow toward Stratos. Stratos spun out of the arrow's path and sent a wave of shadow energy at both Zidane and Maia. Zidane stomped on the ground raising a wall of earth, but this attempt of defense was to no avail as the surge of shadow energy burst through the wall and threw Zidane and Maia backwards several yards. After a moment passed, Zidane opened his eyes to find Maia on her back and her eyes closed. Her bow was at her side and an arrow in the ground.

"Maia? Maia are you alright?!" Zidane called to her while crawling to her. She stirred a little and slightly opened her eyes letting him know that she was only dazed. Zidane then looked from her to find Stratos with a glare of death in his eyes. Zidane picked up his fused Dragon Blade and conjured an aura of flames around the steel. Stratos threw off his dark long coat then drew both of his Dragon Blades fusing the hilts together. An aura of shadow energy surged from the middle of the fused blade to the tips. Stratos's eyes darkened as he gazed into Zidane's flared eyes. Zidane clenched his teeth and tightened his grip on his fused Dragon Blade. He then made a dash at Stratos with a gust of wind behind him. Stratos took a defensive position waiting for the attack. Zidane veered and launched himself off of one of the trees and raised his flame engulfed blade. Stratos stood his ground not flinching. Zidane brought his flame engulfed blade upon Stratos, but Stratos raised his blade to block the attack. A shockwave of fire and shadow was sent throughout the grove as the blades of Stratos and Zidane clashed. This shockwave caused the trees to bend at the base. The power of the shockwave sent both of them backwards but each landed on their feet. Staring into each other's eyes, they began to circle one another crossing in between the rows and rows of trees.

"You are truly pitiful, Stratos," Zidane said with his eyes flaring with fiery embers.

"And why is that, Red Dragon?" Stratos spat.

"It makes sense now. The Ruler of the Shadows is you. You kidnapped my children!" Zidane stopped and set his feet firmly in to the ground.

"I am truly insulted that you would think that I would stoop so low as to kidnap your children to get to you. I need not do so," Stratos said in a disgusted tone.

"Liar!" Zidane roused a chunk of earth and gave a whirling kick to hurl it at Stratos. Stratos held his ground and slashed the chunk of earth in half with his blade. He found Zidane in the air with one end of his blade surrounded by an aura of flame and the other he saw a swirl of wind around it. Zidane began to spin the blade in his hands fusing the wind and fire energies.

"Wildfire Tornado!" Zidane shouted as he released the whirlwind of flames. Stratos gave an evil grin as if he were expecting it.

"Lightning Storm!" Stratos shouted as he spun his blade fusing wind and lightning energies. He released this cyclone of wind and lightning to counter the whirlwind of flames. The two cyclones of flame and lightning clashed with a thunderous clap that echoed throughout the grove and illuminated the shadowy corners. The force of the clash sent both Zidane and Stratos backwards. They both were breathing heavily as they had exerted a tremendous amount of energy.

"It would seem these past years have given your powers a chance to grow," Zidane said as if he admired Stratos for his improved skills and powers.

"It would seem that you have become more like a Dragon over the past decade," Stratos said as he noticed dark puffs of smoke billowing from Zidane's nostrils with each breath.

"Why have you taken my children from me?!" Zidane again accused Stratos of the despicable act.

"You are convinced that I have kidnapped your children. I am better than that, Red Dragon. When I come after you, I come directly at you. There is no third party". Zidane grew angrier, feeling that Stratos was playing mind games. His grip tightened around the Dragon Blade. He lunged at Stratos with a dragon-like growl escaping his throat. The collision of the two blades caused sparks to fly. The fire from Zidane's blade and the shadow energy from Stratos's blade fused to form the dark fire Zidane first saw in the Dragon Valley. Each were attacking and countering each other. They were ducking and weaving between the trees using the trees as shields and to launch themselves at each other. Zidane roused a chunk of earth and gave a spinning kick to it, summoning an aura of fire around his foot in mid-spin. The flame engulfed chunk of earth was hurled at Stratos. Stratos kicked off of a tree to launch himself into the air over the chunk of earth. The flame engulfed earth exploded behind Stratos as he landed. The explosion left a crater and small patches of fire started in the grass around it. Stratos looked up to see Zidane charging at him.

"Tri-Form," Zidane shouted as he got within several yards of Stratos. While charging at Stratos, Zidane split into three separate entities, two being pure energy and the other being the real version of Zidane. Stratos crouched down and grinned.

"Shadow Split," Stratos split into three entities just as Zidane did. Now there were three versions of each. These versions collided with each other and their blades clashed and sparks of fire and shadow energy were flying. The dull thuds of punches and kicks sounded throughout the fray. Maia was slow to get to her feet. There was a slight haze in her vision, she tried to clear it. She then saw multiple versions of both Zidane and their assailant, Stratos. She thought her vision was still blurred, but realized they had both created duplicates of themselves. She drew an arrow from her quiver and took aim but could not decide which of the versions of Stratos to fire at. One by one, the energy duplicates of Zidane and Stratos were destroyed by slashes of the Dragon Blades and blasts of fire and shadow energy.

The real Zidane spun with his blade outstretched ready to slash at Stratos. Stratos had the same idea and slashed at Zidane. Their blades clashed, echoing throughout the grove with sparks flying all around them. They locked each other's blades together pushing against one another. Neither gave any ground with their feet firmly planted into the ground. Stratos gave a thunderous kick to Zidane's chest sending him back several yards. Zidane dropped his blade as he landed on his back. Stratos leapt to the air with his blade, ready to bring it down upon the skull of Zidane. As Zidane looked to see Stratos in the air above him, an arrow pierced Stratos's shoulder as he was about to embed his blade in to Zidane's skull. Zidane rolled away grabbing his own blade. As Stratos landed on his feet, he pulled the arrow from his shoulder. His eyes flared with shadow energy and looked up to see Maia standing several yards in front of him with another arrow ready to release at him. His eyes then slowly faded to their natural hue. A state of serenity struck Stratos as he looked upon Maia. The muscles in his body relaxed. His grip on the Fusion Blade loosened.

"You will not touch him!" Maia shouted as she aimed her arrow at his chest. It was as if he were in a trance. He did not hear her warning; he did not feel the pain that radiated from the puncture wound from the arrow that pierced his shoulder.

"I-Inca?" Stratos said in disbelief as he took a few steps forward toward her.

"You will not come any closer!" she shouted to him. Stratos looked from her intense amber eyes to a shadowy figure that was in the air behind her. His eyes widened and his muscles tensed once again. His eyes then flashed black with shadow energy. He conjured shadow energy into his hand and, with deadly accuracy, hurled several daggers of shadow energy. The daggers of shadow energy embedded themselves in the creature's forehead and it fell with a dull thud to the ground next to where Maia was standing. She slowly took her eyes from Stratos to the creature that landed next to her.

"I-It's... one of those shadow demons!" Maia exclaimed with her panther tail straightening. She then slowly turned to find a whole horde of shadow demons behind her. Her panther-like ears flattened against her head in fear of the horde that stood before her not only on the ground but in the trees above them.

"What evil is this, Red Dragon?" Stratos clenched his teeth as his eyes were fixed upon the shadow demons.

"You should know. You were the one that conjured them. You *are* the master of the Shadows," Zidane retorted.

"Once more Red Dragon, I am not this Lord of the Shadows. I am the one who possesses the Essence of the Black Dragon. I cannot conjure demons of the shadow," Stratos's eyes darkened.

"If you are not the Lord of the Shadows, who is?" Zidane looked from Stratos's darkened eyes to the horde that crept closer and closer to them.

"It does not matter who the Lord of the Shadows is now. We first have to fight through these creatures and survive. Then we can hunt down the one who kidnapped my children and find the cure for Rosey," Maia said to them both as she drew an arrow and took aim.

"It would seem we will need to join forces once more to ward off another evil," Zidane was none too pleased to make a truce with the man who attempted to kill him over a decade ago.

"Only delaying me taking your heart and your powers," Stratos said impatiently. Zidane bore his teeth at Stratos and puffed dark smoke from his nostrils. Stratos gave a grin as he sensed the immense power emitting from Zidane and then turned his focus on the horde of shadow demons.

"Remember Zidane, they are weak at the neck. If you separate the head from the body, they will fall," Maia said as she released an arrow at the head of a shadow demon. The arrow pierced the creature's head and it fell. The rest of the horde looked down at their fallen comrade. They then looked up at Maia, Zidane, and Stratos with anger swelling in their demonic yellow, lidless eyes. Shadow energy fumed from their shapeless bodies. The demons that were poised in the trees began to swing from branch to branch drawing closer to them. Maia took aim and released arrow after arrow with masterful precision, striking the demons in the head. One by one they fell from the branches on to the ground leaving a trail of dark, dead bodies. Zidane and Stratos, who stood behind Maia, looked at each other and nodded to one another. They crouched down and, with Fusion Blades in hand, charged at the horde. They crossed each other's path leaving a trail of fire and shadow energy behind them. They weaved between the rows and rows of trees trying to take the demons' focus off of Maia as she continued to release her arrows into the horde. Stratos suddenly slid to a stop in the middle of the grove in front of the horde. The horde started to charge at Stratos, but Zidane leapt into the air and launched himself off the shoulders of Stratos. In mid-air, Zidane sheathed both of the Dragon Blades and then conjured energy from the Bracelet of Ra in one hand and an orb of fire in the other hand.

"Sunfire!" Zidane shouted as he fused the orbs of raw power from the Bracelet of Ra and the orb of fire into one entity and unleashed it upon the shadow demons. The beam of raw energy came upon the horde with a thunderous explosion destroying many of them and throwing others into nearby trees and branches. As the remaining shadow demons tried to recover, Stratos rushed from behind Zidane. With tremendous speed and agility, he slashed at the demons and swiftly dodged their attacks. In the meantime, Maia shifted into her panther form and leapt to the trees. Shifting back to her human-like form, she began to pick off the shadow creatures, releasing arrow after arrow. One by one they fell victim to arrows to the head or neck. Zidane and Stratos found themselves next to each other in the thick of the horde. They spun around each other slashing, stabbing, and kicking at the demons. They leapt over and dodged under the attacks of the demons. Several of the demons charged at the Dragon Essence Bearers. They both looked at each other and with their free hand they conjured fire and shadow energy. The fire and shadow swirled and fused together into an orb of dark flames.

"Darkfire!" they both shouted as they released an inferno of dark flames. The dark flames scorched and set ablaze the charging demons. Maia spotted them and finished them off by continuing to fire a barrage of arrows. Maia leapt down from the branch that she was perched on. As she landed, she strapped her bow to her back and drew her short sword and joined Stratos and Zidane in the thick of the fray, slashing at and cutting down the shadow creatures that surrounded them. Zidane quickly scanned their surroundings and saw only a few of the creatures left in front of them, "It is time to end this," he said to Stratos and Maia as his eyes flashed with flame. He sheathed both of the Dragon Blades and conjured an aura of flames around his fist. He waited for the shadow demons to draw closer to them. At the opportune moment, he thrust his flame engulfed fist to the ground. He sent a wave of flames surging toward the last few demons. The wave of flames scorched the demons and sent them scattering, bumping into each other in a frenzy to put out the flames that engulfed their shapeless bodies. Zidane rose to his feet and then his ears twitched. From a tree behind him a shadow demon leapt with one of its arms taking the shape of a blade ready to slash at the neck of Zidane. Zidane turned and caught the arm with one hand stopping the blade from cutting into his flesh. The eyes of the demon widened in shock that the blade did not cut into the flesh of Zidane. Zidane grinned and flipped the creature over his head and then placed his foot on what would be the throat of the creature.

"Fortunately for you I am going to let you live only to give your master a message. I am Zidane, Bearer of the Red Dragon Essence and Elf Ruler of the Western Province of Rhydin. Tell your master that I am coming for him to take his head, to take vengeance upon him for taking my children and poisoning my friend. Tell him that I am bringing hell with me," he said with anger in his eyes. His teeth were clenched tightly, dark smoke billowed from his nostrils, and his eyes flared violently. The creature trembled in fear. Zidane lifted his boot off of the creature's throat allowing it to retreat in a hurry, fading into the shadows. Zidane watched the creature flee just before his ears twitched warning him of an attack coming from behind him. He spun, quickly drawing of one the Dragon Blades and blocked Stratos's slash at his neck.

"Attacking from behind? Hardly seems worthy of you, Stratos," Zidane locked eyes with his rival.

"It was only to get your attention, Red Dragon," Stratos retorted with his eyes darkening.

"This is not going to help our children, Zidane! This man said that he did not kidnap Carline and Tritan and that he is not the Lord of the Shadows," Maia pled with Zidane.

"He will not relent in his hunt for my powers and as long as his hunt continues, I will continue to defend myself," Zidane's eyes flashing.

"You are correct, Red Dragon. Your powers will be mine and I will be the one true Lord of All Dragons," Stratos summoned an aura of shadow energy. In the middle of the grove there was a sudden burst of bright blue light that illuminated the whole grove. This explosion of light could be seen for miles.

"Stop!" a voice shouted from the middle of the burst of immense light. The light began to collect in one central point and began to materialize into the face of a woman. It appeared to be young but her eyes showed that she possessed several millennia of knowledge. Her gaze was upon Zidane, Maia, and Stratos who were shielding their eyes from the tremendous light.

"What is this?" Stratos tried to get a glimpse of what was before them. Maia was the first to uncover her eyes. She stood in awe with her eyes widened. Zidane and Stratos soon uncovered their eyes and found the woman's face at the center of the grove. Their eyes reflected the pure light that emitted from this being.

"Maia, who is this?" Zidane did not take his eyes off of the translucent face.

"This is, M-Mesnara. The Spirit of Rhydin and Earth," she responded.

"You seem in shock to see me young Maia," Mesnara's voice echoed throughout the grove.

"I-I a-am," Maia stammered.

"Do you not recall me telling you that I would reappear before you the day you and your comrades took possession of the Sword of Ages?" Mesnara raised an eyebrow at the werecat woman.

"I do now," Maia responded sheepishly with her ears flattening against her head. She then stood slightly behind Zidane.

"Why are you here?" Zidane stepped toward Mesnara.

"I am here to help," she responded.

"Can you really help us?" Zidane asked with hope in his voice.

"I can," she answered with an affirming nod.

"How?" Maia peered from behind Zidane.

"I can put you in reasonable proximity to where your children are being held," she responded.

"Where is that?" Zidane took another step toward her.

"They are being held in the Shadow Fortress at the heart and darkest region of the Shadow Realm," Mesnara's resonant voice was grim at the mention of the Shadow Realm.

"How do we get there?" Maia's ears perked up.

"I will send you there, but you two are not going alone," she responded.

"We do not have time to send for Kulla, Aero, or any of the other officers in the Krystal Kingdom," Zidane gave a shake of his head.

"I do not intend to send them. They have their own missions here on Rhydin to attend to," Mesnara stated.

"Who will you send with us then?" Maia tilted her head to the side in confusion. Mesnara looked past both Zidane and Maia toward one of the few shadows in the grove to Stratos. Zidane and Maia looked back to Stratos and then back to Mesnara with shock on their faces that she would send an adversary of theirs with them.

"You would send *him* with us?! He has tried to kill me numerous times. Why should my greatest adversary accompany me and my wife to rescue our children?!" Zidane protested.

"Although he has attempted to take your Essence, Zidane, and has proven to be a more than worthy adversary, he has also proven to be a great ally. Have you already forgotten the Cyclops in the Dragon Valley or that he saved you from Sekmet's grip and fought alongside you against Sekmet and defeated him," Mesnara responded appearing to grow in size above them. Zidane then glared back at Stratos who had a grin creeping upon the unmasked side of his face as he walked to Zidane's side.

"This is a mistake," Zidane muttered under his breath.

"Keep your friends close and your enemies closer," Mesnara looked upon them.

"We can kill each other when this is over, Red Dragon," Stratos's eyes flashed black.

"Indeed," Zidane responded with his eyes flaring with fire.

"We are all going to have to learn to work together in order to save Carline and Tritan and to help Rosey," Maia said sternly stepping in between Zidane and Stratos, gripping their collars. Zidane looked from her to Stratos, his eyes faded to their natural color.

"We have to learn to work together, for the children," Zidane said as he outstretched his hand to Stratos in a gesture of an alliance. Stratos looked at Zidane then to his outstretched hand, then to Maia whose amber eyes seemed to plead with him. His eyes faded back to their natural color and the anger that was fuming from him subsided. He looked directly into Zidane's eyes and took a step toward him and clasped his wrist firmly returning this gesture. The Bracelet of Ra seemed to faintly glow gold in reaction to the silver Bracelet on Stratos's wrist.

"Now that the Alliance of the two Dragons is sealed, I will open a portal to the Shadow Realm. Heed my warning, you must hurry across the Plains of Shadow," Mesnara's tone changed to that of being stern.

"Why?" Maia asked.

"The Lord of the Shadow is attempting to merge this Realm and the Shadow Realm. If he is successful in his plans, Rhydin, Earth and the cosmos will be plunged into total darkness and eventually die. He will bring his forces to Rhydin and Earth and weaken the forces of good," Mesnara responded.

"Then who will defend Rhydin and Earth?" Maia asked.

"That is the mission I will entrust to Lord Aero and his army, and King Draco and the Four Great Armies of Earth," she responded.

"Will they have enough power to repel the forces of the Shadows?" Zidane asked.

"Have faith, Zidane," Mesnara responded to reassure him.

"We should not linger here, the more time wasted asking questions, the less time we have to find your children and find that cure for your friend," Stratos said coldly.

"Stratos is correct. You must hurry. The fate of the Realm of Light rests in your hands," Mesnara looked to the trio.

"Agreed," Zidane nodded.

"Are you ready?" Mesnara asked.

"We are," Maia responded. Mesnara nodded and then looked to the sky. Her eyes glowed and radiated a pure light. The shadows that engulfed the small grove faded and the full force of the sun's rays shone upon them. Zidane felt refreshed as the sunrays touched his skin. He inhaled a deep breath as if absorbing them. Mesnara closed her eyes and opened a dark portal. It slowly swirled opened underneath her. Zidane hesitantly took a step forward and tried to see to the other side. He could not. The portal was like a dark, bottomless abyss. He then slowly stuck his arm through to his shoulder.

"It is.... cold," Zidane said as a cold shiver ran through his arm and throughout his body. He then took a deep breath and closed his eyes before throwing himself through the portal. Before following him, Maia looked up to Mesnara who smiled at her.

"Be brave. They will both need you," Mesnara continued to smile. Maia returned the smile and then looked to Stratos who stood only a few feet behind her. A chilling shiver ran up her spine as she caught his haunting gaze. She did not let her eyes go from him as she slowly walked through the cold, dark portal. Stratos took a few moments to step toward the portal. He looked at the portal then to Mesnara who looked upon him with sorrowful eyes.

"I know what burdens your heart Stratos, Bearer of the Black Dragon Essence. It is not too late to redeem yourself of the deeds that you have done," she said in a soft, empathetic tone. Stratos then looked from her to the ground and a single tear rolled from the corner of his eye. He quickly wiped it away and gathered himself. He took a deep breath and purposefully walked through the abyss-like portal.

RISE OF THE SHADOWS

I N THE DARKEST CORNER OF the Southwestern forest, not far
from where Zidane and Stratos fought, laid an encampment of
Orcs, Winged Demons, and Abominations. There were makeshift
tents made from the skins of deer and bears they had hunted for
food. Many sat around several small fires sharpening their swords
and battleaxes. The largest of the Orcs stood on top of a boulder at
the center of the encampment. The Orc held his great sword to the
air then let out a roar and beat his chest getting the attention of the
others.

"We must reclaim what was ours! We were feared through all
of Rhydin! We took what we wanted without fear! But now, we
have to cower to shadows at night to hunt for food! For more than
ten years we've lived in the shadow of the Krystal Kingdom! We
must rise and retake what was ours under the rule of Lord Sekmet!"
the Orc bellowed. The entire encampment was in an uproar. The
Abominations beat their cheats, the Winged Demons shrieked and
the Orcs raised their weapons to the night sky roaring. Their roars
and echoes were heard throughout the Southwestern Forest. Then,
their surroundings seemed to suddenly dim and grow darker. The
flames from the scattered fire pits dwindled. The whole encampment
became aware of the sudden change in the environment. Many began
to sniff at the air to try to identify if it was friend or foe that was
coming upon them.

"You will not be able to defeat the Krystal Kingdom without

the aid of the shadows," an ominous voice echoed throughout the encampment.

"Who are you?! Show yourself coward!" the Orc Leader yelled.

"I am a friend," the voice responded as a dark figure emerged from the darkest shadow of the encampment. The figure stood before them. It was that of a man, but covered in the darkest of shadows. He did not take steps, but glided across the ground. An aura of shadow energy surrounded his dark body. He had no definite face but his eyes were yellow and lidless.

"Who are you?" the Orc Leader growled as he readied to attack the unknown figure.

"I am the Lord of the Shadows, Ruler of the Shadow Realm," he slithered closer to the group of former soldiers of Sekmet.

"The Shadow Realm is nothing but a myth," the Orc Leader scoffed. The other members of the encampment shared in the Orc Leaders jest.

"No my misguided fiend, the Shadow Realm is very real. I have been there for over a decade and have indulged in the wondrous powers of the shadows. I have learned its secrets and have seized the Realm so that I may have my long awaited vengeance upon the Krystal Kingdom," the Lord of the Shadows tightened his fist.

"What are you needing us for?" an Abomination scratched his head in confusion.

"I wish to make an alliance with you and the rest of the surviving army of Lord Sekmet," the Lord of the Shadows held out his arms toward these brutish warriors.

"What do we get?" the Orc Leader asked.

"The powers of the Shadows," the Lord of the Shadows responded as the aura of darkness grew and throbbed around his body. The Orcs, Abominations, and Winged Demons looked to each other in bewilderment.

"Prove it," the Orc Leader leaned against his lowered great sword.

"Step forward," the Lord of the Shadows beckoned him to step forward. Still with his guard lowered, the Orc Leader stepped to be within a few feet of the Lord of the Shadows. The Lord of the Shadows slithered toward the Orc Leader then thrust his fist into the Orc's chest. The Orc Leader was momentarily stunned. The Orc's eyes widened as he found the hand of the Lord of the Shadows within his chest. Shadow energy crept from the Lord of the Shadow's arm and hand into the Orc's body. The shadows slowly began to take over the Orc's body and cover him. The Orc began to shiver and convulse.

"Sshhh, do not fight the shadows. Accept it and it will bond with you. It will make you stronger and faster," the Lord of the Shadow's eyes flashed yellow. The rest of the encampment took several steps back as the shadows began to transform the Orc Leader. The Orc Leader slowly began to grow in size. His muscles grew and broadened. The skin of the Orc Leader darkened and fumed the shadow energy his body was absorbing. The Orc Leader's eyes turned to a crimson red and its teeth grew to look like the fangs of a wolf. The Lord of the Shadows removed his hand from the Orc Leader's chest seeing the transformation was complete.

"Yes! Yes!" the Lord of the Shadows cried out triumphantly as the transformed Orc Leader stood before him. The new Orc Leader looked at his hands and clenched them into a fist.

"Try your strength," the Lord of the Shadows was practically licking his lips in anticipation of the raw strength the Orc Leader was about to demonstrate. The Orc Leader walked over to a tree that had the thickest trunk. He looked from its clenched fist then to the tree trunk. He then threw a thunderous punch into the trunk smashing a hole into it, sending splinters of wood into the air and leaving a crack that ran up the rest of the tree from the hole. The Orc Leader pulled out his fist and then looked at it with an evil smile of satisfaction.

"This is only the beginning, my friend. I will give this entire encampment the same strength and power. Then you will spread it to the surviving encampments of former followers of Lord Sekmet. Then we will obliterate the Krystal Kingdom and take Rhydin for ourselves. The Earth will soon follow. The Twin Planets will be overtaken by shadows as the Shadow Realm will merge with this

Realm. There will be no light left," the Lord of the Shadow's eyes brightened at the talk of his plan to take over this land. The Orc Leader let out a thunderous roar that shook the insides of each soldier in the encampment. The rest of the encampment let out shrieks and growls as they saw no flaw in the plan of the Lord of the Shadows. The encampment gathered around the Lord of the Shadows to receive the power of the shadow.

Over the course of the coming days, the newly transformed encampment traveled across the land under the cover of night without the fear of being discovered by the eyes of the Vampire Coven or the Lycans. They traveled to the remaining encampments of the surviving troops who were loyal to Lord Sekmet. They spread the power of the shadows like a plague spreading throughout a village. Being led by the Orc leader, the army of shadow empowered Orcs, Abominations, and Winged Demons grew larger with each passing night. The Lord of the Shadows oversaw the growth of this army.

"Once the Krystal Kingdom has fallen I will merge the land of Rhydin and the Shadow Realm," the Lord of the Shadows saw his plan coming to fruition as he oversaw the shadow empowered army of monstrosities scour the land for remaining encampments that were loyal to Sekmet.

Day slowly turned to night and then night to day as Kulla sat by Rosey helplessly watching the shadow poison ravage her body and take over. She ran a high fever that made her sweat profusely soaking the bed and quilt. Her skin became paler showing the darkened veins throughout her body. Her eyes lost their emerald sheen and began to slowly blacken. Kulla barely ate or slept. Each night he wept, blaming himself for not being there to defend her.

One night as he was muttering a prayer for Rosey's health, a faint blue aura appeared above him. The aura grew and began to illuminate the room. Kulla's ears perked up and he then looked up to the aura that hovered above him. He wiped the tears from his eyes and slowly rose to his feet gazing at the faint aura. He picked up the Scepter of Osiris and gripped it firmly. The hovering blue aura suddenly burst in to a bright blue light illuminating the room and the halls outside of the bed chamber. Kulla shielded his eyes from the blinding light. Once the light subsided, he uncovered his eyes to find a familiar face.

"Mesnara?" Kulla said in disbelief stepping toward the hovering face of made of the combined elements of Rhydin.

"Greetings, Vampire Prince," Mesnara looked upon him.

"What are you doing here?" a look of confusion was on his face.

"Rhydin is in grave danger, Kulla," she shook her head.

"Danger? Danger from what?" Kulla only thought of the threat from the surviving soldiers of Sekmet's army.

"The Lord of the Shadows has shown his face on Rhydin and has mustered an army from the remaining encampments of those who were loyal to Sekmet. He has empowered them with dark shadow energy and now they are lurking in the dark corners of Rhydin waiting for the order from the Lord of the Shadows to unleash their vengeful wrath upon the Krystal Kingdom," Mesnara's tone was grim.

"What am I to do?" Kulla could only think of warning the rest of the Kingdom.

"You are to travel to Earth, to the Temple of Osiris in Philae. There you are to gather the Army of the Undead for they are the best hope for the Krystal Kingdom," she explained. Kulla then looked to Rosey in her helpless state and then let out a deep sigh, "I cannot leave Rosey here by herself. If I am gone, who will watch over her?".

"What you will do is take her to the mountain village of the Earth Shinobi. They will take care of her. They have the best medicine that will ward off the poison from totally assimilating her body. On the way to the mountain village, you will tell Lord Aero that the minions of the Lord of the Shadows are roaming the lands of Rhydin and to muster the Krystal Kingdom to hold off the forces of the shadows until you have returned from Earth and Lord Zidane, Lady Maia, and Stratos have returned from the Shadow Realm. They seek to rescue their children and find a permanent cure for Rosey's condition," Kulla nodded at Mesanara's plan of action.

"Stratos?" Kulla asked.

"There is no time to explain. Time is crucial, Kulla. The fate of this Realm depends upon it," Mesnara's tone conveyed the urgency needed. Kulla looked to Rosey once more and then closed his eyes letting out a deep breath once again.

"I will leave right away," he gripped the Scepter. Mesnara gave a smile then slowly faded away.

Kulla prepared himself to make his long journey starting with warning Aero of the incoming danger from the Shadow Realm. Then to place Rosey in the capable hands of the Earth Shinobi, and then back to the Ruins of Keshnar to utilize the Gate of Caelum to go to Egypt and rouse the Army of the Undead. He first placed on his grieves, wrist gauntlets, and chest armor. He strapped his broad sword to his hip and the Scepter of Osiris to his back. He wrapped Rosey's body in a quilt to keep her body warm while they traveled to the Mountain Village of the Earth Shinobi. As he carried her to the stables, Kulla warned the soldiers to be on alert while they were on patrol of the Kingdom. He told them of the impending doom that seeks to cover Rhydin in Shadow. Once he placed Rosey on his horse, he mounted behind her, then rode off toward the Eastern Palace without resting. Time was of the essence for him, the Army of the Krystal Kingdom, and all of Rhydin.

Once he reached the walls of the Eastern palace, he called for the guard, "I wish to speak with Lord Aero! It is of great importance that I speak with him right away!".

"We will open the gates for you, Prince Kulla!" the guard responded.

"Do not bother! I must leave right away!" Kulla shouted back. The guard nodded and signaled for someone to tell Aero of Kulla's visit.

Several moments passed before the gates of the Eastern Palace opened with Aero walking through them to meet Kulla.

"I am told you have urgent news, Prince Kulla," Aero's eyes could see the urgency and fear in Kulla's eyes.

"I do. It is of the utmost importance," Kulla fought through the fatigue he was starting to feel.

"What is it then?" Aero turned his full attention to his Vampire ally.

"The Shadow Realm will be upon us. The Lord of the Shadows has roused an army from the remnants of the troops who were loyal to Sekmet. He has empowered them with the energy of the dark shadows. They are running wild across Rhydin gathering what remains of the old army. Once this army is at full strength, they will be unleashed upon the Krystal Kingdom and then the rest of Rhydin and Earth," urgency was in Kulla's voice as he explained the Enemy's plot.

"How do you know this?" Aero folded his arms in front of his chest.

"The Spirit of Rhydin, Mesnara, came to me and told me of this plot," Aero's eyes widened at this. It came from the Spirit, herself. It was certainly dire if she called upon them to ward off this evil.

"We must act quickly then. Where are Zidane and Maia?" Aero seemed surprised not to see them by Kulla's side with this dire situation looming on their doorstep.

"They have traveled to the Shadow Realm, along with Stratos to rescue Tritan and Carline. And I cannot help you right now. Mesnara has sent me on a journey," Kulla responded grimly.

"And what journey is that?" Aero asked.

"I am to place Rosey into the care of the Earth Shinobi in the Mountain Village and then travel to the Temple of Osiris in Egypt to rouse the Army of the Undead to aid against the Army of Shadow," Kulla was growing more anxious to be on his way.

"I do not know how long we can hold them off. Paige is not on the mainland, Zidane and Maia are in a different realm, and you go to rouse the Army of the Undead. The Dragon Knights cannot help because they answer to the Horn of Summoning Dragon which is wielded by Zidane. They are so isolated from the rest of Rhydin that it would take a long time for them to respond. And the Earth Shinobi will be guarding their villages as well as taking care of Rosey. That would just leave the Vampire Coven led by your father, Lord Zell, the Lycans and the Elf Army," Aero thought aloud.

"Have faith, Lord Aero. You do have the strength to hold them off. You also have Captains Aldar and Demus to aid you," Kulla attempted to reassure him.

"That is true. Faith in this army is our greatest strength. It got us through the war with Sekmet and it will get us through this one," Aero said with a grin growing on his face as he looked up to Kulla.

"I will return with the Army of the Undead in time to help," Kulla said.

"And do not worry about M' Kara. She is in good hands here," Aero mentioned.

"I know she is," Kulla smiled at Aero's reassurance. "If danger comes her way, she knows how to escape. Her mother taught her. M' Kara is more cunning than we give her credit".

"Very well then," Aero nodded to him. Kulla bade Aero farewell then turned his horse to the north toward the mountains. Aero watched Kulla ride off. He then walked back into the Palace to prepare the Elf Army for the Army of Shadows.

It took a few days for Kulla to reach the mountain village where the Earth Shinobi lived. Kulla ventured to the same village in which he, Rosey, Zidane, Maia, and Master Chen Shun first visited over ten years ago. Once Kulla and Rosey drew closer to the plateau in the mountain, the temperature dropped. The air was cool. Their breaths and the horse's could be seen. Tiny flakes of snow steadily fell to the ground, lightly coating it. Kulla could tell that Rosey was struggling to take in even breaths since the air became thinner as they ventured higher into the mountain. It was close to sunset when they reached the plateau in the mountain where the Earth Shinobi built their village. Kulla rode to the walls and called for a guard.

"Who goes there?" a guard shouted down to Kulla.

"It is Prince Kulla! I am an ally of the Krystal Kingdom!" Kulla responded.

"What proof have you?" the guard asked. Kulla pulled from under his shirt a midnight blue crystal that was attached to a silver chain and held it out. The guard pulled out his gold crystal from his shirt. The two crystals glowed vibrantly in reaction to one another. "You may enter, Prince Kulla," the guard signaled for the gate to be opened. The wooden gate creaked as it was being opened. Kulla spurred his horse onward through the gate and into the Shinobi village. The village appeared the same. The Shinobi were going about their everyday lives. Some were cleaning outside of their wooden huts, some were in small gatherings chatting amongst each other, and others were training. Parents were teaching their sons and daughters to be one with the earth. They were teaching them to take low, deep stances so that they were immovable, just like the earth beneath their feet were. They were taught how to rouse a chunk of dirt and rock, and how to manipulate it from those stances. Kulla looked around the village and then saw a familiar face. It was Raziel, the same young Shinobi who helped them in the battle against Sekmet. On either side of Raziel were two other Shinobi who seemed to be of the same age. One was a woman and the other a man.

"It is good to see you again, Prince Kulla," Raziel folded his hands in front of his chest and bowed. Kulla dismounted and hoisted Rosey from the horse's back still wrapped in the quilt. Kulla then returned the gesture.

"I wish my visit were under better circumstances my friend, but I bring grave news," Kulla sighed.

"What is it?" Raziel asked with concern coming upon his face.

"Where are Karfi, Igboyo, and Roho, they must hear of this as well," Kulla inquired looking around. Raziel looked to the two Shinobi on either side of him and then took a deep breath.

"They passed on a few years ago. We were then appointed to be the new tribal elders of this village. This is Leika and Kalik," Raziel said as he respectively pointed to the young woman and man. Both wore their ebony skin proudly. Like Raziel, Kalik's head had no hair growing from it. Leika's hair was braided and hung to the small of her back.

"I am truly sorry to hear of your losses," Kulla lowered his head.

"Thank you, my friend. They are one with the earth now as we all must be returned to some day. Now what is this urgent news?" Raziel asked.

"The Lord of the Shadow Realm has appeared on Rhydin. He has kidnapped the children of Lord Zidane and Lady Maia. He has empowered the remnants of Sekmet's army with shadow and they are now scouring the lands of Rhydin for more surviving encampments. They are waiting to be unleashed upon the Krystal Kingdom and plunge Rhydin and Earth into eternal shadow," Raziel looked to Leika and Kalik with concern on his face as Kulla told the news

"What are we to do?" Leika looked to the Vampire Prince as if he had the answers.

"Be prepared. Warn the other Earth Shinobi villages. Look out for an army of Orc, Abominations, and Winged Demons empowered by shadow. We know they are weak at the neck. We learned this at a great price," Kulla looked down to Rosey knowing that it was she who discovered the weakness.

"What happened to her?" Kalik looked to the scarlet haired woman.

"She has been poisoned by a shadow demon. Her body is fighting it off, but I do not know how much longer her Shadow Shinobi essence can aid in resisting it. I was told by Mesnara that you have medicine that will slow the spread of the poison even further," Kulla looked to the Earth Shinobi Elders.

"We do have a potion that she can take," Raziel nodded.

"Please, take her and watch over her. I must leave to go to Earth," Kalik motioned for two guards to carry Rosey into one of the huts.

"We will take care of her, Prince Kulla," Leika reached for his hands to hold firmly to reassure him of their healing talents.

"Thank you," Kulla bowed to them, then turned to mount his horse.

"Why do you go to Earth?" Raziel furrowed his eyebrows.

"I must go rouse the Army of the Undead in the Temple of Osiris in Egypt," Kulla responded as he turned his horse and rode through the gates back south toward the ruins of Keshnar.

Ever since Kulla left on this journey, he had not slept. He rode tirelessly through the mountains, hills, and forests of Rhydin. The thought of protecting the ones he loved and thwarting the Shadow Lord's plan to dominate Rhydin drove him to keep going without rest. Once he arrived at the Ruins of Keshnar, he immediately made his way into the Temple where the Gate of Caelum stood. He walked down the dark, narrow corridor to the open room where the Gate stood in front of him. He walked to the pedestal and touched the dials to open the Gate to his destination on Earth. A bright light burst from the opening of the Gate. Kulla then stepped toward the Gate and walked through the portal to his destination on Earth.

Aero was busy preparing the Elf soldiers for an attack upon the Krystal Kingdom. Not too far behind him was M' Kara. She heard every word he said to his troops. She soaked in the tactics that Aero was implementing. At one point in the scramble to prepare for an invasion, Aero was talking with Captains Demus and Aldar, "What should I do?" her question interrupted them. Aero, Demus, and Aldar stopped their deliberations and turned their attention to M' Kara who stood only a few feet away from them. Aero leaned forward to be eye level with her. He looked into her sky blue eyes and saw the eagerness to help.

"I am afraid there is nothing you can do, M' Kara. This is a very delicate and complicated situation we are in," he gave a sigh.

"But, I want to help," M' Kara pled with him. Her eyes seemed to cut directly to Aero's soul and weaken him.

"Find Troy and bring him here. You two cannot help us directly, but you can listen and be mindful of what we are doing and learn from us," Aero's voice held a seriousness that she had not heard from him before.

"Alright," M' Kara responded as she went off down the hall to look for Troy.

She found him in on the balcony of his bedchamber with his mother, Melina. She stood at the doorway and somewhat listened to their conversation.

"Do you think Tritan and Carline are alright?" Troy asked with a look of concern on his face and was deeply rooted in his eyes. Troy was a spitting image of Aero from his sandy, blonde hair and facial features; however his eyes were from his mother.

"I am sure they will be found. Your Uncle Zidane and Aunt Maia are out looking for them. They will be found safe and sound," she smiled reassuring him. Her smile was the smile that could cheer those who were in the darkest and deepest of holes.

"Another war is coming, isn't there?" Troy seemed to sense the danger.

"It would seem so," Melina responded as she looked off to the Northern Mountains.

"It does not look favorable for us, does it?" Troy looked up to Melina. She looked back at him with her light brown eyes and pitch black hair blowing in the wind.

"Have faith, Troy. Things will work out. They did while we were fighting Sekmet and they will work out now," Troy gave a slight grin at his mother's hope and faith in their Kingdom

"Excuse me, Lady Melina and Troy," M' Kara interrupted when there was a break in the conversation.

"Yes, M' Kara. What is it?" Melina turned to face her.

"Lord Aero would like for me and Troy to be by his side," she responded. Melina looked to Troy and then back to M' Kara.

"Very well," Melina sent Troy to go along with M' Kara. From that point on, M' Kara and Troy followed Aero and his Captains around the palace as they spoke to their troops. They were close behind while Aero dispatched scout patrols to scour Rhydin for this growing army of shadow empowered beasts. Troy and M' Kara even sat in on war councils that Aero summoned. They absorbed the knowledge and strategies of war. They learned to turn their weaknesses into strengths and how best to use the tools that they had at their disposal.

Enter the Shadow Realm

O NCE ON THE OTHER SIDE of the portal, Zidane, Maia, and Stratos found themselves in a land where there was very little light. The ground beneath their feet held no live vegetation. There were cracks in the dry ground where auras of shadow energy fumed and crept upward to crawl across the barren ground. The sky was dark, but a hint of light was trying to get through to the ground below. It seemed there was a veil of shadow that prevented the light of the heavens to touch the ground below.

"It's cold here," Maia shivered. Zidane took off his long coat and wrapped it around her.

"It is considerably colder here," Zidane agreed with a nod of his head.

"That is because the sun does not shine here, Red Dragon. There is no light, no warmth," Stratos said grimly as he looked off into the dark land. At that moment, a faint blue light appeared behind them and they turned to find Mesnara faintly glowing.

"Mesnara, y-you don't seem well," Maia was concerned for the Spirit.

"Do not trouble yourself, young one. My powers are not as strong here as they are in the Realm of Light. I cannot go any farther than this point with you. Once I leave you, you are on your own," Mesnara said regretfully.

"Where are Tritan and Carline, and where can we find the cure for Rosey?" Zidane was visibly anxious to get to his children.

"Both of what you seek can be found in the Shadow Fortress at the center of this Realm. It is at the center of all shadows. Be warned, my fighters, there are creatures that none of you have encountered before. You will need to work together as one. And you must be warned Zidane, the power of the Bracelet of Ra will do very little in this Realm, for there is no sun," Mesnara's aura was flickering like the fire of a candle in the breeze.

"How can we find the Shadow Fortress?" Zidane needed that answer before Mesnara faded from their presence. Aimlessly wandering about this Realm was not ideal.

"The one star that shines brightest in any realm will guide you," Mesnara looked to the black sky. Zidane, Maia, and Stratos looked up to find the North Star dimly shining through the blanket of shadow veiling the sky from light. All looked back to find that Mesnara had faded away leaving them alone in this forsaken wasteland.

"We better get a move on. I can already feel the power of the Bracelet fading," Zidane looked to the Bracelet as it faintly throbbed.

"The power of the Bracelet will fade even more as we draw closer to the Shadow Fortress and the strength of the shadows will increase," Stratos began to walk in the direction of the Fortress.

"How do you know?" Maia shivered at the thought of the of the power of the shadows becoming stronger than what it was then.

"I have been here once before," Stratos looked over his shoulder to them, then continued walking on. Zidane and Maia looked to each other, then followed Stratos

They traveled onward for miles toward the Shadow Fortress. The land grew darker the further they ventured. After several hours of traveling, they found themselves in a forest of dead trees. These trees did not grow tall, but had many branches. Not one leaf or needle grew on them. Shadow energy continued to pour from the cracks in the dry ground and hover above the ground like a thick fog.

"A-Are you sure we have to go this way?" an uneasy feeling was creeping about Maia. Her ears had flattened against her head and her tail straightened. The Necklace of Isis began to glow illuminating their surroundings.

"The Necklace is glowing. What do you see, Maia?" Zidane looked from the Necklace to her. Maia placed a hand over the Necklace to absorb the energy. She then placed her other hand to her head and closed her eyes.

"I see... nothing... the vision is clouded... dark," she seemed to strain as she was trying to focus on the vision.

"There is only one way to find out what this vision is and that is to go straight through this barren forest," Stratos drew one of the Dragon Blades then started walking toward the forest.

"Stratos, wait. We do not know what dangers are in this forest," Zidane grabbed his rival's arm.

"More dangerous than that behemoth we fought off in the mountain valley or more dangerous than Sekmet? No Red Dragon, I do not believe that there are any dangers in this forest that we Dragons or wielders of the Ancient Relics need to worry about," an arrogant grin came across the Black Dragon's face. Zidane hesitantly let go of Stratos's arm and nodded in agreement. Drawing one of his Dragon Blades, Zidane followed Stratos into the forest with Maia behind him, holding her bow and an arrow at the ready. After venturing further into the barren forest they came to a wide clearing.

"That is interesting," Zidane stated as he observed a strange rock pile at the center of the clearing.

"What is?" Maia was looking all around them.

"That rock pile. I have never seen anything like it. It looks like someone carefully placed these rocks here," Zidane stepped closer to the rock pile.

"I would not get too close, Red Dragon," Stratos began to reach for his other Dragon Blade. At that moment, Zidane's and Stratos's ears twitched, and Maia's Necklace glowed as the ground shook under their feet. Zidane leapt backwards to Maia and Stratos. The rock pile moved and rose.

"What in the heavens in that?!" Maia exclaimed aiming an arrow at the rocks while they were piling vertically on each other forming legs, then a thick broad torso and then massive arms, forearms, and

61

then thick hands. It seemed the shadows seeping from the cracks in the ground brought the creature to life.

"A rock behemoth," Stratos answered Maia as he drew his other Dragon Blade and crouched in to a defensive stance. The Rock Behemoth roared and slammed its fist into the cracked ground shaking it and leaving a small crater.

"How should we take down this monster?" Zidane drew his other Dragon Blade.

"What other way is there? Head on," Stratos lunged at the creature.

"No, wait!" Maia tried to stop him, but he was already in midair when she reached out to him. The Rock Behemoth saw Stratos's hasty attack and threw its fist at Stratos hitting him in the chest sending Stratos back to the ground next to Zidane and Maia.

"Patience does not become you, does it Stratos?" Zidane asked mockingly while keeping an eye on the Rock Behemoth.

"You are lucky I do not take your heart now, Red Dragon," Stratos shot back, rising to his feet.

"That will have to wait, Stratos. We have a certain behemoth standing before us," Zidane set his feet to ready himself to attack.

"Will you two stop?! We need to work as a team to bring this thing down!" Maia shouted while aiming an arrow at the Rock Behemoth.

"She is right," Stratos groaned.

"Shall we work together to slay a common foe once again?" Zidane asked. Stratos and Maia nodded. Then both Zidane and Stratos ran at the monster with both Dragon Blades drawn. Maia aimed and fired a rapid barrage of arrows at the head of the beast. The Rock Behemoth placed its arms in front of its head to deflect the arrows. This allowed Zidane and Stratos to draw close enough to the beast without falling victim to the massive fists. Zidane leapt to the air and gathered flames around one of his feet and gave a thunderous kick to the torso of the beast. Once Zidane landed, Stratos launched himself off of his shoulders and, with a slash from both Dragon Blades, Stratos released twin beams of lightning at the Behemoth sending it reeling backwards. Maia then leapt from the shoulders of Zidane and then launched herself even higher from the shoulders of Stratos. She took three arrows from her quiver and channeled energy from the Necklace of Isis to the heads of the arrows.

"Tri-Shot!" she shouted as she released the three charged arrows at the Behemoth. The arrows exploded as they impacted on the beast's chest. Maia landed on her feet and the three waited for the smoke to clear. They found the creature had not fallen, but was standing strong in front of them with not a crack on it.

"I do not believe it," Maia's amber eyes widened.

"How is that monster still standing?" Stratos was in disbelief as well.

"We hit that monster with everything we had," Maia drew another arrow.

"Not necessarily," Zidane said with a grin growing on his face as he looked at Stratos then Maia. They both nodded to him. Both Stratos and Zidane stood next to each other. Zidane began to gather flames in one hand and in the other hand lightning surged throughout his hand and flowed through his fingertips. Stratos conjured shadow energy in one hand and in the other he also gathered lightning. Maia took aim with three arrows and gathered energy from the Necklace and focused them into the heads of each arrow.

"Firestorm!" Zidane unleashed a spiraling fusion of flame and lightning.

"Tri-Shot!" Maia exclaimed as she released three energy charged arrows.

"Shrouded Lightning!" Stratos yelled as he unleashed streaks of shadow laced lightning from his fingertips. These three surges of attacks rushed toward the Rock Behemoth and, with a thunderous explosion, they turned the beast to a pile of pebbles and dust. Both Maia and Zidane dropped to their knees in exhaustion while Stratos stood tall.

"I think we need to take a rest," Maia was breathing heavily.

"I agree. It would seem exhausting our abilities in this realm has consequences," Zidane was bent over at the waist trying to catch his breath.

"Alright. It would seem that it has no effect on me, since I draw my powers from the shadows. I feel stronger with each passing moment," Stratos looked from the shadows creeping across the ground. The shadows seemed to be pulling toward the Black Dragon.

"Then you would not mind if you took watch while Maia and I rested," Zidane sat on the dry ground.

"No, I would not," Stratos gave a shake of his head.

"Thank you," Maia forced a smile. Stratos's eyes softened when he looked into her eyes.

While Zidane and Maia closed their eyes and rested against a tree at the edge of the clearing, Stratos stood guard and was watchful of their surroundings. He stood a ways from Zidane and Maia breathing in and absorbing the shadow energy that seeped through the cracks in the ground. He felt stronger and rejuvenated. At the same time though, he felt weak. He thought back to the time before he came to Rhydin and before he went in search for aid from the other Bearers of the Dragon Essences. He was a different person. He was much like Zidane, calm and quiet, but possessed an intense spirit and strong will. He put others before himself and did not crave power. Now, since he had taken the powers of the White, Green, and Gold Dragons, he wanted nothing more than to be the Lord of All Dragons.

"What are you thinking about?" he heard Maia's voice call to him.

"Do not trouble yourself with questions that do not concern you," he responded coldly as he slightly looked over his shoulder.

"What has happened in your life that made you so bitter and cold?" Maia asked with a growing strength in her voice. He turned to face her. She was now standing only a few feet away from him.

"You are a persistent one. Much like your precious Red Dragon there," Stratos nodded his head in Zidane's direction.

"*His* name is Zidane and I know when a good person has been tainted by the lust for power," her eyes never left his nor did she back down from him.

"That good person you believe to be there is no more. That was a long time ago," Stratos scoffed.

"No, that good person is still in there. There is just a heavy emotional burden that is weighing down upon him and it is too heavy for just one person to bear. I sense it," Maia held the Necklace in her hand and took a few steps toward him.

"I have lost everything," he finally said lowering his head and closing his eyes.

"What do you mean?" Maia asked stepping closer.

"The Kingdom I was entrusted to rule and the love of my life are gone, forever," Stratos said through his clenched teeth.

"How did that happen?" Maia was showing her sympathy for his loses through her eyes.

"After I was reborn as a result of the Ritual of Life, my former friend and fellow student of my sensei almost interrupted the Ritual before the fusion could be complete. After I emerged from that coffin, several arrows were released and hit me in the shoulder and leg. As I recovered my beloved Inca was kidnapped, and the rest of us barely escaped. There were too many Orc that rushed into that Temple. And now, she is lost to me. The powers of darkness that threatened my Rhydin took over and submerged that world into darkness. I tried repeatedly to rescue her from the clutches of the Dark Lord, but I was too weak. That was when I discovered there were other universes. I thought that since there were parallel universes, there was the possibility there would be other Dragon Essence Bearers that could come and help me. The White Dragon was the first that I came across. When I came face to face with him, he did not believe that I was him from another universe. He thought it to be a trick of the Dark Lord. I tried to convince him otherwise, but we ended up fighting. I......I ended up killing him," he looked to the ground as if in shame. "After I killed the White Dragon, I heard what I thought to be a heartbeat. It was the power of the White Dragon, the Dragon of

Lightning called to me. Something came over me. I do not know if it was the shadows within me darkening and possessing me, but I have no memory of cutting his heart out and...... devouring his powers," a tear rolled down his cheek. It wasn't because of sadness that he shed a tear, but disgust in himself realizing what he had done. Not only did he do this once, but two more times. "After that, I became obsessed with taking the powers of the other Dragon Essence Bearers and becoming the Lord of All Dragons, then returning to my world and defeating the Dark Lord on my world," he could not make eye contact with her for fear of letting the tears in his eyes stream down his face.

"So, because of this new lust for power, you hunted down fellow Bearers of the Dragon Essences to try to save the one you loved?" Maia tilted her head to the side trying to understand Stratos's rationale.

"Yes," Stratos replied with shame in his voice.

"If Inca is anything like me, she would not want you killing innocents just to save her life," Maia reached out to gently place her hand on his shoulder.

"What would she have me do then?" he finally made eye contact with her. The anger, shame, and frustration he felt shone through his eyes. Maia took a moment to conjure a response, "It is not too late to redeem yourself".

"What do you mean?" he was fighting back the tears.

"You are helping Zidane and I get our children back from this Lord of Shadows. And if we survive this battle, maybe you can go back to your Rhydin and save Inca. Maybe not alone," Maia replied looking into his pitch black eyes.

"Perhaps you are right," Stratos forced himself to grin.

The center of the Shadow Realm was the darkest region. The only light that shone through the darkness was the little light from the North Star. The shadows hung thicker in this region like a thick fog. The cracks in the dry, lifeless earth were wider and deeper in this region. More and more shadow energy crept up from these cracks and hovered above the ground causing the thick fog. Here laid the Shadow Fortress. It was a dark, massive structure surrounded by a tall, thick wall with watchtowers at each corner. Inside of these walls were four immense dome structures. Each iron gate on the walls led to these dome structures. Leading from these structures were stone enclosed corridors. All four corridors connected the dome structures to the one adjacent and another corridor leading to a menacing spire that towered over the dome structures at the center of it all. A thick aura of shadow surrounded this spire.

At the very top of the spire the twins, Carline and Tritan, were being held captive. They were locked in a rather cramped room with only a window that had bars preventing them from escaping through the window. An iron door, with a slit at the bottom for the guards to slip the twin's food through, separated them from the rest of the fortress. Ever since they had been captured, the twins had been surviving on dried, crusty bread and water each and every day. Tritan and Carline huddled together to keep each other warm since there was barely any warmth in this realm.

"How long have we been here?" Carline asked in a weak voice.

"I do not know. I have lost track of the days," Tritan clutched Carline close to him.

"Are we ever going home?" Carline whimpered.

"We have to keep hoping that Mother and Father are on their way to rescue us. I bet you they are following the North Star to find us," Tritan looked out of the only window in their cell at the North Star that dimly flickered.

"Really?" Carline sniffled.

"Yes," Tritan forced a grin.

"We have to find a way to get out of here," Carline looked to the door that kept them inside.

"Yes, but how?" Tritan looked to his sister. Carline thought for a moment.

"I think I know," she responded as she began to whisper her plot into his ear. Once they heard one of the guards passing by their cell, they began to hatch their plan.

"Tritan?! Tritan wake up! Tritan please! Someone help!" Carline cried as Tritan lied motionless in the middle of the cell. A Shadow Demon looked into the cell to see what the commotion was about. "Please help! He is not moving or breathing!" Carline pled to the Shadow Demon looking in. The Demon then opened the cell door and entered the cell to see what was wrong with Tritan. The Demon stood over Tritan cocking its head to the side and looked at him with its yellow, lidless eyes. While the Demon was fixed upon Tritan, Carline slowly rose to her feet and crept behind the unsuspecting Demon. She took a deep breath and dropped into a combat stance. Her eyes were fixed upon what would be the back of the Demon's knee and gave it a swift kick bringing the Demon down to one knee. Once Tritan saw the Demon stumble, he kipped up to his feet grabbing one of the iron plates that their dried bread was served on and swung at the head of the Demon. Even though it was stunned from the shot from Tritan, the Demon saw that Carline and Tritan were on either side of it in fighting stances. The Demon was knocked out by a side kick to the head by both Tritan and Carline on either side. The Demon fell to the ground allowing Tritan to grab the keys. They hurriedly left the cell.

After a few hours of rest, the trio of travelers continued their trek to the Shadow Fortress with their eyes fixed upon the dim North Star guiding them to Tritan and Carline. Their pace had slowed from when they first set out. The shadows were sapping the energy and strength from Maia and Zidane. They grew weaker with each passing moment.

"It would seem that we are drawing closer to the fortress. You both seem weaker than when we left the dead forest," Stratos looked over his shoulder showing the side of his face that was masked. *Thump thump..... Thump thump... Thump thump....* Stratos began to faintly hear that familiar 'thumping'.

"Why do you wear... that mask?" Maia was seemingly out of breath.

"When you, the Red Dragon, and the two others used the combined powers of the Ancient Relics, I moved out of its path in time for it to destroy Sekmet. But the wake of the surge grazed this side of my face. My healing abilities could not fully heal the wound leaving this side of my face permanently scarred," he responded while regaining his focus from the haunting thumping that called to him.

"Where have you been... all of these years?" Zidane tried to catch his breath feeling the strength in him fade.

"I first came in to knowledge of this realm when I researched the Gates of Caelum. I came to find out that any of the Ancient Relics had the ability to open a portal to this realm. Right after you destroyed Sekmet, I opened a portal here and stayed for some years to heal and gather the strength to come back and challenge you. It took me several more years to track you down while you were not in the Palace. Rhydin had changed and developed beyond my recognition," Stratos responded.

"What Ancient Relic do you have... that can open a portal to this... realm?" Zidane furrowed his eyebrows.

"The Bracelet of Mentu. Mentu is the Egyptian god of war. It possesses the power to enhance the strength, agility, speed, and durability of the bearer of this Bracelet. That is why I was able to endure that surge of energy from Sekmet and why I was able to hold him in place while you four conjured the energy you needed to vanquish him," Stratos looked to the silver Bracelet on his wrist.

"How much farther do we have... until we get to... the Shadow Fortress?" Maia asked in between labored breaths.

"It is over that hill," Stratos pointed to a high, steep hill that was nearly two hundred yards away from them.

"That hill leads to... the Shadow Fortress then?" Zidane's steps were visibly labored. Each step took more and more of his energy.

"Over that hill, but then the other side is much steeper. The Fortress stands at the bottom of the hill," Stratos responded. All took several more steps, but then Stratos stopped in his tracks as if he were struck by a thought that passed through his mind like a streak of lightning through the air.

"Why have you stopped?" Maia looked back at Stratos.

"Do not take another step," Stratos warned Zidane and Maia.

"Why?" Zidane turned back to face him.

"Look at the ground. The cracks in the ground have widened and are deeper," Stratos looked to the ground all around them.

"And what does that mean?" Maia slowly backed away from the cracks.

"This is the hazard field. This place is very volatile and dangerous," Stratos's body tensed and his breathing grew heavier.

"How is it dangerous?" Zidane looked at the field trying to see the danger in it.

"A stronger concentration of shadow energy throbs beneath this field and unexpectedly bursts in to geysers of dangerous shadow energy," *Thump thump... Thump thump... Thump thump....* Strata shook his head to regain his focus.

"Can we not just go around then?" Maia felt the Necklace of Isis glowing as if warning her of something, but she did not have the strength to channel its warning to her own mind.

"We cannot. It will take too long. This field stretches for miles either way," Stratos looked to their left and right seeing the hazard field stretch for miles. It would certainly take much more time which they did not have.

"We have no choice then. We have… to go through," Zidane straightened up trying to muster the strength to go through.

"I will go first and you follow in my footsteps," both Maia and Zidane nodded in acknowledgement of Stratos's plan. Stratos inhaled a deep breath before gingerly placing his foot on the hazard field and then placed his full weight into this first step, then waited for a reaction from the ground. Nothing happened. He then took another cautious step onto the field and again, no reaction. Stratos gained more confidence in his steps the farther he got into the field. Zidane and Maia were only a few steps behind him. The farther they got the wider and deeper the cracks in the ground grew. The thick fog of shadow energy seeping from the cracks grew thicker and hung heavier over the ground. *Thump thump.... Thump thump... Thump thump...*

Stratos had to ignore this dark urge that was relentless in pushing to the forefront of his mind. Stratos strained his eyes to see where he was leading Zidane and Maia.

"Why have we begun to slow down?" Zidane's eyes were to the ground in front of him. His focus was on the steps that Stratos took in front of him.

"This thick fog of shadow energy hovering above the ground is not allowing me to see where I am going," Stratos responded keeping his eyes to the ground. At that moment, when Stratos took a step, his ears as well as Zidane's twitched and the Necklace of Isis glowed brightly. The ground beneath their feet began to rumble and shake.

"This is not good," Maia clenched her teeth.

"No, it is not," Zidane stated trying to keep his balance.

"Run!" Stratos shouted as a geyser of shadow energy erupted directly in front of them. He leapt out of the way and ran toward the hill. This eruption caused a chain reaction of geysers to explode. The geysers began to catch up with them and explode right at their heels. Halfway to the hill, the geysers were exploding to either side of them and in front of them. They had to leap to either side or backwards to avoid the explosions of shadow energy. The Necklace of Isis glowed and a vision played in Maia's mind. She slid to a halt and conjured an aura of energy from the Necklace. She used the energy to place a barrier around a geyser that erupted directly in front of Zidane and Stratos to contain it. She struggled to keep the barrier up and contain the shadow energy. Her nose bled the more she used the power of the Necklace. The geyser subsided and Maia lowered the barrier. Her vision blurred and she began to feel a bout of severe vertigo. Her eyes glazed over and then rolled into the back of her head. She then fell to her knees and collapsed onto the dry, cracked ground.

"Maia, no!" Zidane cried out as he saw Maia fall. Zidane ran back to her to pick her up in his arms and then ran toward the hill with Stratos leading the way avoiding the geysers of exploding shadow energy. They were several yards from the foot of the hill and safety from the hazard field. Zidane and Stratos saw shadow energy beginning to build up in an immense pocket just before the foot of the hill. With more and more geysers exploding around them more frequently, they had no choice but to head toward the large pocket of gathering shadow energy. The pocket of energy exploded thunderously just as Zidane, with Maia in his arms, and Stratos leapt into the air. They narrowly landed at the foot of the hill while the geyser nearly scorched their backs. Zidane collapsed to his knees and placed Maia on the ground in front of him. He was breathing heavily and seemed to wane in energy and strength.

"Are you alright, Red Dragon?" Stratos turned his eyes to check on their condition.

"My strength...is waning... but do not... worry about me," Zidane replied in between breaths. Stratos checked for a pulse on Maia's neck.

"She will be fine. She is unconscious for the moment. She pushed her powers while exhausted. Now her body needs time to recuperate from the shock," Stratos reassured him.

"That is a... good idea. I too need... the rest," Zidane collapsed face first to the ground next to Maia.

"I hope your allies are faring better than we are, Red Dragon," Stratos sighed as he watched Zidane's glazed over eyes close. *Thump thump.... Thump thump...* Stratos felt his hand reach for his blade with a trembling hand. The yearning for power was tugging at his mind. The urge to put the Red Dragon out of his misery while in a weakened state gnawed at his very essence. With a clench of his jaw, he tightened his fist and pulled his hand away. "It must be the shadows of this region. They are strong and are affecting me," he looked down to the heavy fog of shadows that crawled across the ground all around his feet and ankles.

A Scattered Kingdom

In the Southeast Province of Rhydin, in the Realm of Light, Zell was in his chambers mulling through various parchments that were scattered on his desk. Many of these parchments were very old and very delicate. While perusing through the documents, he came across a one that immediately caught his attention. He narrowed his eyes upon the words that were written.

"Well what is this?" he asked himself. Then a knock at his chamber doors interrupted his reading. He placed the parchment back on his desk and went to answer the door. It was one of the Vampire guards dressed in a long black coat and a broad sword strapped to his hip.

"Yes, what is it?" Zell looked to the guard with impatience in his voice.

"I apologize for the interruption Lord Zell, but it is a matter of urgency," the guard answered anxiously.

"And what is this matter of urgency?" Zell let out a heavy breath.

"Our spies have spotted a pack of Orc headed our way," the guard responded.

"Send a platoon to dispose of them," Zell dismissively said and then turned to go back to his chambers.

"It is not that simple, Sir," the guard stepped further in to the chambers.

"And why isn't it?" Zell's patience was visibly growing thinner.

"These are not the same Orc we fought in the war against Sekmet. They possess the power of the Shadows," the guard answered. Zell's heart seemed to drop from his chest as the guard spoke.

"Ready the Coven. Raise the alarm. Get the women and children away from the Coven and take them to the Eastern Palace. Give Lord Aero the message that the Orcs are sweeping across the land. Send someone else to ask aid from Craven and his pack. We will need all the help we can muster," Zell's demeanor changed from impatience with the Coven Guard to a sense of great urgency to defend themselves.

"Understood, Sir," the guard bowed and hurriedly left to carry out his orders. Zell then readied himself in his chambers. He strapped on his chest plate, wrist guards, and then strapped his sword to his hip. He took his long coat from a rack while passing the desk that had the parchments he was attentively studying. He took a moment to look at the parchments and then he hurriedly took a satchel and carefully rolled each parchment and placed them inside of the satchel.

"Aero needs to see these documents," Zell muttered to himself as he packed the last of the parchments. He threw on his coat and left his chambers.

Once outside, Zell was on his horse riding around the perimeter of the Coven Mansion making sure that his soldiers were at their stations and ready. Once he was satisfied with the defenses of his Mansion, he summoned for one of his Captains.

"Yes, Lord Zell?" the Captain was at attention in front of the Vampire Lord.

"I want you to take this satchel and ride as fast as you can to the Eastern Palace and give it to Lord Aero himself. There are valuable documents in the satchel. You are to protect it with your life," Zell looked in to the eyes of the Vampire Captain to convey the importance of the satchel's contents.

"I understand, Lord Zell," the Captain nodded. The Captain took the satchel and mounted his horse, then began to ride north toward the Eastern Palace.

"The enemy is here!" one of the guards on the wall shouted pointing to the south. All eyes were to the south. They saw a dark mass marching toward them. The footsteps, the clamor of armor, and the grunts were heard by the Vampire army.

"Captain, you must go now! Lead the women and the children to the Eastern Palace! And you must tell Lord Aero of what has happened here," Zell looked back to the Captain as he was leaving. The Captain nodded and rode off as fast as his horse would take him. He met up with the caravan of horses and wagons of women, children, and adolescents as well as other soldiers as they headed north toward the Eastern Palace. Zell watched as the caravan of his Coven evacuated and made their way north. He turned to face the oncoming shadow empowered Orc army. Looking to the sky above them, he saw a blanket of dark shadows hovering above the army. This shroud of shadow was beginning to cloud the starry night sky. The shadows crept across the sky guiding the Orcs toward the Coven.

"Archers at the ready!" Zell shouted as he drew his sword. The archers aimed their cross bows and had a quiver full of arrows ready to fire upon the enemy. Zell saw the Orcs pick up their pace with their weapons ready.

"Steady!" Zell shouted raising his sword. He waited for the Orcs to get within range of their crossbows and catapults. Now the Orcs let out a battle cry unlike any other and charged at full speed toward the Mansion walls.

"Fire!" Zell shouted as he swung his sword downward. The archers fired their arrows at the front lines of the Orcs. The arrows embedded themselves in to the chests and legs of these Orcs. The Orcs did not fall much to the surprise of the Vampire army. The Orcs merely pulled out the arrows and continued their charge.

"Fire the catapults at will!" Zell looked to those that manned the war machines. They released immense boulders at the charging Orcs. Numerous boulders landed in the thick of the Orc army. The rocks landed and rolled over many Orcs and Abominations. None of the Orcs, nor the Abominations, were killed and seemed to not be scathed by the boulders. With the power of the shadows, the Orcs possessed the ability to flatten against the ground and slither across the ground much like the shadow demons. The soldiers, even Zell, became disheartened. To them, these Orcs seemed to be invincible.

Zell then looked to the north and saw the last of his Coven disappear into the northern hills. He turned back to face the charging Orc army that was bearing down upon them. His eyes narrowed and focused on them. His grip on his sword and the reins of his horse tightened. He led his horse to the frontlines of the Vampire army. All eyes of the soldiers behind him were upon him, waiting to see what his orders would be. Zell raised his sword to the air, "For Rhydin and our people!" he spurred his horse toward the Orc army. Letting out war cries, the Vampire army followed Zell on to a collision course with the Orcs. The sound of steel clashing against steel and the war cries of both armies echoed and carried for a great distance.

The Captain leading the caravan of the refugee Vampires heard this disturbing sound and turned toward the south only to see the sheet of shadows creeping over the night sky. His heart dropped to the pit of his stomach and feared the worst for the fate of Rhydin. But when he looked to the sky, he did see though a glimmer of hope. The sheet of shadows could not keep out the light of the North Star.

It was almost dawn when the caravan reached the walls of the Eastern Palace after traveling day and night in their cramped covered wagons. The gates were opened to allow the refugee Vampires into the Palace's walls and then soon into an underground shelter that helped them avoid the light from the rising sun. Aero met with them and, with the help of several Elf soldiers, made sure the needs of the Vampires were met with M' Kara and Troy by his side.

M' Kara went to check on the rest of her Coven.

"What is your name?" Aero asked the Captain stepping toward him.

"Damien, Captain Damien," he answered seemingly shaken up.

"What happened?" Aero placed his hand on Damien's shoulder to calm him.

"They came," he responded looking to the ground.

"Gather yourself, Captain. You have to be an example for your people," Damien nodded at Aero's words and gathered his wits. "Now tell me exactly what occurred," Aero looked into his eyes sensing his distress.

"The Army of Shadow Orc and Abominations marched upon the walls of our Mansion. Arrows from our crossbows did not harm them nor did the boulders launched from our catapults crush them. They continued their charged upon our front lines and did not stop," Captain Damien responded. Aero's hand fell from Damien's shoulder with a look of disbelief on his face.

"What is the matter, Father?" Troy took notice of the troubled look on his father's face.

"I thought we had more time before they began their invasion. We have to make haste and ready the defenses. Captain Damien, I know you and your people have had a long journey, but when the sun sets you have to lead your people, along with the villagers of this Province, through the woods and to the Western Palace," Aero's voice was stern to stress the importance of his plan to protect the Vampire people.

"I understand, Lord Aero. Lord Zell wanted me to give these documents to you. He said they were of the utmost importance," Damien reached into his satchel and pulled out the parchments to give to Aero. Aero took them and began to read them. His eyes widened in shock.

"W-Where did you get these?" Aero looked from the documents to Captain Damien.

"Lord Zell was reading them in his chambers. I assume they came from his personal library," Damien responded.

"What are those, Father?" Troy tried to stand on his toes to see. At that moment, M' Kara walked over to them.

"Where is my grandfather?" she asked with sorrowful eyes. Aero knelt down to her and looked into her misty blue eyes.

"He stayed behind to defend the Mansion and give time for the rest of your Coven to escape," Aero gave a deep sigh.

"Is he going to meet us here or at the Palace?" Aero looked to

Damien at M' Kara's question, but he averted his eyes as if there was no hope.

"Pray that he does," Aero said in a calm voice. Tears rolled down M' Kara's cheeks. Aero gave a hug to M' Kara to comfort her.

"Captain Damien, give a message to Captain Demus to lead a scouting party to find out all they can about this army. Also, tell Captain Aldar to begin with the evacuation of those who are not soldiers from the Palace and the neighboring villages in this Province," Aero said still holding M' Kara. Captain Damien nodded and went through a hatch to enter the Palace. Troy felt the pain M' Kara had in her heart. Her mother was deathly sick, her father was not around, and her grandfather was in battle with the Shadow Orc and Abominations, possibly dead by now. This was a turbulent, emotional time for her.

The day quickly passed and dusk was upon Rhydin, and the palace was nearly empty. There was no life within the stone halls. No sound emitted from any of the rooms. It was deserted and nearly everyone was on their way to the Western Palace, except for M' Kara. She stood on a balcony facing the south where her Coven was. She watched the hills hoping that her grandfather would appear at the top of one of those hills. Tears did not stop flowing from her eyes since the arrival of the members of her Coven. Troy and his mother, Melina, walked into the room to find her staring off toward the hills.

"M' Kara, it is time to go," Melina called to her in a soft voice.

"I don't want to go," M' Kara sniffled.

"Why? You have to," Troy chimed in.

"My grandfather will be here. You will see," she began to sob.

"M' Kara dear, it will be unsafe for you to stay here. I am sure your grandfather will know to meet us at the Western Palace," Melina walked toward her and wiped away her tears. M' Kara forced a grin and nodded.

As Melina, Troy, M' Kara and others loaded some of their belongings into a wagon preparing to leave, Aero met them. He gave a farewell hug to Troy and M' Kara and then a warm embrace and a kiss to his wife.

"Please be careful and come back to us," Melina looked into his eyes.

"I will," confidence was in his eyes, "I need you to do something".

"What is it?" Melina looked to him as he had rolled parchments in his hand.

"I need you to take these documents to the Western Palace to keep them safe and hidden. These documents are of the utmost importance. They hold the key to Rhydin's most treasured secrets," Aero's gaze stressed how important it was to safeguard them.

"I promise I will," she took the delicate parchments in her hands. They gave each other one last kiss and then Aero turned back to the Palace to prepare for the coming battle. Melina, M' Kara, and Troy watched him return to the Palace before embarking on the travel to the Western Palace with the last of the civilians of the Province.

It was well into the night when the last of the caravan reached the center of the Woodland Realm. All were asleep, except for M' Kara. The thought of her grandfather still out there kept her awake and her mind racing. She constantly peered out of the back of the wagon to see if she saw a glimpse of her grandfather behind them. She saw nothing. She looked back to the people who were all asleep in the wagon and then back to the woods behind them. She bit her lip and then rose from her spot. She prepared to jump out of the wagon when she felt a pull at her ankle. She looked back to find Troy grasping at her ankle.

"What are you doing?" he whispered.

"My grandfather is still out there and I have to find him. I am going back to the Eastern Palace," she tried to jump out again, but Troy held her back.

"Are you mad? It is dangerous back there," Troy's voice raised a bit hearing what M' Kara was planning to do.

"What would you do if it were your mother?" M' Kara asked looking past Troy to Melina. Troy looked from M' Kara back to his mother who slept peacefully. He let out a sigh, "I would be jumping out as well," he released her ankle.

"I know," she turned to jump.

"I am coming with you. You will need help," Troy said as he carefully rose from his spot being careful not to wake anyone. M' Kara nodded and then they both jumped from the wagon and landed in a bush.

"Where do we go from here?" Troy asked as they placed the hoods of their cloaks over their heads.

"Follow me," Troy followed her north farther into the woods.

"Where are we going?" Troy asked as they reached a clearing.

"You'll see," M' Kara grinned.

At the middle of the clearing, an inn stood. They walked toward it and in front of the door was a wooden slab that read, '*Welcome to the Red Dragon Inn*'. M' Kara pulled on the iron dragon head door handle opening the wooden door. She led Troy in and found the inn was nearly vacant. Only a few patrons were lounging in the chairs near the fireplace and some were seated at the bar counter drinking. M' Kara led Troy to the bar counter. The bartender looked over the counter.

"Aren't ya two a bit young to be in here?" the Barkeeper scratched his scraggly, dark beard.

"My mother use to work here," M' Kara said from underneath her hood.

"And who might that be, Lass?" the man further asked as he crossed his arms in front of his chest.

"Her name is Rosey," M' Kara answered. The eyes of the man widened then lowered his head to see the young vampire's face.

"Oh, Lady M' Kara. I'm sorry, I didn't recognize ya. You've grown up so," the man said as he lifted a part of the bar counter to let them pass.

"That is alright," she said with a slight grin.

"Who is your friend?" the man looked to her traveling companion.

"I am Troy, son of Lord Aero," Troy responded in a somewhat mature voice.

"My liege, please forgive my ignorance," the man said with a slight bow.

"You are forgiven," Troy said with a smile on his face.

"What can I do for ya two?" the man folded his hands in front of him looking at the two youngsters.

"My mother told me there was a passage that leads from here to the other Palaces. We wish to go to the Eastern Palace," M' Kara looked to the man from underneath her hood.

"But Lass, have you not heard? Those dark Orcs and Abominations are roamin' these lands. It's too dangerous for ya," concern was in his voice.

"That is why I am also asking you to show us where my mother kept the Shadow Shinobi armory," M' Kara said in a hushed tone. The man hesitated to tell them. He looked from M' Kara to Troy.

"Are you going to show us where it is, or would you rather us cause a ruckus? It would make you look bad as a barkeeper that two children even came into this establishment while you were here," Troy threatened narrowing his eyes upon the man.

"Alright, alright, follow me," the man finally said. The man led them into a medium sized room in the back. There were shelves stocked with various brands of brandy, ale, wine and beer. The man walked to the far end of the room and pulled on a lever that was set behind one of the shelves. One of the shelves on the wall to his right slid open. The man led M' Kara and Troy down the dimly lit stairway. The air was dusty and stale. Cobwebs lined the ceiling and walls. Their footsteps echoed faintly from the cobble stone lined stairs. This staircase led to a larger square room. On one side of the room, the wall was lined with weapons such as katana, kunai, sai, shuriken, daggers, arrows, bows, rope, and bead-like orbs. The opposite wall was lined with racks of dark body suits, masks, light wrist gauntlets, shin guards, and light chest plates. M' Kara and Troy stood in awe of the various weapons that were laid before them. Something had caught the eye of M' Kara. Her eyes were fixed upon the weapon as she walked to the wall. Her gaze was upon a metal ring shaped weapon.

"Sir, what is this?" M' Kara asked without removing her eyes from the weapon.

"That, Lass, is a chakram. It is a most useful weapon in the hands of a skilled Shinobi. It can ricochet off of many walls of any surface with a single throw. This chakram is extremely special because at the handle in the middle there, it splits into two half moon blades," the man responded.

"How do you know so much about these weapons?" Troy tilted his head to the side. The man looked from M' Kara to Troy and then disappeared into a cloud of shadow and then reappeared on the other side of the room. He then disappeared and then reappeared in the same manner in front of them.

"You are a Shinobi of the Shadow," M' Kara smiled with widened eyes.

"Aye, I use to be many years ago and many pounds ago," he patted his rounded belly as they all laughed.

"So you worked alongside my mother?" M' Kara asked.

"Aye. I was the one who took her in when she came from Earth. That's why she trusted me to watch this Inn and the weapons that are hidden underneath," he said.

"You never told us your name, Sir," Troy just now realized the fact.

"Oh, please forgive me young master. My name is Duncan," he gave a slight bow.

"Do you mind if I take this?" M' Kara pointed to the chakram.

"I suppose you can, but I suggest that you also take the glove that goes with it," Duncan took the glove off of the rack.

"Why do I need the glove?" M' Kara narrowed her eyes on to the glove.

"The edges of the chakram are extremely sharp and if you try to catch it with your bare hand, it will give a nasty cut," Duncan shook his head at the thought of having the young girl severely cut by the weapon.

"But wouldn't the edge cut through the glove?" Troy walked to them to get a look at this glove.

"The inside of this leather glove is lined with mythril which is almost as hard as dragon scales and is as flexible as cloth," Duncan showed the inside of the glove to them both.

"May I?" M' Kara held out her hand to receive the glove.

"Certainly," Duncan handed it to her so she could slip it on her right hand.

"It's a bit big," she laughed lightly.

"You will grow into it," Duncan nodded.

"Can I take these?" Duncan turned to find Troy holding a belt of shuriken.

"Do you know how to use them, young master?" Duncan walked toward him.

"Yes, you just throw them," Troy gave a shrug of his shoulders as if it were an easy task.

"No Lad, you don't just *throw* these. There are many techniques that one uses to throw these simple looking weapons. And if ya want to master these weapons, then you will need to learn how to feel the movement of the wind around ya and use the current to choose the path of this weapon," he took one of the shuriken into his fingers.

"When this is over, will you teach me?" Troy asked humbly.

"It will be an honor my Prince. But, I will allow you to take them for now. It is best to learn to be somewhat comfortable with them in your hands," Duncan said.

"Thank you," Troy wrapped the belt of shuriken around his waist, but then the belt fell to the ground around his ankles.

"It would seem it is a bit big for me," Troy held a sheepish expression. Duncan then walked over to the weapons rack and took a smaller belt. Troy took the belt and put it on. Duncan stood back and saw two little warriors stand before him.

"You both need to be careful. You have the element of surprise, use it to your advantage," Duncan said just before he led them to the tunnel. Troy and M' Kara both took satchels from the rack against the wall and slung them over their shoulders.

"Where does this tunnel lead?" Troy asked.

"This tunnel will lead us to just under two miles within the town of Belnar. We will make our way to the palace from there," M' Kara looked back to him.

"Your mother has taught you well," Duncan said.

"Yes, she did," she said as she started on her way down the tunnel with Troy behind her.

In the meantime, the front lines and battle formations of the Elf Army had been set. They stood poised ready for battle. Their eyes attentively watched the south for the Shadow Orc Army. Tension was in the air. Stories of these creatures withstanding a barrage of arrows and enduring the crushing weight of hurled boulders from catapults were still on their minds. Anxiety struck their hearts. They were unsure of themselves. They did not know if they would be able to defeat this army.

"The scout party is back," a soldier shouted back to Aero. Aero looked and saw a single soldier riding back on his horse. The Elf soldiers looked to each other to find only a single scout returning. He rode past the frontlines to where Aero was stationed. Aero dismounted and helped the scout from his horse seeing that he was severely wounded. Another soldier helped Aero lower him to the ground. Blood trickled from the soldier's mouth and there was a deep puncture wound in the soldier's stomach.

"Soldier, what happened? Where are the other Scouts and Captain Demus?" Aero knelt beside the injured soldier.

"We were... discovered, Lord Aero. We fought... but they...were too... strong. I barely... escaped," the scout spat blood.

"What happened to the Vampire Mansion?" Aero's voice was distressed. The Kingdom was starting to crumble at the hands of remnant soldiers from Sekmet's reign in the southwest.

"They have enveloped... that region... of Rhydin... in shadow," the scout responded in between gasps of air.

"Soldier, take this man as far away from the battlefield as possible. Get his wounds healed immediately," Aero turned to one of the soldiers. The soldier nodded and hoisted the wounded scout onto a horse and then they rode off toward the woods. As Aero rose, his fist was clenched and shaking. His head turned toward the south. His eyes narrowed and focused. Anger swelled within him as the shadows were approaching.

The sun set behind the Western Mountains and night covered Rhydin. The night sky was even darker than the previous night. The shadows began to envelope Rhydin as the Shadow Orc and Abominations ravaged the land. Bit by bit the Shadow Army was overthrowing the rule of the Krystal Kingdom. After each conquest, the Shadow Lord was merging the Shadow Realm with the overthrown regions of Rhydin. Toward the south, a dark mass was marching toward them. The Shadow Army was massive. The darkness from the shadow energy seeping from their skin could be seen for miles.

"The enemy is here!" Captain Aldar's voice carried to the Elf soldiers on the front lines.

"Ready the catapults!" at Aero's orders, capsules were loaded and readied to launch at the oncoming Shadow Army. The clamor of their armor and weapons was heard by the Elf Army and it rattled their nerves.

"Steady troops!" Captain Aldar shouted. The Shadow Army drew close to within two hundred yards of the Elf frontlines.

"Fire the catapults!" Aero shouted. Each of the catapults released the large, clay capsules at the frontlines of the Shadow Orc Army. The capsules burst upon the enemy frontlines splattering a dark, oozing substance on them.

"Argh! What is this?!" the Orc Leader looked about him as the dark substance clung to his rough skin. Aero gave a grin as more of the capsules were being released and splattered further among the ranks of the Shadow Orcs and Abominations. The Shadow troops were stopped in their march stunned and confused looking at the thick liquid substance that clung to their skin and armor.

"Release arrows!" Aero ordered. The ranks of archers readied their arrows and aimed. The tips of the arrows were engulfed in fire. A barrage of fire arrows was released and showered upon the Shadow troops. The eyes of the Shadow Orcs and Abominations widened in shock realizing what the thick black substance was that clung to them. Once the flames of the arrows landed upon the ranks of Shadow Army, they immediately burst into flames. The thick black substance that was held in the capsules was oil. The fire from the arrows spread among the Shadow troops like a wildfire through a forest of dry deadwood. The confidence and morale of the Elf Army began to rise tremendously as they saw the Shadow Orcs and Abominations scatter trying to extinguish the flames that ravaged their shadow covered bodies.

"Load the catapults with boulders!" Aero pointed to those soldiers who manned the catapult, "Archers continue to rain fire upon them. Fire at will!" Aero did not want the assault to stop. The Elf archers continued to release fire arrows into the ranks of the Shadow Army. Boulders began to rain down upon and crush the Shadow Orcs and Abominations. "Shield Guard, slow march forward!" Aero pointed his sword toward the lines of the enemy. The four lines of Elf troops carrying tower shields and spears began their unison march upon the frontlines of the Shadow Army. When the Shield Guard drew within one hundred yards, Aero spotted a dark mass in the sky above them.

"Winged Demons!" an Elf soldier shouted. These shadow empowered Winged Demons were poised and ready to swoop down upon the Shield Guard.

"Archers, concentrate your fire on the Winged Demons!" Aero pointed to the sky. The archers on the walls and on the ground turned their attention up to the Winged Demons above.

"They are weak at the necks!" Captain Aldar shouted before the archers released their arrows. Arrows flew up into the air. Many pierced the necks of the Winged Demons which only enraged the survivors. The Winged Demons swooped down upon the archers who were set on the palace wall. They clawed at the archers while others lifted the Elven archers into the air and then dropped them to the ground. While the Elf Archers were being attacked by the Winged Demons, the frontlines of the Elf Army was being charged upon by shadow empowered Abominations. They charged from the inner ranks of the Shadow Army. They crashed upon the tower shields scattering many of the Shield Guard. Many Elf guards were thrown back by the sheer power of the Shadow Abominations. The Shield Guard protected themselves from the bludgeoning blows of the Abominations by taking cover behind their tower shields and, using their spears, they jabbed at the chests and necks of the Shadow Abominations. The frontlines of the Elf Army were failing. The Shadow Orcs, who were set ablaze, were now beginning to gather themselves. The shadow energy that engulfed their bodies slowly extinguished the flames. The volley of oil capsules and fire tipped arrows only delayed these Shadow Orcs from crashing through the now weakened frontlines of the Elf Army. The number of archers on the palace walls dwindled as a result from the continuing onslaught from the Shadow Winged Demons. Aero and Aldar looked to each other and then drew their weapons.

"Captain Aldar, sound the charge," Aero ordered as his eyes narrowed and the grip on his sword tightened. Aldar inhaled a deep breath and blew into a conically shaped horn. The low, bellowing sound that emitted from the horn signaled for the rest of the ground troops of the Elf Army to charge upon the Shadow Army. Aero and Aldar rode side by side with the rest of the Elf Army close behind them. Aero rode past an Abomination and slashed at its knees bringing it down and then Aldar slashed at its neck severing the head from the rest of the body.

"Remember, these beasts are weak at the neck!" Aero yelled as he turned his horse to face the other Elf troops behind him.

"Lord Aero!" Aldar cried out trying to warn Aero. Aero turned to find an Abomination behind him with its arm shaped like a club ready to attack. Aero kicked off his horse in time for him and his horse to dodge the clubbing blow. In mid-air, Aero spun and slashed at the knee of the Abomination. When the Abomination was brought down to its knee, Aero spun and slashed at its neck splattering shadow energy. Once the Abomination was dead, Aero turned to observe the carnage around him. The Elf Army was being annihilated. Only a handful of corpses of the Shadow empowered Orcs, Abominations, and Winged Demons laid at the feet of the Elf soldiers but many bodies of Elf soldiers fell to the blows and slashes of the Shadow Army. A wave of Shadow Abominations was charging at the remaining Elf troops.

"Captain Aldar, sound the retreat! We are falling back to the Western Palace! We cannot win this battle!" Aldar reluctantly took the horn and sounded the retreat at Aero's order. The remaining Elf troops retreated west toward the woods. To buy them some time, Aero gathered energy into the steel of his blade. He then cut the air with his sword sending a beam of energy from the sword at the swooping Winged Demons. They fell to the ground, some on top of charging Orcs and Abominations. Aero again gathered energy into the steel of his blade. He then thrust the point of his sword into the ground. A surge of energy rushed into the ground and an explosive wave of energy surged through the ground toward the Shadow Troops. The explosions sent the Orcs and Abominations into the air. Aero whistled for his horse. His horse galloped to his side and, without stopping, Aero swung himself onto its back. While riding toward the woods, Aero took a quick glance to the Eastern Palace as it was being overrun by the Shadow Army.

All were gathered within the walls of the Western Palace. Tents were set for the villagers and other refugees who were evacuated from the regions of Rhydin overrun by the Shadow Army. Aero and the rest of the Elf Army rode through the gate of the Western Palace. The civilians gathered around the returning troops to find only half had survived. Melina, who tended to the needs of the refugees, made her way through the gathering crowd to meet her husband. She rushed to him and gave an embrace, relieved to find that he survived the battle.

"Not many returned from the battle," she looked about those soldiers that did return.

"This battle cost us many of our Elf Troop lives. The Shadow Army is near invincible. I thought we had an opportunity to stop their rampage across our lands. We know their weakness, but there were too many of them and so few of us. The Kingdom is split," Aero said with his head lowered. Melina brought him closer to comfort him. Aero's eyes widened as if a sudden jolt had streaked across his mind. He then looked into Melina's eyes to find a deep hurt and sorrow.

"What is the matter?" Aero placed his hands on her shoulders. Tears began to form and stream down her cheeks, "M' Kara and Troy are not here," she forced from her lips.

"W-What?! Where are they?" Aero's eyes widened and his grip tightened on her shoulders.

"All of us were asleep in the wagon while passing through the woods and when I awoke, they were not there," she buried her face in his chest crying. Aero held her tightly.

"Where could they have gone?" Aero asked under his breath.

"Lord Aero," Aldar called to him.

"Yes, Captain?" Aero's eyes went to the Elf Captain.

"Perhaps Master Troy and Lady M' Kara found a way to slip back into the Eastern Palace. Lady M' Kara did want to wait for her Grandfather," Aldar looked from Melina to Aero.

"We must do something," Melina tightened her grasp on Aero's armor as if pleading with him.

"I know. We will think of something," Aero kissed her on the forehead.

"Sir, there have been whispers of a underground passageways that run to the Eastern Palace. If Master Troy and Lady M' Kara took those tunnels, they should be exiting them at any moment now," grim was Aldar's voice.

"May the Heavens be with them," Aero looked to the darkened sky.

Outside the deserted town of Belnar, a trap door in the ground opened. M' Kara and Troy emerged from the underground tunnels to find the region now darkened with shadow. The air was cool for that time of the year.

"What happened here?" Troy's eyes widened at the dismal sight of the region.

"The Shadows," M' Kara responded flatly. Staying low and silent, the Elf Prince and Vampire Princess made their way toward the Eastern Palace. No presence of the Shadow Orc Army was seen on their way there. Despite not seeing any of the enemy, they were still careful for fear of being discovered by any of the Shadow Army's agents. When they arrived, they stopped and leaned their backs against the outer wall.

"Where do we go from here?" M' Kara looked to her friend.

"There is a trap door that leads to the stables," Troy turned to head in that direction.

At the corner of the wall, Troy leaned down and pulled on the handle to the trap door. It was a dirt tunnel that was dug under the wall of the Palace leading to the stables. No stone or brick lined the walls. There was a torch every twenty feet that dimly lit the tunnel. This tunnel led to a dirt wall where there was a ladder that led up to the surface. Troy was the first to climb to the surface. With one hand, he opened the trap door cautiously as to not allow for it to make any noise. In the other hand, he had two shuriken ready to throw. M' Kara was behind him with the chakram in hand.

"It is safe," Troy looked back to M' Kara. They entered the stables to find it abandoned. M' Kara peered down the hall from the doorway of the stables and found no one. The hallway was dark and uninviting. They cautiously made their way down the hall staying close to the wall. One could barely see ten feet in front of them because of the thick shadow.

"It is good I have my father's night vision and not my mother's," M' Kara whispered. They continued their covert adventure through the shadow enveloped Eastern Palace. At each corner they peered around to see if any of the Shadow Troops were patrolling; so far they saw none.

"There is my father's armory," Troy whispered pointing to the door at the end of one of the hallways. M' Kara followed Troy down the hall to the wooden door. "It is too heavy," Troy tried to open it himself. M' Kara stepped up and helped him pull it. The door creaked and it echoed in the hall. They both stopped and stood motionless. They looked behind them to see if any Shadow troops heard the creaking of the door and were headed in their direction. They heard no movement in the halls and quietly entered the armory. They breathed a sigh of relief once they were inside of the room.

"That was too close," Troy breathed a sigh of relief.

"It's a little dark in here," M' Kara squinted despite having better vision at night.

"I am sorry, I left my flint and steel on the wagon," Troy said sarcastically. M' Kara gave a harsh elbow to Troy's side. They searched the room for a torch. Troy found one and M' Kara took out her flint and steel and scraped them together to create sparks. The torch was lit and gave them some light in the almost pitch black room. They saw all of the rare weapons Aero collected. Weapons were in glass cases, and on racks, while suits of armor hung against the wall. A book on a pedestal caught the eye of M' Kara. She walked over to the far side of the room and stood before it.

"M' Kara, what is it?" Troy watched as she took the book in her hands.

"It looks like a book of spells. Ancient spells," she responded flipping through the pages. At that moment, they felt the floor shake. They stood motionless trying to hear where it was coming from.

"Footsteps?" M' Kara asked. Troy nodded. They began to breathe heavily. From fear of being discovered, tension struck their limbs not wanting to move a muscle. Finally, Troy mustered up the courage to put out the torch and M' Kara put the ancient spells book in her satchel. Troy took shuriken in both of his hands and M' Kara had the chakram ready. The footsteps drew closer causing the floor shake more. The grip on their weapons became tight and tense. Their hands shook with fear coursing throughout their bodies. The footsteps stopped at the door. They heard the heavy grunts of whatever was at the door. They felt their hearts pounding rapidly in their chests. There was a hush, M' Kara and Troy stood motionless and silent, near holding their breaths. The Shadow soldier stood at the door, listening for any signs of intruders. Hearing nothing the Shadow soldier left and walked down the hall. Troy and M' Kara let out their breaths to ease the rigidness in their bodies and lowered their weapons.

"That was really close," Troy looked to M' Kara while his ear was still listening for approaching enemies.

"Yes it was," M' Kara nodded.

"We need to leave," Troy put the shuriken back on the belt.

"No we can't. I need to find my grandfather," M' Kara protested.

"He will not be here. If he was here, I think we would have seen him," Troy took her by the wrists. M' Kara's eyes began to tear up, then dropped to her knees. Troy sat next to her and wrapped his arm around her. "It will be alright. If the Shadow Army got to him, he is in a better place and is watching over us right now. We were lucky to get into this Palace without being seen. I think Lord Zell was with us," Troy said in attempts to ease her inner pain. M' Kara looked from the floor to Troy and nodded. They both slowly rose to their feet and quietly made their way to the door. They slowly opened the heavy wooden door and then Troy peered his head out to see if there were any guards lurking about. Troy led M' Kara down the hall once they were satisfied it was safe. They quickly and quietly made their way through the maze of dark stone hallways. To them it seemed that there were more guards patrolling the halls than when they first entered the Palace. They were forced to hide behind pillars, in dark corners, and under tables.

"There seem to be more guards now," Troy whispered.

"Yes, we need to be extra careful," M' Kara whispered back.

"Easily done," Troy turned a corner only to bump into something broad and massive. Troy was stopped in his tracks and M' Kara was close behind. The massive Shadow soldier turned with its eyes glowing yellow.

"I-It's a....," M' Kara stammered.

"S-Shadow Ab-bomination," Troy finished her thought also stammering. Troy and M' Kara quickly jumped backwards without taking their eyes off of their enemy. The Shadow Abomination tightened its fist and took several steps toward the ant-like children in front of him.

"W-What do we do?!" M' Kara's hands trembled looking at the beast. Troy looked around. The hall became more narrow the farther they went back.

"Ready your chakram, and follow my lead," Troy whispered. A confused look came on M' Kara's face then she looked to her surroundings and then gave a nervous nod. She took the chakram from her belt and held it tightly. Troy took several shuriken from his belt and held them between each finger. The Shadow Abomination continued to stalk the two small children. Troy dashed at the Abomination with a sudden burst of speed. The Abomination gave a low growl and stood its ground. Troy veered to the wall and leapt toward it. With one foot he launched himself at his enemy. The Abomination was ready to swat Troy out of the air like a fly, but his knees buckled under him. While Troy was distracting the Abomination, M' Kara charged at it head on. With the chakram separated into half moon blades, she slid under the Abomination's legs and slashed at his knees. While the Abomination toppled, with a snap of his wrists, Troy threw the shuriken which embedded themselves in the head and neck of the Abomination. With a dull *thud*, the Abomination fell to the stone floor of the darkened hall.

"That was easy," Troy said with a triumphant smirk. M' Kara said nothing but shook her head. They left their fallen foe and continued on their way out of the Palace.

"We need to get out of here. Someone will see that Abomination and know someone is in the Palace," M' Kara said while they hurriedly made their way through the halls.

"Wait. I hear something," Troy stopped in his tracks and listened.

"What is it?" M' Kara stopped as well looking to her friend.

"It is not clear, but someone who seems to be the leader is giving orders," he responded trying to listen to where it was coming from.

"We need to get out of here," M' Kara attempted to pull him by his arm.

"Do you not want to get information on the enemy? Is that not what my father taught us? 'Know the strengths and weaknesses of your enemy in battle and use them to your advantage'," Troy reminded her of one of the strategy lessons given to them by Aero. M' Kara released her hold on his arm and nodded.

"Where is it coming from?" M' Kara reluctantly asked.

"It sounds like the Palace War Room," Troy concentrated on the origin of the voices. Troy followed the sound of the voices down a few dark hallways.

"You have good hearing," M' Kara calmly commented.

"Thank you," Troy smiled.

"If that is the fact, then why can you never hear when your mother says to take care of your chores," she said with a smirk.

"Hush," Troy said sharply. They came to a large wooden door with the Family Crest hanging above it. Troy gazed at it for a moment and, in his forefinger and thumb, held the crystal that hung around his neck. M' Kara put her ear to the door to listen for the voices. Troy did the same and they heard several voices in the room.

"That has to be the leader," M' Kara whispered.

"I think you are right," Troy whispered back.

"How can we see if it is him?" M' Kara asked in a hushed voice. Troy looked around and saw the window behind her. He walked to it and opened it. There was a narrow ledge that led to the window of the War Room. Troy turned and gave a smile to M' Kara.

"No," M' Kara refused with a shake her head.

"What? Are you afraid? Come on," Troy said as he stepped out onto the ledge and carefully walked across with his back to the wall. M' Kara hesitated for a few moments, then decided to step onto the narrow ledge. She looked down and gave a little yelp seeing how high up they were. Troy whipped his head to her and made a motion for her to keep quiet.

"Don't look down, don't look down, don't look down," M' Kara chanted to herself as she followed Troy across the ledge. Troy came to the window of the War Room. He peered in and then quickly withdrew.

"What did you see?" M' Kara focused her eyes on Troy.

"A very large Orc, an Abomination, a Winged Demon, and I think the leader," Troy then crouched down and walked under the window to the other side so M' Kara could see. She carefully walked to the window and quickly poked her head in. She nodded her head to Troy in agreement with him. Both peered inside to see and to listen to them.

"The Merger of the Shadow Realm and Rhydin will be complete. We only have a few more regions of Rhydin to conquer," the Shadow Lord was pacing about the room.

"The Merger?" Troy whispered. M' Kara shrugged her shoulders and they both continued to listen.

"The Winged Demons will fly to the Northern Mountains and destroy the Earth Shinobi villages. The Abominations will sweep through the Woodland Realm and when there, overrun the Keshnarian Ruins. No one will escape through the Gate of Caelum. The Orcs will be with me. We will take the Western Palace and destroy the last of the Elf Empire. My revenge on this Realm and Zidane is almost complete," The Shadow Lord gave a maniacal laugh.

"What does this fiend have against Uncle Zidane?" Troy whispered to M' Kara.

"I don't know," she answered with a shrug of her shoulders.

"Argh! Pull the curtains on those windows! I hate that cursed North Star! Too much light!" the Shadow Lord exclaimed.

"He doesn't like light," M' Kara and Troy said in unison. At that moment, M' Kara's foot slipped and a loud gasp escaped her lips. The Shadow Lord and the rest of his Generals whipped their heads to the window and saw Troy and M' Kara peering through the window.

"Uh oh," Troy uttered with widened eyes.

"Um, hi," M' Kara sheepishly waved to them.

"Get them!" the Shadow Lord shouted with his eyes glowing yellow, the shadow energy around him furiously grew. The Generals rushed to the window to grab them. Troy looked down below them and saw a tree.

"Jump!" Troy shouted as he leapt from the ledge down. M' Kara looked back through the window and saw them closing in and then she finally jumped before her cloak was grabbed. They safely landed in the top branches. They both looked up and saw the Winged Demon fly from the window heading down to them.

"Down!" Troy shouted. With great quickness and agility, M' Kara and Troy leapt from tree branch to tree branch going downwards. Once they landed on the ground, they saw the Winged Demon almost upon them. They ran toward the front gate as quickly as they could. Troy looked back and saw that the Winged Demon was only a few yards behind them. He took a couple shuriken from his belt and whipped around to throw them at the Winged Demon. The shuriken embedded themselves into its wings and it dropped to the ground. They continued to the front gates. From each door, they saw Orcs rush out giving chase.

"We are in big trouble!" Troy grit his teeth as he was trying to will his legs to move faster.

"Keep running," M' Kara shouted back.

"That is not good!" Troy pointed to the main gate as they saw it closing. They quickened their pace and as the gate was about to close, both dove through the narrow opening and landed on the other side rolling.

"We made it!" M' Kara shouted triumphantly.

"Open the gate!" a voice shouted from the other side. The gates slowly began to reopen. Troy and M' Kara saw a small platoon of Orcs approaching the gate.

"We spoke to soon," Troy said as they turned to run toward the forest. Up and down the hills they ran from the angered Shadow Orcs.

As they almost reached the edge of the forest, something suddenly jerked M' Kara back.

"Troy!" M' Kara yelled. Troy slid to a halt then turned to find a spear had been thrown and pinned her cloak to the ground. He ran back and tried to take the spear out from the ground but it was too far in and he did not possess the strength to pull it out. He saw the Shadow Orc closing in. He took a few shuriken in his fingers and whipped his wrist throwing them. They embedded themselves in to the legs of the Orc Leader. The Orc Leader merely looked at the shuriken in his leg and then to Troy who stood between him and M' Kara. The Orc Leader took the shuriken out and tossed them aside. It then gave a thunderous roar at Troy and M' Kara. The Orc Leader raised its great sword to bring down upon Troy. In mid-swing, a loud neigh was heard. The Orc Leader and the other Orcs turned to find a flame engulfed horse charging toward them. The horse charged through and trampled over them. M' Kara gave a strong tug on her cloak ripping it free from the spear.

"It's Sundancer, Lord Zidane's horse!" M' Kara rejoiced. Troy and M' Kara leapt on to Sundancer's back and he rode off into the woods.

"It appears we are in the clear. Thank you, Sundancer," Troy leaned forward to say in the horse's ear. M' Kara then looked back and saw Winged Demons weaving through the dense forest.

"You spoke too soon, Troy. We have Winged Demons after us!" M' Kara shouted.

"When will they rest?!" Troy looked back as well. Sundancer quickened his pace trying to outrun and out maneuver the Winged Demons. Sundancer veered left and right, weaved in between trees, galloped under low branches and leapt over dead trees all in attempts to be rid of the Winged Demons. All attempts were to no avail. The Winged Demons were quite nimble flyers and were able to keep up with Sundancer. One of the Demons flew beside them and then maneuvered to be in front of Sundancer. The Demon swiped at Sundancer's legs tripping him. M'Kara and Troy were thrown to the ground. They slowly rose to see the Demons hover over Sundancer as he rose to a vertical base and began kick his hind legs at the Demons.

"Get away from him!" Troy shouted as he took several shuriken and threw them at the Demons. The shuriken hit the Demons in the arms and legs. A few of the Demons withdrew from attacking Sundancer and flew toward the children. Troy and M'Kara stood together with weapons ready to fend off the Winged Demons. When the Winged Demons began to bear down upon them a chilling, haunting howl was heard. The Winged Demons stopped and looked around. Seeing nothing they continued their attack on the two children, but then another haunting howl was heard and then a huge, dark figure tackled one of the Demons from the air and once on the ground it ripped at its neck. It was a huge wolf that saved M'Kara and Troy. The wolf stood on its hind legs. Around its neck was a gray crystal attached to a gold chain.

"Craven?!" M'Kara took a step toward the Wolf ally.

"I will protect you Vampire Princess and Elf Prince," Craven growled. Craven then gave a howl that echoed throughout the woods signaling for the rest of his pack to attack the Winged Demons. They attacked the Demons hovering over Sundancer freeing him for M'Kara and Troy to mount.

"We will be behind you. Run!" Craven turned to finish off the others. Sundancer neighed and galloped west with other Lycans on either side and behind them.

Aero returned to the Western Palace after searching for Troy and M'Kara in the woods. It was late into the night and his soldiers grew weary. Searching while fatigued would do them no good, especially if they were to run into any of the Shadow empowered Army. After leaving his horse in the Palace stables, he found Melina on one of the eastern balconies looking off toward the woods. She was watching and waiting for the children to return.

"I am truly sorry," Melina said when she heard Aero approach.

"For what?" his fatigue could be heard in his voice.

"For letting the children out of my sight," she said with tears in her eyes. That was when a creature with the body and face of a woman, and wings like an eagle flew from the east and perched on the edge of the wall. This was one of Melina's summons. Melina had summoned this Harpy to search for M' Kara and Troy. The Harpy shook her head with a discouraged expression upon her face. "I have even sent one of my Summons to search for them and she has found nothing," Melina said with great pain and sadness in her voice. The Harpy bowed her head and faded away.

"Do not blame yourself, Melina. I am sure they are alright," Aero gave an embrace of comfort. A faint howl on the wind was then heard from the east.

"What was that?" Melina asked turning her head toward the chilling sound.

"A howl... from a wolf?" Aero furrowed his eyebrows in confusion. He stepped to the edge of the balcony and kept his eyes watchful of the grasslands to the east. Another haunting howl was heard from the grasslands.

"It sounds like a...," Melina said walking to the edge of the balcony.

"Lycan howl," Aero finished. They then saw a pack of Lycans running on all fours escorting a horse toward the Western Palace.

"Is that Sundancer?" Melina focused her vision.

"Yes, carrying Troy and M' Kara with Craven and the rest of his pack. Guard, prepare to open the gate!" Aero shouted with a smile.

Sundancer, with Troy and M' Kara on his back, along with Craven and the Lycan pack entered the gates of the Western Palace. They were met by Aero, Melina, Aldar, and several other soldiers. Troy dismounted and rushed to hug his mother and father. M' Kara dismounted and stood by Sundancer with her head lowered.

"M' Kara come here, child," Melina said with open arms. M' Kara looked at Melina and then lowered her head again. Sundancer nudged M' Kara into Melina's welcoming arms. Tears streamed down her cheeks.

"I am sorry, Lady Melina. I did not mean to put us both in danger. I was only trying to find my grandfather," M' Kara said with tears in her eyes.

"I understand, M' Kara. It is alright. You are safe now," Melina hugged her tightly. Aero also gave a hug to M' Kara to comfort her.

"Father, M' Kara and I found out what the Shadow Lord is planning to do," Troy said trying to make the situation better.

"And how did you manage to do that?" Aero asked with a raised eyebrow.

"You taught us the lesson to find out the strengths and weaknesses of your enemy and use them to your advantage. What we found out was, they are planning to take over the Shinobi villages, the Keshnarian Ruins, and come here. They are taking over all of Rhydin to merge it with the Shadow Realm. The Shadow Lord also wants revenge on Uncle Zidane," Troy was trying to recall all that they had heard.

"If they take the Keshnarian Ruins then there is no way for the villagers to get away from them. We cannot go any farther west because of the mountains. We are stuck," Aero said grimly.

"But we also found out that they do not like the light from the North Star," M' Kara interjected.

"They do not like light. That is why the shroud of shadow hangs over them while in battle. If only there was a way to harness that. There is barely any light left in this land other than the dim light from the North Star," Aero said thought aloud.

"You two had best get inside and rest. You have had quite an ordeal," Melina said. Both Troy and M' Kara nodded and headed for the main Palace door escorted by Elf soldiers.

"I am sorry I got you in to trouble," M' Kara said with her head lowered.

"Do not worry. It is alright. Besides, it was fun," Troy chuckled while M' Kara forced a grin.

"Thank you for watching over them, Craven," Aero turned his eyes to his Lycan ally.

"You're welcome. We have come to honor our pledge to fight alongside you," Craven transformed back to his human form as did the rest of his pack.

"What happened?" Melina looked to Craven.

"We were on our way to visit the Vampire Coven when we saw the region covered in shadow. Shadow empowered Orc, Abominations, and Winged Demons were roaming the land. The leftovers of battle still riddled the region. Then we set out to investigate and found out this new army began to ravage Rhydin. We soon discovered they were weak at the neck and head so we used the element of surprise and weakened some of their forces," Craven recalled their journey up until that point.

"We are truly thankful that you protected the young ones and brought them here," Aero placed his hand on the man's broad shoulder. Sundancer stomped his hoof to the ground creating a small flare.

"And we thank you, Sundancer," Melina reached forward to stroke his mane.

"I just hope Kulla, Zidane, and Maia can get back in time to help," Aero looked up to the North Star.

ARMY OF THE UNDEAD

ONCE HE STEPPED THROUGH THE Gate of Caelum, Kulla felt the blistering heat of the desert. He was in Egypt, the sand was hot under his boots. The oppressive heat beat down upon his brow, the hot wind felt like fire lashing at his skin. To Kulla, it felt like the dry heat itself sucked the moisture from his body. After gathering himself and scanning his surroundings, Kulla found where he was.

"Karnak," he said to himself as he looked to the ruins that stood in front of him. He first looked upon the three main temples of this conglomeration of edifices. Then he saw the ruins of smaller temples that were set along the perimeter. All of them were enclosed by a stone wall that seemed to be strong when it was first built, but time and the unrelenting elements wore on it. Portions of the wall had fallen into a pile of rubble. Kulla had seen parchments of this mass of temples when it was first built. He could only imagine the magnificent sight it must have been. He took a map from his satchel and oriented his position. He faced east then began to walk through the hot sand of the desert.

As the sun crept higher in the sky, Kulla felt more of the oppressive heat press upon him. Through the sweltering heat, over sand dunes, and fighting off the feeling of collapsing from the elements, he traveled for miles onward with the goal of rousing the Army of the Undead to help save Rhydin. He reached the top of one of the tallest sand dunes and saw off in the distance a river.

"The Nile," he said with a grin. He continued his walk to the Nile and from there he would travel south to the Temple of Philae, where the Army of the Undead rested. Halfway down the sand dune, his vision began to blur, his knees weakened then buckled under him, and the strength in his body faded. His body went limp as he collapsed into the scorching sand and slid to the bottom. His vision blacked out, his body motionless, and his breathing ragged.

It was well into the night when Kulla awoke from his unconscious state. He found himself on a cloth cot with a cold, damp cloth on his brow. He slowly sat up pushing the cold cloth from his head. A pail of water was set next to the cot for him to draw from with a ladle. Once he quenched his thirst, he rose from the cot and walked about the tent. He found his sword and Scepter leaning against the opposite wall. He took his sword and strapped it around his waist and took the Scepter of Osiris. He walked out of the tent and found there were guards on either side of the opening. Their skin was dark like the earth and their eyes were focused. They wore gold scaled armor with gold greaves on their forearms and shins. They held spears and had scimitars strapped to their hips. Once they saw Kulla walk out of the tent, the guards stood at attention as he passed them.

"Where am I?" Kulla looked the guards.

"You are in the Egyptian Army encampment near Luxor," a voice responded from within the camp. Kulla tracked that voice to a man sitting near a fire. The man stood and faced Kulla.

"Ahmaar," Kulla immediately recognized the Egyptian General who aided in the final battle against Sekmet. They clasped wrists with each other.

"What are you doing here, my friend?" Ahmaar asked as he invited Kulla to share the fire with him.

"I am on my way to Philae, to the Temple of Osiris," Kulla responded as he sat down.

"And what is there awaiting you?" Ahmaar asked with a raised eyebrow.

"The Army of the Undead," there was an eerie hush among the soldiers who stood and sat in close proximity to them. Kulla looked around as the eyes of each of the soldiers were on him.

"Why do you search for them?" Ahmaar leaned forward in his seat.

"I need to summon them to aid us in the fight against the Shadow Army," Kulla's voice held the burden he felt in his heart. This mission was of great importance.

"Shadow Army?" Ahmaar was visibly confused as to what the shadow army was. They had not reached Earth yet.

"Yes. The Shadow Lord has shown his face on Rhydin and has empowered the survivors of Sekmet's army with dark shadow. Their only weakness is severing their head from their body or slashing their neck. Their bodies cannot be injured by arrow, blade, or boulder," Kulla's voice trailed off in thought. The price of that information was high.

"That is most discouraging. Where are the other two sides of the pyramid?" Ahmaar asked, "We only found you in the desert."

"Zidane and Maia are in the Shadow Realm rescuing their children who have been captured by Shadow Demons. They slipped into the Western Palace while we were away. My wife, Rosey, was poisoned by these dark shadows and now she is in the care of the Earth Shinobi. We are fighting a losing battle, Ahmaar. The Krystal Kingdom needs the Army of the Undead," Kulla said almost pleading with him.

"It is written that the Army of the Undead will only answer to the one who wields the power of Osiris and if one were to summon them without it, they would forfeit their soul and serve as an Undead Soldier in that Army," Ahmaar's voice was grim.

"How did the Army of the Undead come in to existence?" Kulla asked.

"They were the greatest army of their era. They defended this country and conquered many. In the Temple of Osiris, they pledged their souls to him to serve in an eternal army. They vowed to answer the call of whoever summoned them in the name of Osiris," Ahmaar looked from the sand to Kulla.

"So whoever calls upon them using Osiris's name and who wields the power of Osiris will be in command of this Army," Kulla thought aloud.

"That is correct," Ahmaar confirmed with a nod.

"Will this help?" Kulla held the Scepter of Osiris toward him.

"The Scepter of Osiris will aid you if you believe in its power and are accepting of it. If not, your soul will be taken," Ahmaar warned.

"Will you help me?" Kulla pled with his eyes.

"We will take my vessel down the Nile to Philae at first light tomorrow," Ahmaar patted Kulla on the shoulder.

"Thank you," Kulla sighed with relief.

As the sun rose over the horizon, Kulla, Ahmaar and several Egyptian soldiers prepared to make the journey to the Temple of Osiris. They gathered their weapons and took rations of food and water. Ahmaar's boat was docked on the bank of the Nile River. All gathered in the boat. There was enough room to fit twenty full grown men.

"What news do you have on purging Earth of the former soldiers of Sekmet?" Kulla asked as they were being rowed down the river.

"We have come across only a few encampments since we defeated that army. Sir Galidan, Lioneus, and Raoko Shun have reported the same. King Draco has made valiant efforts in eradicating those survivors," Ahmaar was proud of what they accomplished.

"The same has been happening on Rhydin. Only we did not find all of them as you may have concluded with the Shadow Army ravaging the lands as we speak," Kulla said.

"That is most unfortunate, my friend. We must hurry then if what you say is true about the Shadow Army being near invincible. You will need all of the help you can get," Ahmaar said.

"Agreed," Kulla looked toward the south down the Nile River.

The sun crept across the sky and mid-afternoon came upon them as they saw an island ahead of them. It was lush with vegetation. Behind the island were rolling hills that stretched for miles beyond what the eye could see.

"Is that…?" Kulla started to ask with his eyes widening as he rose to his feet.

"Yes, my friend. That is the Temple of Osiris," Ahmaar smiled when he saw his response to seeing the Temple for the first time. As they drew closer to the bank where the Temple stood, Kulla could see the carvings and hieroglyphics on the front wall. He was the first out of the boat when they docked.

"I assume you have never seen the Temple of Osiris before," Ahmaar walked to Kulla's side.

"I have only seen drawings of it in charts, but never in person like this," Kulla continued to gaze upon the architecture. The other Egyptian soldiers soon joined them once they secured the boat to the bank. As they approached the brick stairs to the main door of the Temple, an arrow cut through the air passing Kulla and pierced the shoulder of one of the Egyptian soldiers. Kulla looked to the brush alongside the Temple and saw their attackers.

"Orcs! Take cover!" Kulla shouted. Ahmaar and the wounded soldier took cover behind a stone column, as did Kulla and the other soldiers. Ahmaar pulled the arrow from the soldier's shoulder then took his bow and drew an arrow to aim into the brush.

"How many are there?" Ahmaar shouted to Kulla.

"I count around twenty five!" Kulla shouted back.

"We are at a slight disadvantage! There are only ten of us!" Ahmaar said as an arrow flew by his face. Kulla then looked into the Temple entrance and then to the brush where the Orcs were.

"How long can you hold them off?" Kulla shouted to Ahmaar.

"How much time do you need?" Ahmaar dodged another arrow.

"As much as you can give me!" Kulla shouted back. Ahmaar nodded then looked to the rest of his soldiers shouting orders in an Egyptian dialect. Kulla took a deep breath drawing his sword. He turned and as fast as he could ran toward the entrance to the Temple. As Kulla was doing this, Ahmaar and the other Egyptian soldiers were releasing a barrage of arrows into the brush trying to cover Kulla's advance to the Temple. Arrows flew past his feet and head as he ran up the steps. Once inside he found himself in a small courtyard with two stone columns on either side of the room. He continued through the stone courtyard and into a hall. He was searching for a doorway that would lead him to the chambers in which the Army of the Undead slumbered. He searched through the rooms and halls, but found no stairway that led to the chambers. He found himself in what seemed to be the sanctuary of the temple. On the far side, he looked to the wall and saw what seemed to be a hidden door built into it. He wiped away the accumulation of dirt and dust to reveal the door. Kulla searched for a lever or door handle to open it, but found none. A loose brick in the wall caught his attention. He walked to it and removed the brick. In the vacant space, he saw a small lever. Kulla gripped the lever and pulled back on it. A moment later, he heard what seemed to be some sort of mechanism unlocking. The hidden door slowly slid open to reveal a dark narrow stairway that led downward. Even with excellent vision during in dark places, Kulla's eyes could not pierce the darkness that awaited him below. He took one of the torches that lined the wall and walked down the stairs.

The air was stale and full of dust and dirt. His footsteps echoed in the narrow brick stairway. Kulla kept his free hand to the wall trying to feel where he was going. He could tell the staircase was spiraling downwards. From the echo of his footsteps in the stairway, he was far below ground level. He finally reached the bottom of the stairwell and tried to feel around for some sort of pedestal, but found nothing to brace himself on. He looked around and found only a darkness that seemed to go on endlessly. He whistled and listened for the sound to ricochet off of the walls and get an idea of how large the room was. The sound of his whistle went on and on, echoing throughout the chamber. Kulla took a deep breath realizing he was in an immense room. As he inhaled that deep breath, he caught the scent of something unusual and seemed to be out of place. He was drawn to the smell. With his hand in front of him, he went off to his right trying to figure out where the smell was coming from. He bumped into what seemed to be a brick well. He stuck his hand into the well and felt that it was some sort of liquid. It was thick and was the origin of the pungent odor that hung in the air.

"Oil?" he lowered the torch to the well. The air around the dark liquid flared from the flames of the torch. Kulla jumped backwards so as not to be caught in the flame. He took a moment to think and looked from the torch to the well. He tossed the torch into the well and in a bright flare, the oil ignited and a trail of fire cut from the well to a narrow brick pool. The pool lined the walls and as the fire trailed across the oil, the chamber began to be illuminated. Hieroglyphs covered the entirety of the walls. Four stone columns were in each corner of the room, each with the image of Osiris holding the Scepter. Kulla's eyes widened as he saw the thousands of stone sarcophagi that were laid side by side in numerous rows. All led to a risen platform that overlooked the chamber. As he began to walk toward the platform, his eyes fell upon the number of soldiers that committed themselves to Osiris. On each sarcophagus was a face that had a blank and empty stare carved in it. The arms were crossed across the chest with a spear in one hand and a scimitar in the other. Kulla looked up to the stone platform and a feeling of intimidation and anxiety came across him. His heart was throbbing and his hands began to tremble. He shook the feeling from his mind and body then began to climb the stairs to the top of the platform. As he reached the top, he could see each and every one of the sarcophagi of the soldiers who devoted their souls to Osiris. He also saw a hole in the platform that was not very wide. He looked around for some clue as to what was supposed to go in it. As he faced the wall behind him, he saw an image of Osiris with his arms outstretched and the Scepter stuck in the ground in front of him. What appeared to be souls were emerging from the head of the Scepter. Kulla looked from the Scepter of Osiris to the hole that was in the ground. He slowly approached the hole with the Scepter of Osiris in hand. With both hands he raised the Scepter into the air and plunged the Scepter into the hole. The head of the Scepter began to glow brightly and steadily throb with pulsating energy.

"Souls of the Ancients, souls who vowed your lives to Osiris, I Kulla, Wielder of the Scepter of Osiris, call upon you to rise from your eternal slumber," Kulla said with a voice that resounded. His arms and hands were outstretched as if beckoning to these spirits. As these words were uttered, there was a burst of light from the head of the Scepter that illuminated the whole chamber. The walls and the floor shook from the power of the Scepter. The souls of the soldiers began to pour from the Scepter's head and fly around the chamber. They weaved between each other as the souls began to fill the chamber. Soon they began to fade into the sarcophagi that held their bodies for several generations. Kulla dropped to his knees as he watched the last of the souls fade into their bodies. There was silence for a few moments. Kulla rose to his feet and walked down to the sarcophagi.

"Nothing," he exhaled a deep sigh. The sarcophagus to his right began to rock back and forth. A loud moan was heard from within. Then, one by one, all of the sarcophagi began to rumble. The doors of the sarcophagi began to slowly be pushed away and fell to the ground with a crash that echoed through the chamber. Kulla first saw the mummified hands of these soldiers reach up to the sides to pull themselves out. He took several steps away from the sarcophagi and watched the mummified soldiers rise from their long slumber. Kulla was in awe of the soldiers who stood before him. There were males and females of varying in heights and sizes. They wore gold chest plates, greaves on their shins, and gauntlets on their wrists. What Kulla found intriguing was that they wore golden masks that resembled the face that was carved into the sarcophagi. They were blank and expressionless. One of the mummified soldiers stepped forward toward Kulla.

"What is thy bidding, Wielder of the Scepter of Osiris?" the soldier gave a bow of his head. Kulla looked from the Scepter to the thousands of soldiers that stood before him and gave a wide grin showing his fangs.

Outside of the Temple, Ahmaar and his soldiers were being pushed back by the ambushing Orcs. The Egyptians soldiers were greatly outnumbered and overpowered. They continued to fight despite the fact they were fighting a losing battle. Several soldiers suffered wounds from flying arrows.

"We have run out of arrows!" one of the soldiers shouted.

"Perhaps today is a good day to die," Ahmaar drew his scimitar and prepared to charge at the enemy. The Orcs knew they were out of arrows and charged out of the bushes. Ahmaar and the other soldiers charged from their hiding places behind columns and fallen stone. Swords and axes clashed as the Egyptian soldiers and the Orcs collided. Ahmaar and his men were in the middle of a mob of Orc troops. The Orcs surrounded them, leaving them nowhere to go. One of the Orcs glared at Ahmaar and stepped toward him.

"You are the stinkin' human who wounded me in that battle," the Orc pointed his sword at Ahmaar.

"I cannot say that I remember you. I killed so many of your comrades that night," Ahmaar gave an arrogant smirk.

"You'll remember me once you're in the afterlife," the Orc raised his sword to strike Ahmaar. A whistle was heard coming from the Temple. All eyes went to the origin of the whistle that cut through the air. Kulla was standing several feet from the main entrance.

"Leave those men alone!" Kulla shouted to them as he casually walked toward the mob of Orcs.

"What are you going to do if we don't?!" one of the Orcs shouted back.

"You will not have to worry about me. You will have to answer to them," Kulla pointed to the top of the Temple with the Scepter. At that moment, the mummified soldiers emerged from hiding with bows and arrows aimed at the Orcs. More soldiers emerged from the entrance behind Kulla. The rest of the mummified soldiers rose from trap doors around the Orcs troops. The Orcs cowered as they saw the Army of the Undead emerge.

"Where did this army come from?!" one of the Orcs exclaimed.

"You are gazing upon the Army of the Undead," Kulla walked down the steps of the Temple.

"You may kill us now, but our brethren will have no mercy on you!" one of the Orcs shouted.

"Your brethren will not have the chance. They will receive the same mercy that you showed our soldiers and our villages! You will receive no mercy, and neither shall they," Kulla said as he was within a few feet of the Orc horde. Enraged, one of the Orcs raised its axe ready to attack Kulla. As the Orc was swinging its axe, one of the Undead Soldiers cut the arm from the Orc's body and another slashed it from navel to chest. Kulla ordered the archers on the Temple roof to fire. They released a shower of arrows at the Orcs, not hitting any of the Egyptian soldiers who were in the middle of it all. Each of the Orcs fell to either an arrow or a blade leaving only the Egyptian soldiers in the middle of the Orcs' corpses. Ahmaar looked around him and saw only the bodies of the Orc on the ground around him and his soldiers. Kulla ordered the Undead Soldiers to be at ease.

"I see you were successful in rousing the Army of the Undead," Ahmaar grinned as he looked to the impressive army of mummified soldiers that stood behind Kulla.

"My journey only begins with this Army. We must go back to save Rhydin and cleanse it from the Shadows that have overtaken it," Kulla's confidence seemed to be renewed with the awakening of these mummified followers of Osiris.

"May the Heavens guide you and protect you," Ahmaar placed his hand on Kulla's shoulder.

"You are not coming with us?" Kulla's voice held his disappointment.

"I cannot my friend. I have an obligation here on Earth to defend against Orc hordes such as this," Ahmaar looked to the bodies of the Orc soldiers that littered the sand.

"I thank you, my friend, for everything," Kulla's gratitude was clear on his face and eyes.

"No thanks are needed," Ahmaar responded as he reached for the Crystal around his neck. Kulla did the same and as the midnight blue Crystal of Kulla and the Lilac Crystal of Ahmaar were out, they glowed in reaction to each other. They all made their way back to the encampment farther north on the Nile. From there Kulla led the Undead Army to the Gate of Caelum in Karnak.

LOST STARS FOUND

H OURS PASSED SINCE ZIDANE AND Maia lost consciousness
after pushing their powers to their very limits while in the
darkest region of the Shadow Realm. They lied on the dry, cracked
ground recuperating from the shock of exhaustion. Stratos sat nearby
keeping a watchful eye for any danger. He often looked down to Maia
reminding him of the love he had back on his own world. He relived
the moment his love, Inca, was taken from him. The pain of Inca
being captured was infinitely worse than the arrows that pierced his
flesh that day. His thoughts were interrupted by Zidane's stirring
and waking.

"It would appear you are done resting, Red Dragon," Stratos
looked from Maia to his Dragon rival.

"Yes, I do believe so. How long were we asleep?" he gave a groan
as he sat up.

"A few hours. This is the darkest region of the Shadow Realm.
The Shadow Fortress is on the other side of this steep hill," Stratos
nodded his head toward the hill that stood between them and their
children. Looking at and speaking to Zidane did not rouse the urge
within Stratos to take the power of the Red Dragon for himself.
The few hours of reflection and mediation to control himself greatly
benefited him. He breathed a sigh of relief that he was rid of it. It
was at that moment that Maia awoke. Her eyes fluttered opened and
she yawned. She stretched in her cat-like manner. Stratos's eyes once
again softened as he watched Maia wake. Zidane caught his gaze and
rose to his feet and walked to Stratos's side.

"Does she remind you of her?" Zidane stood by him.

"She does," Stratos nodded without looking at Zidane.

"What happened?" Zidane looked down to his rival.

"When I was reborn as Stratos, there were many Orcs that flooded the room. Many arrows pierced my body rendering me helpless as they captured Inca and took her away from me," Stratos looked to the ground as if in shame.

"I am sorry to hear that. Maybe you and I are not so different," Zidane crouched down beside the Black Dragon.

"No, we are not. We are the same person, but just from a different Universe. You were correct, Red Dragon. I was corrupted by power when I had my first taste of it. Killing the White Dragon sent me down the path of the darkest of shadows that many would not return from. I was lost and alone," Stratos clenched his teeth and balled his fist.

"Well you are not alone anymore. You still have the Dragons within you. Their thoughts and powers are with you. And if you wish, I can go back with you. Two Dragons are better than one," Zidane placed his hand on his shoulder.

"Thank you, Zidane," Stratos forced a grin on the unmasked side of his face.

"I apologize for interrupting you both, but I think we have an immense task ahead of us," Maia called to them from the top of the hill as she was looking down. Zidane and Stratos joined her and looked down. The hill was high and steep, nearly vertical. They saw the Shadow Fortress two hundred yards away from the foot of the hill, but between the foot of the hill and the entrance to the fortress were thousands of shadow demons blocking the entrance. It was as if they were overlooking a sea of shadow below.

"What are we to do?" Maia asked with anxiety creeping into her voice. Several moments of silence past as they thought of many possibilities.

"I believe I have a plan," Zidane and Maia crouched down beside Stratos as he etched his strategy into the ground.

Once they were ready, Zidane and Stratos took their places at the top of the steep hill. They were ten feet away from each other. Looking downward, they saw the sea of Shadow Demons below them waiting to swallow and drown them. Zidane began to conjure an aura of flames around his hands and Stratos roused an aura of shadow energy around his hands. They both hurled balls of fire and shadow energy down at the horde of Shadow Demons. Several explosions erupted within the army of Demons and all of their attention fell upon the intruders who stood on top of the hill. Their yellow lidless eyes flashed with anger.

"Well we have their attention now. The first part of your plan is working," Zidane inhaled and exhaled deep breaths to control the nervousness running through his body.

"It would seem so," Stratos tightened his fists to stop them from shaking.

"Remember they are weak at the neck and head," Zidane focused his vision on the enemies below.

"I remember," Stratos looked down as well.

"Shall we?" Zidane looked over to the Black Dragon with a half-smile on his face.

"We shall," Stratos returned the smile to his new ally. At that moment, Zidane and Stratos jumped down the hill then, while keeping their balance, began to slide down the hill with both of their feet under them. The Shadow Demons saw the two sliding down the hill and thought they would be easy targets seeing they had nowhere else to go but down. Using their shadow energy, the Demons conjured spears in their hands. They then hurled them in the air at the interlopers.

"Look out!" Zidane shouted to warn Stratos of the incoming spears. With quick movements of their hands, Zidane and Stratos moved the earth beneath their feet in such a way that they avoided each of the spears. Once the spears hit the ground they exploded leaving small craters. The two Dragon Essence Bearers then motioned for the earth to mold into inclines that would send them from side to side and forward allowing them to gain momentum. They also roused the earth to block the spears of shadow energy and used the earth to launch them into the air. All while keeping their tremendous momentum down the steep hill.

Meanwhile, Maia was at the top of the hill watching for the point in which she would descend. This plan of Stratos's required impeccable timing. When Stratos revealed his plan, he pointed to a spot on the hill. When he and Zidane reached that point Maia was to make her descent. She waited and once they reached that point, she leapt down the hill with bow and an arrow ready. She slid directly in the middle of the paths Stratos and Zidane created. The Shadow Demons were so occupied with the weaving and dodging of Zidane and Stratos that they did not notice Maia. She began to conjure energy from the Necklace of Isis. Zidane and Stratos looked to each other seeing they were close to the bottom and motioned for the earth to form a steep incline into the air. They both were sent straight into the air and were aiming to land in a large grouping of Shadow Demons.

"Arrow of Isis!" Maia shouted as she released the energy charged arrow into the frontlines of the Demon horde. The arrow surged through the middle of the sea of Shadow Demons leaving an opening for Stratos and Zidane to land. With dragon blades drawn, they began to slash and stab at the Shadow Demons around them. Their backs were facing each other with an opening for Maia to slide in and release another Arrow of Isis attack. They continued through the Shadow Demon Army toward the entrance of the Shadow Fortress. The massive stone doors of the gates were closed to them.

"Maia, use another Arrow of Isis to open the gate," Zidane said as he countered an attack from a Shadow Demon. Maia took another arrow and conjured energy from the Necklace to the head of the arrow.

"Arrow of Isis!" she shouted releasing the arrow to the doors. A massive hole followed by a deep trench in the ground was a result of Maia's attack. Maia was the first one to get to the other side of the front wall. Stratos sheathed his blades and from behind Zidane, he roused a high wall of earth between them and the Shadow Demons. Zidane also sheathed his blades and he too roused a wall of earth to reinforce the wall Stratos roused. They turned to find Maia doubled over in exhaustion.

"Maia, are you alright?" Zidane rushed to her side.

"I think I overexerted myself with so many powerful attacks," her breathing was heavy and labored, but she still fought to stay upright.

"You will lose strength more quickly in this region of the Shadow Realm, but we have to keep moving now. The Shadow Demons know we are here and will relentlessly hunt us," Stratos looked around for any sign of an attack.

"Can you keep moving?" concern for Maia was in Zidane's voice.

"Yes, I can," Maia straightened up. They found an enormous dome structure in front of them that led to the towering spire in the middle.

"Do you think Tritan and Carline are being held in the spire?" Maia looked up to the intimidating structure.

"There is only one way to find out," Stratos drew one of his blades and rushed toward it. Zidane and Maia were close behind him heading for the entrance to the dome structure. Zidane conjured a ball of flames in both of his hands and hurled it at the heavy iron door blowing it open. It was dark inside of the Fortress. Fortunately, their impeccable vision cut through the dark halls.

"We have to be cautious in these halls. They know we are here and will most certainly add more guards," Stratos's voice was hushed. Stratos and Zidane had their blades drawn while Maia had her bow drawn and an arrow ready to release at a moment's notice.

Elsewhere in the fortress, Carline and Tritan were making their way through the cold, dark halls. They traveled silently, hiding in dark corners and empty rooms to avoid the Shadow Demons who were patrolling. Their hearts were pounding for fear of being discovered covertly roaming through the halls. As they turned one of the corners, they saw several sets of yellow lidless eyes at the opposite end of the hall. Carline and Tritan quickly opened the nearest door and entered the room. In that dark room were several rows of long tables where racks holding flasks of various sizes and vials of glowing liquids. The room smelled of the mixture of these liquids, it was almost nauseating.

"What is this room?" Carline whispered covering her nose.

"I do not know, but we better find a hiding place," Tritan whispered. They huddled together in a corner opposite of the door keeping a watchful eye on it. They kept their breaths quiet, listening for the footsteps of the Shadow Demons. The footsteps drew closer to the door and then they heard the doorknob turn. Two Shadow Demons entered the room. Carline was about to let out a gasp, but Tritan placed his hand over her mouth to suppress it. The Shadow Demons walked to opposite sides of the room and began to walk down the rows of tables. Tritan and Carline silently rolled under one of the tables narrowly escaping being discovered by one of the Demons. As the Demons walked by the table Tritan and Carline were under, Tritan crawled to the adjacent table. Carline was starting to follow, but found one of the Demons turning the corner into that row. She crouched silently holding her breath as the Demon past her. She then quickly rolled to be under the next table to be with Tritan. The Demon quickly turned its head as if it heard something. Seeing nothing, the Demons made their way to the door and exited closing the door behind them. When they heard the footsteps of the Demons get to the end of the hall, they let out a sigh of relief.

"That was too close," Carline tried to calm her breathing.

"Yes, it was. We need to find a way out of here," Tritan kept his eyes on the door. Carline nodded her head and then they got from under the table to go to the door. Tritan slowly opened the door and cautiously poked his head out to look to both sides of the hall trying to see if there were any signs of Demons.

"It looks safe," Tritan whispered. He then signaled for Carline to follow him down the hall. Again, Tritan peered his head around the corner and saw a stairway that led down.

"I see the stairs," there was a glint of hope in Tritan's voice.

"Are there any Demons?" Carline was hesitant in her steps behind him.

"I see nor hear any," Tritan shook his head. Tritan led Carline to the stairs so they could make their descent. Tritan and Carline went down several flights, the staircase seemed to be never ending. Once they reached the bottom they turned the corner and ran into a tall, dark figure who knocked them backwards to the floor. Carline and Tritan gasped looking up at the figure and began to back track when they saw two more walk up behind the first dark figure.

"Tritan.... Carline?" the one stepped closer to the youngsters.

"Father?" Tritan stopped to strain his eyes to cut through the shadows.

"Is that you, Momma?" Carline's eyes brightened at the voice she heard.

"Thank the Heavens you two are safe!" Maia rushed to them and wrapped her arms around the two of them. Tears welled in Tritan and Carline's eyes as they hugged Maia and Zidane. Stratos was a few feet behind them keeping a watchful eye for any Shadow Demons.

"We knew...," Carline started to say. "You would come," Tritan finished.

"How did you two escape?" despite his excitement, Zidane's voice was still hushed.

"The Shadow Demons are strong...," Tritan started. "But not too smart," Carline forced a smile through the tears of relief she was shedding.

"We are proud of you," Maia shared in the tears her children shed.

"I am sorry, but we cannot linger here. Now that we have found your children, might I suggest we look for that cure for the shadow poison," Stratos was growing anxious while within enemy territory. The urgency to move was within him.

"Who is that?" the Twins looked to the Black Dragon curiously.

"There is no time to explain. We need to find that antidote," Zidane too felt the urgency to move from that place.

"Where should we start looking? This fortress is massive," Maia looked to Statos and Zidane.

"Tritan and I saw a room…," Carline started to say. "With a lot of strange liquids," Tritan finished.

"Do you remember where it is?" both of the Twins nodded to their father's question.

"Take us there," at Maia's words, the Twins led them up the stairs. They climbed several stories with no resistance. When they came close to the landing where the room was, Carline and Tritan stopped in their ascent when they saw several pairs of yellow eyes heading down toward them.

"Tritan, Carline, stay back. Maia, stay with them and be ready with your bow. Stratos, you are up with me," Zidane rushed up the stairs drawing both of his blades.

"Why could this not be easy," Stratos commented to himself drawing his blades as well. The Shadow Demons formed their arms to be double edged blades and were ready to strike at Zidane as he rushed at them. Zidane sidestepped one of the slashes and let its momentum drive him down to Stratos who slashed at the Demon's knees and then its neck. Zidane ran one blade straight through another Demon and then slashed at the neck with his other blade. Maia aimed and released arrow after arrow at the necks of the Demons who were at the rear of the group. They dropped straight down the middle of the spiraling staircase to the bottom floor. Zidane and Stratos continued to sidestep and counter the attacks of the oncoming Demons making their way up the stairs. Carline and Tritan stood several steps behind Maia staying out of danger's way. Stratos and Zidane slashed their way through the last of the Demons and came to a landing.

"That is the landing," the Twins pointed, then took the lead and led them down the hall to the room. Once there, they saw the many vials and flasks of various liquids.

"Which one is the cure?" Maia began to search through the racks and shelves.

"Would it not be labeled?" Stratos was searching the opposite side of the room. Frustration built within them as they found none of the vials or flasks were labeled. They did not know if what was in that room helpful or lethal. Zidane stopped for a moment then looked from Stratos to the vials that sat before them.

"Stratos, do your abilities allow you to sense shadow energy?" Zidane raised a questioning eyebrow.

"They do, but what help does that do?" Stratos furrowed his eyebrows in confusion at Zidane's line of thinking.

"Shadow energy was most likely how it was generated in the Demon's body and it took energy to pass it to Rosey. Would it not make sense for shadow energy to make an antidote?" Zidane pointed to the many vials racked within the room.

"You are right, Zidane," with that, Stratos closed his eyes and focused his energy. He opened his eyes to reveal they were as black as the deepest abyss with shadow energy seeping from them. His eyes went from vial to flask of liquid scanning them for any traces of shadow energy. His eyes then fell upon a small rack, with thin vials mounted on it.

"These are it," Stratos took one of the vials to examine it more closely.

"Are you sure?" Maia approached him to look at the vial as well.

"I am positive," Stratos's eyes faded to their normal hue.

"Let us go then," Zidane turned to the door, but then heard several sets of footsteps marching down the hall.

"What is it, Poppa?" Carline froze in place.

"Shadow Demons," he responded with his eyes flaring red and embers sparking from his dreadlocks.

"Stratos, can you open a portal to Rhydin?" Maia turned her head to him.

"I do not know if I can in this region of the Shadow Realm," Stratos gave an uncertain shake of his head.

"You are going to have to try Stratos because here they come," Zidane drew both of his blades and readied for the oncoming Shadow Demons. Stratos held out the Bracelet of Mentu and focused his energy. The Bracelet faintly glowed silver and began to throb with energy. Behind him, Carline and Tritan stood watching their father fight off the Shadow Demons and Maia releasing arrows over Zidane's shoulders into the hall. A beam of silver light emitted from the Bracelet of Mentu opening a small, faint portal.

"I do not think this portal will hold for very long," Stratos called to his comrades.

"Carline, Tritan, go now!" Zidane shouted back to them as he fought off the Shadow Demons with Stratos joining at his side. The Twins jumped through the portal with no hesitation. "Maia, you are next, go!" Maia released one more arrow hitting a Demon in the head then rushed back to the portal and went through. The portal faded as Zidane and Stratos fought off the Demons while making their way to the portal.

"Zidane, you must go now before it is too late," Stratos put a vial of the antidote in Zidane's belt.

"What about you?" Zidane glanced at Stratos from the corner of his eye.

"I will be right behind you," Zidane hesitated, but then sheathed his blades and leapt through the portal that faded even more after he reached the other side. Zidane, Maia, Carline, and Tritan found themselves back on Rhydin close to the foot of the Western Mountains just south of the Western Province. Zidane looked back and found that Stratos was not behind him. The portal faded more with each passing moment.

"What happened...," Tritan started to ask. "To him?" Carline clutched her mother's arm.

"I thought he was right behind me," Zidane eyes never left the waning portal. Several moments passed and the portal grew smaller and Stratos was not through. The portal finally disappeared in a flash and at that moment Stratos flew through and rolled across the ground. All breathed a sigh of relief.

"I thought you were right behind me," Zidane helped Stratos to his feet.

"I am sorry. I was occupied," Stratos said with a grin from under the mask.

"Mother, is it day...," Tritan started to ask. "Or is it night?" Carline finished asking as they both looked out to the land and saw nothing but shadow. A thick aura of dark shadow hovered in the sky above letting very little light touch the earth below.

"I-I do not know," Maia looked upon the land with fear in her eyes.

"What has happened?" Zidane stood in awe of the darkness that was enveloping his home.

"The merging of the Shadow Realm and this Realm is almost complete. Once the two Realms are one, there is no turning back. Rhydin with look as barren as the Shadow Realm does," Stratos's voice was grim as he spoke of Rhydin's fate.

"How do we stop this?" Maia looked to Stratos.

"Defeat the Shadow Lord," Stratos said as if it were a simple task.

"And defeat him we must. We are going to need as much help as we can get. Hopefully Aero and the others are holding out," Zidane continued to survey the darkening land.

"Where are we going to get aid now?" Stratos asked. Zidane looked to the Western Mountains that were directly behind them, "The Dragon Knights and the Red Dragon, Tufar". The others looked to the Western Mountains behind them as well and all gave a nod to Zidane.

A Dragon's Redemption

WHEN THEY REACHED THE SUMMIT of the Western Mountains, they overlooked the lush valley where the Dragon Knights, Dragons, and their civilization dwelt. It was quiet and tranquil. No war had touched this region of Rhydin, nor had any shadows overtaken the lands. When they looked to the east, the land was dark. It was shrouded in a blanket of shadow; the east had become dark and unwelcoming. No light touched the earth or shone through the thick fog of shadow that loomed over the land. Despite the land being overtaken by shadows, a glimmer of hope continued to shine in the sky above. The light of the North Star persistently fought to cut through the darkness.

"It appears the land has grown darker since we climbed this mountainside," Zidane observed as he looked off to the east.

"The power of the Shadow Lord has overtaken much of Rhydin. The Western Province is the last hope for Rhydin," Stratos looked out to his rival's home.

"We have to hurry then. Aero and whoever else is left will need our help," Maia said as she turned to walk down the mountain valley.

When they reached the center of the lush forest, they came to a clearing. A tree stump sat at the middle of the clearing. The wood of the trunk was different from the other trees that were around.

"Do you remember this place, Zidane?" Stratos looked to the forest around them as if a river of memories streamed into his mind.

"I do," Zidane simply responded looking to his right hand as if he could feel the dagger that pierced through it all those years ago.

"I never apologized for what I did and no mere words could remedy what I did not only to you, but to the White, Green, and Gold Dragons," Stratos said as a tear rolled down the cheek that wasn't covered by the mask.

"What you are doing now will redeem you," Maia reached out and gently touched his shoulder. Stratos gave a grin from under the mask then looked to the Twins seeing what could have happened if he had not been corrupted by power.

"You are fortunate to have a family to look after who unconditionally love and support you," Stratos looked to Zidane.

"We can be your family too," the Twins approached the man that resembled their father.

"Carline and Tritan are right. In a way, we are family. We are just from a different universe," Maia said with a simple shrug of her shoulders.

"Thank you," Stratos placed his hands on the heads of Carline and Tritan as he gave them a grateful smile.

"We need to move on toward the mountain. That is where the village is," Zidane pointed to the their destination.

"Agreed," Stratos said as they followed Zidane deeper into the forest.

They soon saw the two tall stone dragon statues that were set on either side of the entrance to the village as if standing guard and watching for intruders. Stratos, Maia, and the Twins gazed in awe upon the stone wall that encircled the village. They saw the stones were not cemented, but were fused together.

"How were these stones put together?" Stratos ran his fingers across the wall, just as Zidane did.

"The fire of the Dragons fused the stones together," Zidane replied as he led them into the village.

The people in the village were going about their daily lives; some were cleaning, others talking, the young children of the village were playing. Once the villagers saw Zidane and his comrades, they immediately halted their business. A hush fell upon the village as all eyes fell upon them. All bowed their heads in reverence.

"It is good to see you again, Lord Zidane," a voice was heard from the gathering crowd. Zidane looked to find Afelina with her head still bowed.

"Afelina?" Zidane took a few steps toward the woman who was the first to greet him on his first visit.

"Yes, Lord Zidane, it is I," she responded slightly raising her head to make eye contact with him.

"It is good to see you again," Zidane gave a pleasant smile to the woman.

"Thank you Lord Zidane. To what do we owe this visit?" she and the other villagers raised their heads.

"We must have an audience with the Dragon Council. We need to gather the Dragon Knights. An army of Shadow empowered Orcs, Abominations, and Winged Demons have overrun Rhydin. They are being led by the Shadow Lord," Zidane's words caused an anxious muttering among the villagers.

"I will escort you, Lord Zidane," Afelina turned to lead them through the crowd to the mountain entrance. Her eyes glanced back to the group and saw how fatigued they were. It seemed as if they had been through an ordeal. "But first, I will get you something to eat," she smiled just before leading them to her hut.

Her hut was just as Zidane remembered it. It was simple yet cozy. Afelina and the five of them were able to fit inside. Each found a place to sit while she gathered some wooden bowls and spoons for them. "I hope you like stew," Afelina looked to the Twins. Carline and Tritan looked to one another and shrugged, "We have never had it before". Afelina smiled and ladled some of the stew into their bowls. There were chunks of beef, chopped vegetables, and potatoes within a thick broth.

"I was cooking for the evening just before you arrived. Thankfully, I have enough," Afelina ladled the stew into the bowls for the others. Each were grateful for the meal. Battling within the Shadow Realm had drained them of energy. Zidane, Maia, and Stratos had nothing to eat since they embarked on the rescue mission. The Twins had eaten nothing but crusted bread and water to faintly sate their appetites. After serving her guests, Afelina ladled her own bowl and sat at the table.

"Where did this Shadow Lord come from, and why is he attacking our land?" she looked to Zidane.

"As to where he came from, his realm is of the Shadows. It is separate from this realm in which we live. It is a barren wasteland fuming with shadow energy. It is taxing upon the body to just be in it, unless you are of the shadows," Zidane glanced to Stratos.

"The deeper into the realm you go, the more strenuous it becomes upon the body," Stratos added.

"We do not know why the Shadow Lord is here other than to take over this realm," Maia sighed, "His minions kidnapped our children. He must have known we'd go to find them. We left this world vulnerable to his plot".

"We are going to rid this land of the shadows as one Kingdom," Zidane's eyes flared. Afelina sensed the determination within them all. It was stronger now than it had been when she first met the Bearer of the Red Dragon Essence. After they ate and rested for a little while, Afelina led them to the opening in the mountain.

Afelina stood to the side as Zidane and the others looked upon the cave's opening. After thanking Afelina for her hospitality, they entered into the dark cave with the smell of ash hanging heavily in the air. As they ventured deeper in the cave, the light began to fade making them focus their vision to cut through the darkness. As they turned the corner, they saw a dim light at the end of the tunnel. At the end of the tunnel, they saw two Dragon Knights standing at attention with their eyes focused and unwavering. They held their spears firmly and their shields in front of them. The eyes of Stratos, Maia, and the Twins fell upon the massive brass door the Knights were guarding. They saw the image of the winged dragon breathing an inferno of flames into the sky. Their eyes went to the top of the door where the

Eye of Ra was engraved. As they approached, the eyes of the Knights fell upon Zidane and it seemed they stood straighter.

"Lord Zidane, it is good to see you again," one of the Knights said in a forceful voice.

"Please be at ease. It is good to see you two again as well," Zidane replied.

"Who is this, Lord Zidane?" the second asked pointing his spear at Stratos. The others looked to Stratos.

"This is the Bearer of the Black Dragon Essence. There is a story as to why he is here in this universe, but there is no time for that. We must speak with Lord Tufar and the Dragon Council," Zidane replied after a moment's thought. The Knights looked to one another then turned to pull a lever that would open the brass door. As the door opened, the smell of ash and brimstone hung thicker in the air causing Maia, the Twins, and Stratos to almost choke. Once they walked through the brass door, they found themselves in a civilization that was built inside of the mountain. They followed the one Knight toward the other end of the mountain village. The Twins closely walked with Zidane and Maia. Their eyes were wide as they saw a dragon for the first time in close proximity to them. Their eyes never left the dragon. They felt the ground shake with each of its steps. They felt the rumble of its voice in their chests. Zidane and Maia chuckled as they saw the reaction of the Twins to the dragon. Stratos's eyes wandered as well. This could have been his fate if he stuck to the path he was supposed to, like Zidane did. As they were being led down the main path of the civilization, they walked past numerous dragons and Dragon Knights. Each dragon and knight recognized that it was Zidane, the Dragon Lord, and in reverence bowed to him as he passed by.

"You command the dragons and Dragon Knights?" Stratos was in awe of the reverence being demonstrated for the Red Dragon.

"They answer my call. I am the Dragon Lord of Rhydin," Zidane looked to Stratos.

"And the Elf Ruler of the Western Province," Maia added proudly.

"This could have been my fate," Stratos looked to a Dragon Knight walking alongside his dragon companion, talking as they went.

"Yes, but it is not too late. You do have time to redeem yourself. You have already started to make your way back to the path by helping me save my children and getting the antidote for my friend's ailment," Zidane said with a reassuring smile. As they passed a pavilion, the Twin's eyes fell upon young men training with tower shields and spears. They heard their trainer shouting orders to them.

"Will we be...," Carline started to ask. "Training like that?" Tritan finished.

"You will be going through a different type of training. They are training to become Dragon Knights," Zidane followed the eyes of the Twins and saw what they saw.

"Will we be...," Tritan started. "Learning to fight like you?" Carline finished.

"You will be going to the man who trained me," Zidane replied. The Twins smiled and nodded. It was on the other side of this mountain civilization the Dragon Knight stopped. In front of them was a set of massive brass doors identical to the ones they first entered, with the exception of them being large enough for a dragon to walk through and be amongst the other dragons and Dragon Knights. On both of the doors was the same engraving of a Great Dragon breathing an inferno of flames into the sky. The Knight walked to the door and with a closed fist knocked four times. Soon the door opened and another Dragon Knight emerged. He immediately bowed when he saw Zidane, "It is good to see you again, Lord Zidane".

"It is good to see you as well," Zidane replied with a bow to the Knight.

"What business do you have with the Dragon Council?" the Knight asked.

"The services of the Dragon Knights are needed. Rhydin is in grave danger," Zidane's tone turned more serious.

"Very well," the knight nodded. "Knight, you may return to your post," he said. The first knight bowed and turned to return to his post at the first door.

"Who is this?" the Knight pointed his spear at Stratos.

"This is Stratos. He is the Bearer of the Black Dragon Essence," Zidane replied. There was a look of confusion that crept upon the face of the knight.

"There is no time to explain. We must hurry," Maia interrupted. The knight gave a nod sensing the urgency in her voice and led them through the brass doors. They were being led down a long, dimly lit corridor. Further and further into the mountain they went. It was humorous to Zidane when he saw Stratos run his fingers along the smooth wall just as he did when he first walked this corridor. He remembered the anxiousness that was in his heart. He knew that he would meet Tufar that night and was nearly overcome with nervousness. Zidane wondered if Stratos was feeling the same way that he did.

Before them was a high archway, it was high enough for the tallest of dragons to walk under. This archway was lined with golden adornments that were intricately engraved in the stone wall. It took masterful craftsmanship to carve such designs. If it was not by the hands of dwarf, then it was one who rivaled the skills of the dwarves. When their eyes lowered from the archway. they beheld the tallest and seemingly strongest of all of the Dragon Knights. His armor was thicker than the others. His spear and heavy shield were tightly held within his grasp. His eyes were expressionless, yet held an intense focus. This Dragon Guard was quite aware of the presence of Zidane and his companions.

"What is it, Knight?" the Dragon Guard asked in a booming voice.

"I present Lord Zidane and his family," the knight said with a bow. The eyes of the Dragon Guard then focused their attention upon them. They then went to Stratos who strangely resembled Zidane.

"Lord Zidane, who is this?" the Dragon Guard's eyes never left Stratos out of suspicion it seemed.

"This is Stratos," Zidane replied. "He is the Bearer of the Black Dragon Essence".

"How can this be?!" the man exclaimed as his eyes widened in shock. Zidane had never seen this Dragon Guard waver in his demeanor.

"Please, we don't have time to discuss this. Rhydin's fate is hanging by a thread," Maia pleaded.

"Very well. Back to your post, Knight," the Guard calmed from his shock. The Knight bowed and took his leave back down the hall

"Follow me to the chambers, Lord Zidane and guests," the Archway Guard said as he turned and walked into the Chambers of the Dragon Council. Zidane, Maia, Stratos, and with the Twins clinging to their parents followed the Guard into the chambers. As they entered the chambers, they immediately saw the dark abyss of a tunnel on the opposite side of the chamber. On either side of the council chamber two long tables were set where the members of the Dragon Council sat. Behind each one there was a dragon. All were of varying heights, shapes, and appearance. The Twins stood in awe of the dragons who stood before them. They had never seen a dragon up close, only in books and manuscripts. The members of the council stood as they entered the chambers and all bowed to them in unison. Even the dragons bowed their heads in respect.

"To what do we owe this visit, Lord Zidane?" one of the councilmen asked.

"The Shadow Lord has appeared on Rhydin and has conjured an army from the remnants of Sekmet's forces. He has empowered them with dark, shadow energy. They have taken over most of Rhydin. They plan on merging this Realm with the Shadow Realm," Zidane stepped upon the Eye of Ra that adorned the center of the chamber floor. There was a certain glow that surrounded Zidane as he spoke strongly to the men and dragons of the council.

"This is most disturbing. We must gather the Dragon Knights," one of the Dragons looked to his comrades. The other Councilmen nodded in agreement.

"Who is this, Lord Zidane?" one of the dragons asked looking at Stratos.

"There is a peculiar resemblance to you," one of the councilmen stated.

"This is because he is the Bearer of the Black Dragon Essence. He is from a parallel universe to our own. His name is Stratos. There is no time to explain the reason why he is here. What matters now is that he is here to help us as best he can," Zidane looked into the eyes of each of the councilmen. They all looked to each other in confusion.

"Zidane is right," a thunderous voice sounded from the dark tunnel. All looked to see billows of dark smoke hang heavy in the air. Then they saw eyes the color of a raging wildfire. Carline and Tritan took a hold of Maia's arms out of pure fear. They felt the floor quake under their feet as the thunderous footsteps drew closer to them. The enormous foot of a dragon emerged from the dark corridor with the razor sharp talons digging into the floor of the chambers. His massive head with two horns jutting from the crown of his head emerged from the corridor. The eyes of the Twins widened as they beheld the Red Dragon, Tufar. All of the councilmen and dragons bowed as Tufar emerged from his cave. Tufar's fire wreathed eyes immediately went to Stratos who was stunned with fear. Tufar then leaned his head down and came within inches of Stratos's face. Dark smoke billowed from Tufar's nostrils with every exhale.

"Your eyes tell a very sad story Stratos, Bearer of the Black Dragon Essence," Tufar's voice was low and rumbled within Stratos's chest. Stratos then lowered his head as if in shame. "Why do you lower your head?" Tufar asked.

"I am not worthy to be in the presence of a great dragon such as you," Stratos continued to avert his eyes from the Red Dragon.

"Mesnara has told me of why you are here, but also told me that you helped your counterpart in successfully rescuing his children from their prison. I do not think young Zidane and Maia could have accomplished that without your aid. The Heavens have a plan for each and every one of us. Sometimes we wander off of the path we are to travel to only find out who we are not, but then get back on the path to find out who we truly are," Tufar gave a slight smile. Stratos then raised his head and looked into the eyes of Tufar.

"Thank you, Tufar," Stratos said and bowed his head. Tufar then saw the Twins holding firmly to Maia's arms not taking their eyes off of him.

"Do not worry little ones, I prefer to protect you, not eat you," Tufar's laugh bellowed and echoed within the chamber.

"Tufar, we need the Dragon Knights. The Shadow Lord is on Rhydin with his Shadow empowered army. Much of Rhydin has fallen to the Shadows," Zidane stepped to Tufar.

"What do you plan to do, Zidane?" Tufar leaned his head to him.

"Stop the Shadow Lord. He is the source of this plight," Zidane said with growing intensity.

"Do you believe that you alone can stop him?" Tufar raised a brow. Zidane took a moment to answer. He turned to look at Stratos and Maia then back to Tufar.

"No, not alone," Zidane gave a shake of his head.

"You are not alone, Zidane. We are with you," Maia walked to be by his side.

"It is time that I redeem myself," Stratos placed his hand on Zidane's shoulder.

"And you will have the aid of the Dragon Knights," Tufar said.

"I thank you all," Zidane looked into the eyes of those who were around him.

"The Wildfire Dragon Armor is here, Lord Zidane," one of the councilmen said standing beside the rack with the crimson armor. Zidane walked to it and, with the help of Maia, he readied himself. Zidane strapped on his shin greaves and wrist gauntlet. Maia was behind him and strapped on his chest plate and cape. Carline stood in front of Zidane and handed to him his helmet while Tritan held the Horn of Summoning Dragon. Zidane took his helmet from Carline and the Horn from Tritan. He knelt to them and gave them both a hug and kiss on the forehead.

"No matter what happens this night, you two have been nothing but a blessing to me and your mother. We both are very proud of you," Zidane looked into their light brown eyes. He stood and faced Maia. No words were spoken, but they knew what the other was thinking. 'I love you' was the thought. Zidane took her in his arms with her head resting on his chest. Stratos stood at the middle of the chamber with Tufar standing next to him.

"You will need armor, Stratos," Tufar leaned down to him.

"Where am I going to get armor here?" Stratos looked up to the Red Dragon. Tufar turned his head to a rack in a dark corner on the far side of the chamber. It was covered by a dark veil. Stratos looked from Tufar to the rack then walked to it. He slowly reached out to the veil and pulled it away. On the rack there was a suit of armor. That armor was silver with gold trimming the edges. The chest plate and shoulder armor were crafted to fit the body of its wearer. The leg armor and wrist gauntlets were broad and thick with leather gloves fastened to the wrist gauntlets. The helmet covered the entire head, but left only a long, thin slit for the eyes to see.

"This armor appears to be old," Stratos ran his fingers across the metallic armor.

"It is over a thousand years old," Tufar stated.

"Over a thousand years old?!" Stratos turned his head back to Tufar in amazement that the armor lasted that long.

"It belonged to one of the great Dragon Lords," Tufar's tone softened when he spoke of him.

"Who did it belong to?" Stratos looked back to the armor.

"Do you recognize the armor, Zidane?" Tufar turned his head to face Zidane. Zidane took a moment and walked to the armor. Zidane ran his hand across the chest plate and helmet. His mind flashed back to a memory of him seemingly putting on the armor. A moment later, he regained his focus then looked to Stratos.

"This armor belonged to Giltia. The one whose soul fused with

Fid to create me. He was the knight who helped start this civilization," Zidane said. Tufar nodded in approval.

"You kept Giltia's armor even after he died?" Maia looked up to Tufar.

"Yes. Giltia and I were very close friends. After he died, the armor was one of the things that would remind me of him," there was a faint smile on the dragon's face.

"You are allowing me to wear his armor?" Stratos took a step away from it.

"It is not as strong as the Wildfire Dragon Armor, but it will prove sufficient for battle," Tufar replied. Stratos hesitated, then nodded and took the armor from the rack. Piece by piece he strapped on the chest plate with shoulder armor, then the armor that covered his shins and legs. He only put on one wrist gauntlet since he already had the Bracelet of Mentu on his right wrist. He looked at the helmet and hesitated in taking it. He brought his hand to the mask that covered half of his face. He let out a deep breath before slowly taking the mask off. He then took the helmet from the rack and replaced it with the mask he wore for thirteen years. With the helmet under his arm, he turned to face Tufar, Zidane, Maia, and the Twins. They saw the scars that covered half of his face. It was as if someone had set a fire to his flesh leaving unforgiving marks on that side of his face.

"Are we ready?" Tufar asked as he looked down to Zidane, Stratos, and Maia. They looked to each other taking a deep breath and nodded.

"Are the knights gathered?" Tufar turned to ask one of the Councilmen.

"They are, Lord Tufar," the councilman replied with a bow.

"Then let us make haste and save Rhydin," Zidane said. Zidane, Stratos, Maia, the Twins, followed by Tufar walked out of the chambers to meet the Dragon Knight army.

Shadows in the Distance

SHADOWS IN THE DISTANCE

OUTSIDE OF THE BRASS DOORS, the entire Dragon Knight army waited for Zidane, Stratos, Maia, Tufar, and the Twins. They stood in several single file lines. The Dragon Knights stood with their shoulders pinned back, chests out, chins up, and eyes forward at attention. Their massive shields and helmets were in one hand while their spears were in the other. Their double edged swords were strapped to their waists. To the right side of each knight their dragon companion stood. All stood straight and proud with their wings folded and tucked to their sides. Their eyes were focused and possessed a calm intensity. From the ranks of the Dragon Knight army, a familiar soldier approached them.

"Captain Antillus?" Zidane almost did not recognize the Knight who he fought beside against Sekmet's forces.

"*General* Antillus, Lord Zidane. I was granted a promotion in rank a few years after the battle against Sekmet," Antillus responded with a slight smile.

"It is good to see you again," Zidane reached out his hand to the knight.

"Likewise, Lord Zidane," Antillus clasped wrists with him.

"We need one of your captains," Maia approached him.

"Gladly, what is the task?" Antillus turned his eyes to Zidane's spouse.

"Once we fly over the Western Palace the Twins are to be dropped off, and then they must fly to the Northern Mountains to give this antidote to a friend of ours who is in the care of the Earth Shinobi.

This mission is to be entrusted to one of your best captains. There may be danger along the way. The Shadow Lord may be sending a contingent to wipe out the Earth Shinobi villages," Zidane took the vial of antidote from his belt.

"Captain," Antillus called. From the ranks a young man stepped forward and stood in front of Antillus.

"General, is that...?" Zidane started to ask.

"Captain Arteus. Yes, this is my son. A Dragon Knight," Antillus said proudly. Zidane approached Arteus and examined him from toe to head. Arteus wore the Dragon Knight armor proudly. He stood strong and with purpose.

"You have grown strong since I last saw you," Zidane still seemed in shock over how time passed by him.

"Thank you, Lord Zidane," Arteus said strongly.

"As we fly over the Western Palace, you are to safely drop off Tritan and Carline. Then you are to deliver this vial of antidote to the Earth Shinobi in the Northern Mountains. Our friend Rosey has been poisoned by the Shadows. It is important that she get this right away before she is lost," Zidane held out the vial for Arteus to take.

"I understand, Lord Zidane. I will not falter," Arteus took the vial and put it in his waist belt. Zidane and Maia then turned to Carline and Tritan looking into their eyes.

"Be brave. Arteus will look after you," Zidane looked from Tritan to Carline with softened eyes.

"Everything will be fine. Have faith," Maia gave a tight, warm hug to them both.

"We want...," Tritan started to say. "To help," Carline finished.

"I'm sorry, but you can't," Maia said holding back a tear.

"Why not?" they both asked.

"You both are too young. And, Heaven forbid, if anything were to happen to your mother and me you both are the future of this world. They will need you," Zidane reached forward to wipe away the tears that rolled down the cheeks of the Twins. They hugged each other. Arteus then escorted the Twins to Chaakar, his dragon companion.

Carline and Tritan climbed onto Chaakar and sat at the base of his neck.

"When in the air, hold on tightly," Chaakar turned his head to them. Stratos walked to Zidane and Maia's side and placed his hand on Zidane's shoulder.

"They will be fine. They survived a cell in the Shadow Realm," Stratos was attempting to ease his mind.

"I do not worry for them," Zidane gave a shake of his head.

"Who then?" Stratos asked.

"I worry for us," Zidane looked to Stratos. For the first time, Stratos saw what seemed to be fear in the eyes of Zidane.

"Why do you say that?" Stratos was confused by the look of fear in Zidane's eyes.

"If the Shadow empowered Orcs are more powerful and are in larger numbers than the demons we faced in the grove and at the fortress's entrance, our chances of surviving are slim," Zidane said to Stratos in a hushed tone so that the Dragon Knights would not to hear.

"Zidane is right. From the look of Rhydin, we don't have a great chance," fear had also touched Maia's heart, it seemed.

"I cannot believe what my ears hear. Zidane, you looked death in the face and were resurrected. I nearly killed you in the Western Mountain Valley, and both of you ventured into the Shadow Realm defeating a Rock behemoth and fought off an army of shadow demons. You both gave me hope that I could return to my universe and save the ones that I love. This is just one more challenge that we must face," Stratos looked deeply into the eyes of Zidane and Maia.

"Stratos is correct. You must band together like you did over a decade ago against Sekmet. You will need to utilize all of your abilities to face the Shadow Lord and his Army," Tufar leaned his head to the trio.

"We will need to be brave," Maia nodded at Tufar's words. Zidane took a deep breath looking to the ground. He clenched his jaw, his fist tightened, and a great intensity grew in his spirit and radiated from his eyes. Dark smoke billowed from his nose and his eyes flashed silver. He then put on his helmet as did Stratos. Maia readied her bow and quiver of arrows. Zidane turned and looked upon the army of dragons and Dragon Knights that stood before him.

"Tonight, we face the horde that emerges from the Shadows! Tonight, we defend Rhydin from the demons that would dare invade our land! These beasts are not invincible. Take their heads and you will slay them. The Shadow Lord has brought anarchy to our land! It is war he wants and we, as the Dragon Knights, will give him war!" Zidane exclaimed with the Dragon Knights rallying with him.

"Dragons and Dragon Knights, what is our creed?!" Tufar roared.

"We the Dragon Knights of Rhydin, pledge our hearts, our souls, and our bodies to protect those who are in need; to uphold and enforce the laws of this land; to vanquish any evil that may threaten or plague the land," all dragons and Dragon Knights said in unison. Tufar then reeled his head back and letting out an inferno of flames into the air and along with him the thunderous roars of the dragons.

"Dragon Knights, take flight!" Zidane shouted as he, Maia, and Stratos climbed on the back of Tufar. The Dragon Knights followed suit by putting their helmets on and climbing on to the backs of their dragon companions. With Zidane, Maia, and Stratos on his back, Tufar took the lead and was the first to take off up and toward the opening in the side of the mountain. He was closely followed by Antillus and his dragon. Then Chaakar, with Arteus, Carline, and Tritan on his back was next followed by the rest of the dragons and Dragon Knights. The ground of the mountain valley was shrouded by the shadows of the dragons flying overhead. Afelina, with many other villagers, stood at the entrance of the village watching the Dragon Knights fly east to battle.

In the war room of the Western Palace, Aero, Craven, Captain Damien, and Captain Aldar gathered around a wooden table with a map of Mainland Rhydin at the center. They were devising a scheme of how to defend the land from the Shadow Army.

"What are we to do, Lord Aero? We are severely outnumbered in this fight," Craven said, stroking his full beard in thought.

"The Lycan is correct. We cannot win this battle through brute strength," Damien gave a shake of his head.

"You both are correct. We will need tactics to at least slow these beasts down," Aero looked to each person in the room.

"Are you saying we are to hold out until Lord Zidane, Lady Maia, and Prince Kulla return?" Aldar raised an eyebrow to his elf lord.

"Yes, Captain Aldar. Without the Ancient Relics, we do not have any advantage. But, what we do have is knowledge of the terrain and knowledge of their weaknesses," Aero responded.

"And what are those weaknesses?" Damien folded his arms in front of his chest.

"We all know that they are slain when beheaded. I have also heard the Shadow Lord is weakened by the light from the North Star," Aero pointed upward as if the North Star was right above them.

"How are we to get light from the North Star?" Craven stood confused by the mention of the celestial object.

"We cannot. But we do have another option that will stall them," Aero looked to his Lycan comrade.

"And what is that?" Aldar asked.

"In our last battle, fire seemed to slow them down significantly. We will use that to our advantage," Aero said with a slight grin on his face.

"How will we do that?" Damien looked from Aero to the map.

"It is called the Ring of Fire," Aero responded with a flash of excitement in his eyes.

"The Ring of Fire?" Aldar asked even more confused.

"Yes. We will need as much oil and dry hay and rope as we can possibly get. Gather your pack, Craven. We will need your strength for this battle. Aldar and Damien, rouse all of the elf and vampire soldiers. Tell them to gather the rope and hay. We have much work to do before the Shadow Army bears down on us. We make our last stand here," Aero pounded his fist into the map in front of them.

They nodded then left to complete their assignments. Aero stayed in the war room for a few moments looking at the map of Rhydin.

Within the walls of the Western Palace, groups of elf and vampire soldiers were gathering bundles of hay and dry tinder into numerous piles. Other groups of vampire and elf soldiers were gathering the piles of hay and tinder to tie it all together into a six foot sphere with thickly woven rope. In their beast forms, the lycans were gathering heavy clay capsules that were being crafted in the furnaces of the Western Palace by many of the villagers and members of the Vampire Coven. There was a small hole made in each of the clay capsules so that the lycans could lift barrels of oil and pour it in the capsules. Once filled, the lycans put a cork in the hole to seal it. Numerous clay capsules were filled with oil and were being set next to the catapults in front of the palace. Two hundred yards outside of the Palace walls, a small group of lycans, vampires, and elves were pouring the thick oil on to the ground, saturating the soil. Aero was walking along the palace grounds, overseeing the progress of his plan to make sure that everything was to his standards.

"Aero, where are the villagers and children to go once the battle starts?" Melina asked as they were walking among those making the spherical bundles of dry hay and tinder.

"I think they will be safest in the underground chambers. I will have a small platoon on guard there. If anything goes wrong, there is an underground tunnel that leads to the Northern Mountains. You will need to lead them there," Aero turned his eyes to her.

"I am not going to stand by to wait for the fate of my husband. You will need all of the help you can get on the battlefield. The only ones you have are Captain Aldar, Captain Damien, and Craven. There is no one else here that equals your ability. You will need my summoning abilities" she pled looking into his eyes.

"I know we will be outmatched physically, but if anything were to go wrong on the battle field, you will have to lead our people to safety and possibly start anew. You will also need to take Troy and M' Kara into your care. They are the future of our kingdom," Aero placed his hands on her shoulders.

"Shall I send word to the villagers to come here and bring only what they need?" Melina gave a reluctant nod, conceding to his wish. Aero did not answer, but held her in his arms.

In the dojo style training room in the Western Palace, Troy and M' Kara kept themselves busy by honing their skills. There were wooden logs hanging from the ceiling of the dojo that were controlled by a mechanism that made them sway from left to right. On the sides of the logs were targets. Troy stood ten yards in front of the undulating targets. Troy took a shuriken from his belt and threw it over handed with all of his strength. The shuriken embedded itself in the opposite wall, missing his target. Frustration built within him and his eyes flashed white. On the other end of the dojo, M' Kara was sitting in a wooden chair with her legs crossed and the book of Ancient Spells sitting in her lap. She intently read through the tattered pages. It would seem that after each incantation, a mishap would occur. One spell was to conjure fire in one's hand. She conjured the fire, but it slightly burned her hand. Another incident was her attempting to levitate. She closed her eyes and focused her thoughts. She levitated, but once she opened her eyes, she found that she was too far in the air. She panicked and lost her concentration to only fall to the mat below. Troy saw this and quickly rushed to her to see that she was unharmed.

"How are you doing with your exercises?" M' Kara groaned and got herself into a sitting position.

"In total, I have hit none of those targets," he presented the 'unharmed' swaying targets and numerous shuriken embedded in the opposite wall.

"I have not done better. I can't control the spells," M' Kara said with frustration building in her voice. At that moment, Melina, with a few elf soldiers escorting her, entered the dojo. Troy and M' Kara stood as they entered.

"So this is where you have been all this time," Melina looked to the two younglings.

"We are training," a discouraged tone was within Troy's voice.

"And how is that faring?" Melina tilted her head to the side.

"Not good," M' Kara said as she took the spell book from the chair.

"You two are young. You have plenty of time to develop your abilities," Melina said to reassure them.

"Alright," both Troy and M' Kara said.

"We need to get to the underground chambers, away from the battle," both nodded and followed Melina and the soldiers out of the dojo to the underground chambers.

THE LAST STAND

OFF IN THE DISTANCE, TOWARD the east, the shroud of shadows crept closer and closer toward the west. The shroud covered the night sky and casted the Woodland Realm into a shadow. The merging of the two realms was nearing. All the Shadow Lord had to do was overtake the Northern Mountains and the Western Province; the last of the surviving regions of the Krystal Kingdom. The legions of the Shadow Army marched through the woods destroying whatever laid in their path. There was but one army that stood between the Shadow Legions and the rest of Rhydin. That Army was made of the remnants of the Southeast Vampire Coven led by Captain Damien, the Lycan Pack led by Craven, and the Elf Empire led by Captain Aldar and Aero. Catapults were set on either side of the palace. Several rows of archers were positioned on the walls and others were in the windows of the palace. Their eyes were fixed upon the grasslands to the east. There were several scattered wooden walls set fifty yards from the palace walls. These wooden makeshift walls were eight feet in height. Behind these walls were the lycans readied in their beast forms. Each lycan held the rope to spheres made from tied tinder and hay. Aero was at the head of what was left of the Krystal Kingdom Army. Aldar and Damien were alongside him with the vampire and elf troops mounted on horses behind them in front of the palace walls. Their eyes narrowed as the shroud of shadow overtook the woods and were hovering over the grasslands.

"The shroud of shadow is near!" Aero shouted. The elf and vampire ground troops drew their weapons, the archers on the palace walls readied their bows and arrows waiting for their orders, and the lycans on the field tightened their grip on the roped spheres. Aero drew his sword and raised it to the sky signaling for the catapults to be readied. The lycans, in their beast forms, hoisted massive stones onto the catapults with the elf and vampire troops readied at the levers to release at the oncoming Shadow Legions. Aero's eyes were fixed upon the grasslands waiting for the Legion of Shadows to draw closer.

The shroud of shadow was finally drawing within range. The grunts and growls of the shadow empowered orcs and abominations were heard. The ground beneath the lycans' feet rumbled with the footsteps of the oncoming army. The sky continued to darken as the Shadow Army marched across the grasslands. Hundreds upon hundreds of shadow empowered orcs and abominations marched onward toward the Western Palace. The eyes of the Krystal Kingdom Army widened as they beheld the massive Army of Shadow. Several horses reared up to their hind legs for fear of this incredible evil.

Aero turned his horse around to face the army behind him, "Elves, Vampires, and Lycans of the Krystal Army, steady your horses, still your hearts, ease your bodies, and quiet the doubting voices that speak to you! Do not fear these beasts, for they are not invincible! These Orcs and Abominations *can* be defeated! We are Rhydin's last defense against these demons! We shall not let them overcome us! After this night, Rhydin shall be a free land from the horde of Shadow! With hope in our hearts and faith in the Heavens above, we shall not fear the Sea of Shadows!".

The spirits of the vampire, elf, and lycan troops were livened; their hearts were strengthened and their bodies were empowered. They shouted their war cries letting the Shadow Legions know that they did not fear them. They were standing tall and strong in the face of their evil. Aero turned his horse around to face the oncoming Shadow Army that continued to march across the grasslands. Aero raised his sword once more to the sky and waited for the Shadow Army to come within range of the catapults. The troops at the catapults waited for his command. When Aero saw a great number of the Shadow Army march into range, he cut his sword toward the ground signaling for the catapults. The elf and vampire troops pulled on the levers and released a barrage of heavy stones at the Shadow Army. These stones were not aimed in the thick of the Shadow Army, but were aimed to the right and left flanks of them. The orcs and abominations were moving inward to avoid the oncoming stones. Aero grinned as he watched the Shadow Troops moving inward creating a large group toward the middle of the battlefield. Again, Aero raised his sword to the sky. At this signal, the archers on the palace wall, and in the scattered windows, drew arrows that had the heads engulfed in flame. Aero waited for the Shadow Troops to draw closer to them. The Army of Shadow continued to march forward, despite the continuing barrage of heavy stones. Once they reached the middle of the battlefield, Aero gave a grin.

"They are now in place," he said as he again cut his sword toward the ground to signal the archers. The archers released their arrows into the air. A shower of flame engulfed arrows fell all around the Shadow Army. To the surprise of the Shadow Orcs and Abominatons, none of the arrows pierced any of them, but stuck into the ground around them. Soon, they found themselves encircled by a wall of flames. The flame tipped arrows ignited the oil saturated ground and burst into a wall of flame. The Shadow troops became anxious and backed away from the wall of flames, bunching closer together toward the middle.

"Prepare the capsules!" Captain Aldar shouted back. The lycans adjusted the catapults to aim for the Shadow Troops in the ring of fire. The others then loaded the clay capsules onto the catapults.

"Release the capsules!" Captain Damien ordered. The Vampire and Elf troops pulled on the levers and released the capsules into the air toward the Shadow Orcs and Abominations. As these capsules crashed and shattered upon the Shadow troops, thick oil splashed and clung to the skin of the Shadow troops.

"Oil?!" an Orc exclaimed as it tried to wipe the thick liquid off, as did his comrades. More of those capsules were released into the Shadow Army, spreading more among the troops.

"Lycans!" at Aero's order, the lycans on the field emerged from behind the makeshift walls, dragging the roped spheres of dry tinder and hay. Once the Lycans were clear of the walls, they began to spin in place with the rope clutched tightly in their massive paws. Gaining speed and momentum, the lycans let loose the spheres. Rolling toward the wall of flames, the spheres immediately burst into flames. The Shadow Troops saw these balls of flame roll toward them but they did not react in time to avoid them. They were overtaken. The orcs and abominations were engulfed in flames as the oil on their bodies was ignited.

"Archers, fire!" Aldar shouted. The archers on the walls and in the windows released arrows into the air and down upon the encircled orcs and abominations. A barrage of arrows showered down upon the Shadow troops. The fiery shower of arrows embedded themselves into the skulls and necks of their targets. The numbers of the Shadow Army dwindled as this unrelenting attack from the Krystal Kingdom Army continued.

"Your plan is working, Lord Aero. The Ring of Fire has slowed them down significantly," Damien rejoiced.

"This will give Lord Zidane, Lady Maia, and Prince Kulla time to arrive," Aldar's eyes never left the battlefield in front of him.

"I hope this strategy will hold them," Aero remembered the previous battle he was in with the Shadow Army. His eyes surveyed the battle. He saw the flight of the arrows continuing to rain down upon the Shadow Army. The Shadow orcs and abominations were struggling to fight off the flames that were set to their bodies. Many bodies of the Shadow Army littered the grounds within the Ring of Fire. Others were fighting off the flames or were severely wounded with arrows in their necks. The confidence of the Krystal Kingdom Army began to rise as they observed the Shadow Army shrink in size.

The rejoicing did not last for much longer. The ears of the Elf soldiers heard a horn sounding from within the woods, many yards away, and all the eyes of the elf soldiers searched the tree line for any adversaries. Aero then spotted several catapults being pulled by abominations out of the woods and onto the grasslands to enter the battlefield. Close behind the catapults were several lines of orc and abomination troops.

"They had reserves waiting and watching," Aldar drew his sword.

"They waited for us to use our resources?" Damien looked to Aero as if searching for an explanation for the rationale of the Shadow Army.

"They are also using the catapults from the Eastern Palace against us," Aero clenched his teeth and tightened the grip on his sword. By now the Shadow Orcs and Abominations who were trapped in the Ring of Fire were all vanquished in that massacre. The numbers of those caught in the Ring of Fire did not compare in size to the army that was emerging from the woods. Aero saw that in addition to the Shadow Orcs and Abominations, there were Shadow Demons mixed into the Army.

"The Shadow Lord has summoned his Demons to join this army. Captain Damien, quickly get a report from the catapult contingent," Aero turned his eyes to the Vampire Captain.

"Yes, Lord Aero," Damien turned his horse and quickly turned to the catapult troops.

"Captain Aldar, quickly get a report from the archers," Aero shifted his gaze to his Elf Captain.

"I will, Sir," Aldar responded as he quickly turned his horse. Aero's eyes then became fixed upon the growing number of the Shadow Legions. The sea of Shadows poured out of the woods, spread across the grasslands, and marched toward the palace poised to swallow it whole. In the back of Aero's mind, he came to realize that he may not last through this battle. He came upon an enemy that was near invincible and seemed to have no end. Both Aldar and Damien returned to his side.

"There are a dozen boulders for each of the catapults and only a few capsules of oil, Lord Aero," the vampire reported.

"And the archers have a half a quiver of arrows left," Aldar added.

"Very well," Aero nodded his head. "Aldar sound for the lycans in the field to return. Damien, signal for the catapult contingent to ready the oil capsules with torches in hand and tell the archers to light the heads of their arrows".

"Yes, Lord Aero," Damien returned to the catapult units and gave the orders, while Aldar blew a deep breath into a conical horn sounding for Craven and the lycans to return. Craven and the lycans who manned the spheres of hay and tinder immediately returned to the palace and took their place among the ranks of the Krystal Kingdom Army.

"What are we to do, Lord Aero?" Craven transformed to his human form.

"We will use what is left of the oil capsules and light them and release flamed arrows," Aero responded. Craven nodded and left to take his place at a catapult. Aero faced the battlefield and raised his sword once more to the sky. The lycans loaded the oil capsules onto the catapults then took out the corks of the capsules and replaced it with a piece of cloth so that the vampire and elf troops could light the oil within. The archers lit the tips of their arrows and waited for the order from Aero. Aero narrowed his eyes as he was poised waiting for the Shadow Army to draw closer.

"Release the Rain of Fire!" Aero shouted as he saw the Shadow Army come within range of their catapults and arrows. The elf and vampire troops at the catapults placed the flame of their torches to the pieces of cloth. The oil capsules were then released upon Aero's command. The archers released their flamed arrows into the air following the oil capsules. Once the capsules crashed upon the ground, they shattered and burst into flames spreading among the main forces of the Shadow Army. Many Shadow orcs, demons, and abominations were set on fire while others were pierced by the rain of flame tipped arrows. Many of the Shadow Legion fell to the relentless Rain of Fire. Despite the Rain of Fire being unleashed and creating casualties, many of the Shadow Army endured and continued their march toward the walls of the Western Palace.

"What are we to do now, Lord Aero? All of our oil capsules have been launched and the archers are running out of arrows," Aldar looked to Aero for his next orders. Aero turned his eyes to the Army that was bearing down upon the walls of the Western Palace. His grip on the hilt of his sword tightened as he closed his eyes.

"Lord Aero?" Damien called to him.

"Captain Aldar, sound the charge," Aero said through his teeth as he opened his eyes.

"Sir, are you certain?" Aldar asked as he hesitated to sound the charge.

"We cannot allow the courage in our hearts to fade away, Aldar. Our enemies are bearing down upon us relentlessly. They mean to destroy all that we hold dear in our hearts and swallow it in dark Shadow. All that is beautiful and good will be extinguished. We cannot allow them to pass us. We must fight. We will hold them as long as we can until Zidane, Maia, and Kulla return to us. The Trinity will be here. Until then, we must muster the strength that is in each and every one of our hearts and hold off this evil," Aero's eyes seared into those of his Elf Captain. "Aldar, sound the charge," he raised his sword to the sky once more with his hand firmly gripped on the hilt. Aldar nodded his head with a renewed strength in his heart. He inhaled a deep breath and blew into his conical horn that sounded throughout the hills and echoed so much so that the Shadow Army heard and almost halted in their march. Aero spurred his horse to a slow gallop followed closely by Captains Aldar and Damien. They were then followed by the other elf and vampire troops on foot, along with the lycans who one by one were slowly shifting into their wolf-beast form. The Orc Leader pushed his way to the front of the Shadow Army and looked upon the charging army of the Krystal Kingdom.

"They are far inferior to us," an Abomination said in an arrogant tone.

"We will easily wipe them out," another Orc hissed.

"That's what we thought over ten years ago. They beat us then and almost wiped us out. Stay focused!" the Orc Leader barked.

In the meantime, Aero continued to lead the Krystal Kingdom in a slow gallop toward the Shadow Army with his sword raised to the sky. Craven was alongside Aero, as were Aldar and Damien. Aero brought down his sword signaling the archers on the walls of the palace to release the last of their arrows upon the front ranks of the Shadow Army. The arrows flew into the air and down onto the front lines of the Shadow Army. Many of the Shadow troops were struck in the head and neck by the shower of arrows, wounding them while others were pierced in the arm or chest. While the Shadow troops were recovering from the rain of arrows, Aero and the Krystal Kingdom Army were bearing down on them. The distraction of the bombardment of arrows did not allow the Shadow troops to form any type of defensive formation. This allowed for the Krystal Kingdom Army to crash through the front lines of the Shadow Army.

Aero, Damien, and Aldar rode through, slashing to their left and right at the heads and necks of the shadow empowered orc, abominations, and shadow demons. Craven and the rest of the lycan pack leapt at the Shadow troops, slashing at their necks with their razor sharp claws. The lycans used their pure strength to not only bring down the massive abominations, but to also pick up and use the shadow demons to throw at other Shadow troops. The Orc Leader was knocked backwards on his back by Aero's horse and was nearly trampled by the other horses of the troops of the Krystal Kingdom Army. Aero, Aldar, and Damien followed by the elf and vampire troops continued their charge through the sea of Shadow Troops. An abomination stepped in the path of Aero's horse and hoisted it in the air, throwing Aero off and into a group of shadow demons. As Aero hit the ground, he rolled up to his feet drawing a dagger and had his sword in the other hand. He slashed and stabbed at the necks of the demons. The Shadow Demons surrounded Aero and greatly outnumbered him. Aero quickly side stepped and ducked under each of their attacks.

Aldar and Damien continued riding through the army of Shadow troops with the elf and vampire troops riding by their sides. A small grouping of Shadow Demons stood in front of Aldar and Damien. Both narrowed their eyes and tightened the grip on their swords. The Shadow Demons did not flinch and stood their ground against the oncoming troops. As Aldar and Damien drew within fifteen yards of the Shadow Demons, the Demons outreached their hands and released a barrage of shadow spikes at the Krystal Kingdom troops. Aldar was pierced through his left shoulder and thrown off his horse while Damien was struck in the leg. The other troops were severely wounded by the shadow spikes and were either thrown off their horses and struggling to get to their feet, or they remained laid out on the ground. Aldar slowly rose to his feet and took the spike from his shoulder. His left arm felt dead and heavy to him, almost useless. He bent his arm at the elbow and kept it close to his body as he raised his sword to defend himself.

Damien too was slow to get to his feet. He found the spike had gone straight through his leg and was showing on the other side. Damien pulled the spike out from his leg. He had no feeling in his leg. Much like Aldar's arm and shoulder, Damien's leg felt dead to him. He could not even force it to move.

Aldar fought his way to Damien and a few other Vampire and Elf troops. They were soon surrounded by shadow orcs and demons. Shield bearing Elf troops stood between the surrounding Shadow troops and Aldar, Damien, and the other Krystal Kingdom troops. A haunting howl was heard echoing from the frontlines of the Shadow Army. The Shadow troops turned to see several charging lycans with Craven leading them. Craven leapt to the air and landed on three Shadow Demons taking them to the ground then slashed at their necks. The other lycans leapt over the surrounding Shadow troops and stood with the rest of the soldiers of the Krystal Kingdom.

"Where is Lord Aero?!" Craven shouted as he hurled a Shadow Demon into an oncoming Abomination.

"We have not seen him since the charge!" Aldar responded as he stabbed at the neck of an Orc. The Elf troops bearing shields crouched down with their shields in front of them and aimed their

spears and swords outward over their shields. These Elf troops
formed a circle around Aldar, Damien, and the other Elf and Vampire
troops. The Shadow Demons and Orcs crashed upon the shields and
were immediately met with the tips of swords and spears.

"This enclosure will not hold them for long!" Aldar shouted to
Damien as he slashed at the neck of a Shadow Orc.

"We have to act now if we are to have a chance!" Damien
responded as he struggled to stay on his feet. Damien surveyed the
battlefield and found scattered pockets of troops from the Krystal
Kingdom Army surrounded by troops from the Shadow Army.

"We have to make our way to those small groupings of our
troops!" Damien shouted pointing to the small pockets of soldiers
from the Krystal Kingdom.

"Form the Phalanx! Shield bearers, face north! Everyone else get
behind the wall of shields! Lycans, cover the rear!" at Aldar's orders,
the shield bearing soldiers formed a wall of shields from the circle
formation they were in. Then, the Vampire and other Elf troops
took their places behind the shields. The Lycans, led by Craven,
acted as the rearguard for the phalanx. Shadow Demons and Orcs
crashed upon the shields, attacking them with ferocity. The attempts
of the Shadow troops to break through the phalanx failed. They only
received the points of swords and spears to their heads and necks.
The phalanx of Elf shields moved forward leaving a trail of Orc
and Shadow Demon corpses. While the phalanx marched through
the battlefield, they gathered the small pockets of Krystal Kingdom
troops, enlarging the phalanx.

"Do you see Lord Aero?!" Aldar shouted to Damien. Damien was
still struggling to stay on his feet.

"I do not see him!" Damien responded as he thrust his sword
over the shoulder of an Elf soldier, stabbing a Demon in the neck.
Aldar scanned the battlefield in front of him, and found a wave of
Abominations charging straight at the wall of Elf shields. Aldar's eyes
widened as he saw the mammoth creatures.

"Brace yourselves!" Aldar firmly planted his feet into the ground.

The Elf shield bearing soldiers tightened their lines and braced themselves for the massive creatures. Their eyes were fixed upon the Abominations. Their feet were firmly planted on the ground. The Shadow empowered Abominations tightened their grips on their massive clubs and war hammers. The ground underneath the army of the Krystal Kingdom shook.

"Steady!" Damien shouted.

"Hold your ground!" Aldar added as he clenched his teeth. Moments later, the Abominations crashed through the wall of shields, sending Elf and Vampire troops backwards. Damien rolled out of the way of the Abomination charge as did Aldar. Still wounded from the shadow spikes, Damien and Aldar struggled to defend themselves from the constant onslaught from the Shadow Legions. They watched Elves, Vampires, and Lycans fall to the attacks of the Shadow horde all around them. Very few of the Shadow soldiers fell to the blades of the Krystal Kingdom.

"We cannot hold out much longer!" Damien shouted now noticing they were greatly outnumbered. He turned to find an Abomination with a battle axe raised over his head. With his leg incapacitated, Damien could not move quickly enough out of the way of the incoming attack. The battle axe was being brought down, but was blocked by the sword of Aldar. He stepped in front of the Abomination and locked his sword with the blades of the axe. With a roar, the Abomination kicked Aldar in the chest sending him back into other Elf soldiers. Damien took a dagger from his belt and threw it at the Abomination, hitting it in the shoulder. The Abomination looked at the dagger and pulled it out. The Abomination swung its fist at Damien and sent him back into Aldar and the other Elf soldiers. As Damien and Aldar were on the ground, they saw the Abomination loom over them. The Abomination placed its foot on Aldar's chest and was about to deal the final blow when a shadowy figure leapt into the air from behind the Abomination and thrust its sword in its neck. The Abomination fell backwards with a dull *thud*.

Aldar and Damien discovered the shadowy figure was Aero. Aero held out his hand to help Aldar and then Damien to their feet.

"What happened to you, Lord Aero?" Aldar winced from the pain in his shoulder.

"I was occupied by several Shadow Demons," Aero responded out of breath.

"What is our plan of action?" Damien asked while other Elf, Vampire, and Lycan troops gathered together.

"At this point, we need to get back to the Palace walls and not let them pass," Aero's eyes surveyed the battlefield.

"Where is Craven?" Aldar searched their surroundings.

"I do not know. I did not see him while I was fighting my way to you. We might find him on the way back to the walls. We need to move now," Aero responded. At his order, the group of Elf, Vampire, and Lycan troops, led by Aero, Damien, and Aldar fought their way through the Shadow Orcs, Abominations, and Demons toward the walls of the Western Palace. Aero gathered energy into the steel of his sword and thrust it to the ground creating a wave of energy to surge through the ground underneath the feet of a group of Shadow Demons. The ground exploded from under the Demons, throwing them in different directions of the air. From the smoke of the explosion, an Abomination charged through straight at Aero. Aero slid to a stop and braced for an attack from the Abomination. A howl was heard just before the Abomination could attack Aero. Craven leapt at the neck of the Abomination clawing and slashing at it, bringing it to the ground.

"Well done, Craven," Aero said.

"You're welcome, Lord Aero," Craven growled as they continued to fight their way through the sea of Shadow troops. Many Elf, Vampire, and Lycan troops fell to the hands of the Shadow Army. Aero, Craven, Damien, and Aldar with the remaining troops of the Krystal Kingdom broke through the front lines of the Shadow Army and made their retreat toward the walls of the Western Palace with the Shadow Army giving chase.

Within fifty yards of the palace walls, Aero stopped in his retreat with his eyes and head lowered. Aldar stopped as he noticed Aero was not running at his side. With his arm still tucked to his body, Aldar made his way back to Aero.

"Lord Aero, what are you doing? We need to get back within the Palace walls," Aero's sudden change in demeanor confused the Elf Captain.

"We cannot," Aero simply said.

"What?! Why not?!" Aldar questioned him.

"We have to stall them. If we go back within the walls they will break through and eventually into the Palace where our elders, women, and children are taking shelter from this carnage. There are not enough of us to stop them within our walls. We must make a stand here," Aero said sternly as he raised his head to face Aldar. Aldar looked from Aero then to the charging sea of Shadow troops bearing down on them. Aldar took a deep breath and stood next to Aero facing the oncoming Shadow Army. Aero tightened his grip on the hilt of his sword with energy flowing from his arm into the steel of the blade. Soon Craven, Damien, and the rest of the Krystal Kingdom stood in three rows, all were shoulder to shoulder, spanning the front wall of the Palace, standing tall between the Shadow Army and the gates to the Western Palace. The Shadow Army drew closer to the front line of what was left of the Krystal Kingdom Army, the last resistance of the Realm of Light. The catapults on the lines of the Shadow Army released massive boulders toward the Krystal Kingdom troops. All eyes were fixed upon the boulders in mid-flight.

"May the Heavens be with us," Aero muttered to himself as he watched the boulders draw closer and saw the Shadow Army bear down upon them. Aero crouched down and crossed his forearms in front of him to brace for the massive boulders. Closer and closer the boulders came and each of the soldiers on the side of the Krystal Kingdom held their breath as they anticipated the crushing blow of the boulders. Aero closed his eyes as he saw a boulder bear down on him. Moments passed and Aero found that he was not crushed by the massive boulder. He slowly opened his eyes to find the boulder had stopped only a few feet above his head as did the other boulders that were hurled at them. Aero and the other soldiers of the Krystal Kingdom found a strange aura surrounding each of the boulders hovering above them. Then a bellowing horn was heard from just beyond the Western Palace and a thunderous roar was heard throughout the western hills. Aero turned and looked to the sky to see an armada of dragons with their Dragon Knights. At the front of the army of dragons was Tufar and on his back were Zidane, Maia, and someone who was unfamiliar to Aero. The Shadow Army halted in their march upon the gates of the Western Palace seeing the fleet of dragons flying from the west.

"Lord Zidane and Lady Maia have returned!" Aldar shouted triumphantly.

In the sky, Zidane, Maia, and Stratos looked upon the battlefield in front of the Western Palace. They saw the carnage that was the result of an immense battle. Many bodies of Elves, Lycans and Vampires littered the grounds of the Western Hills and very few, in comparison with Krystal Army, of those were from the Shadow Army. Maia's eyes were glowing brightly as she held out her hand using the power of the Necklace of Isis to stop the boulders from crushing the Krystal Kingdom Army.

"There are so few," Zidane said grimly.

"The Shadow Army is stronger and grows stronger with each territory it conquers," Stratos looked to the shadows that spread across the skies.

"And the Western Province is the last threat to them," Tufar growled.

"Aero and the Krystal Army are not going to last long, we have to act fast," Maia used the power of the Necklace to hurl the boulders back at the Shadow Army, crushing several of the catapults.

"Arteus leave the Twins in the courtyard and make your way to the Northern Mountains to help the Earth Shinobi!" Arteus nodded at Zidane's order and directed Chakaar to the ground. Tritan and

Carline hopped down to the ground from Chakaar's back, "Get to safety and let the people know Lord Zidane and Lady Maia have returned with the Dragon Knights," the Twins nodded and ran to the main doors of the palace. Arteus made sure they made it inside before he and Chakaar made their way north to prevent the attack upon the villages of the Earth Shinobi.

"Circle above the Palace, Tufar," Tufar did as Zidane asked of him and the rest of the Dragons followed Tufar.

"Maia, I want you to tell Aero to make a charge toward the Shadow Army," Zidane turned his head to face her.

"But that is suicide, Zidane!" Stratos protested.

"Trust me," Zidane looked into the eyes of both Maia and Stratos.

"I will," Maia responded hesitantly. She closed her eyes and placed her hand on the Necklace concentrating its energy to her mind, "*Aero, Zidane wants you to lead a charge toward the Shadow Army,*" her voice resonated in his mind. Aero nodded and raised his sword to the sky signaling a charge.

"Lord Aero! What are you doing?!" Craven growled placing his massive paw on Aero's shoulder.

"Zidane wants me to lead a charge into the Shadow Army," his eyes were fixed upon the sea of Dark Shadow who resumed in their march toward the gates.

"But that is suicide!" Damien exclaimed.

"I have faith in Zidane," Aero calmly responded, still with his eyes fixed upon the Shadow Army. Damien, Craven, and Aldar looked to each other and then to the Shadow Army who were nearing the palace walls.

"As do I," Aldar inhaled a deep breath and tightened the grip on his sword. Damien and Craven clenched their jaws and both nodded their heads to Aero and Aldar. They readied themselves as did the rest of the army of the Krystal Kingdom. Aero started with a steady run toward the Shadow Army. From above the palace, Zidane, Maia, Stratos and Tufar saw Aero lead the steady charge at the Shadow Army.

"They have started their charge like you said. What do you plan on next?" Stratos's fists were clenched tightly to the point they were trembling. Zidane sending his allies charging at the front lines of the Shadow Army caused his body to tense with anxiety.

"Draw your Dragon Blades and ready yourself, Stratos. We are in for a wild ride," Zidane drew his Dragon Blades with his eyes flaring red. Maia readied her bow and arrows. Tufar then led several Dragons down to the battlefield while the others, led by Antillus, flew higher above the battlefield. Tufar soared just above the heads of Aero and the charging Krystal Kingdom. Tufar gathered a ball of flames in his mouth and his eyes began to seep with ferocious flames.

"Tufar, release your fury!" Zidane's voice boomed and resonated in the air above the Krystal Kingdom Army. Tufar blew a fireball as did the other Dragons alongside him at the frontlines of the Shadow Army. There were several explosions of flames as the fireballs hit the troops of the Shadow Army. As soon as that line of Dragons released their fireballs, they climbed higher into the sky allowing the company of Dragons led by Antillus and his Dragon to fly in closer toward the ground and release another barrage of fireballs. This barrage of fire greatly crippled the frontlines of the Shadow Army allowing for Aero and the Krystal Kingdom Army to charge fully toward them and attack relentlessly. Aero slashed his way through the burning front lines along with Damien, Craven and Aldar by his side.

"Very good, Zidane. But, when do we get to fight?" Stratos's demeanor changed when he saw the front lines of the Shadow Army scorched by Dragon flames. His eyes were wild with lust for battle.

"I am to assume very shortly," Tufar said.

"Why do you say that?" Maia looked to the Red Dragon.

"Look at the tree line," Tufar nodded his massive head in the direction he spoke of. Zidane, Maia, and Stratos focused their vision and saw ranks of archers emerging from the tree line and onto the battlefield with arrows seeping with shadow energy. Close behind them, giant crossbows were being rolled out by several Shadow empowered Abominations.

"That does not favor us. Those giant crossbows look like they can kill a Dragon. We had best be careful," Stratos tensed once more seeing the menacing iron crossbows.

"Did I not say we were in for a wild ride? Hang on!" Zidane leaned forward in his seat on Tufar's back. Antillus and the remaining Dragon Knights joined them.

"Antillus, be careful of the Shadow Archers!" Zidane shouted to him and pointed to the tree line.

"We will dispose of them!" Antillus shouted and led a group of Dragon Knights and Dragons toward the tree line. As they drew closer, the Abominations loaded the giant crossbows with steel pikes.

"Zidane, they are loading the giant crossbows! Antillus and his company will be in trouble!" Stratos's eyes had been focused on the tree lines scouting their predicament.

"The Young Dragon is right, Zidane," Tufar concurred, "We Dragons cannot withstand a shot from those giant crossbows," Tufar blew a fireball down upon the Shadow Army causing an explosion throwing many Shadow troops in to the air.

"Maia, can you reach Antillus telepathically to warn him and his company to fall back?" Zidane asked.

"I can try," Maia said as she touched the Necklace with her fore and middle fingers. She concentrated the energy into her mind and searched for Antillus's, "*Antillus, pull back. They are waiting for you and your company with the giant crossbows. Your Dragons cannot withstand that type of attack*". Antillus raised his spear signaling for his company to turn back, but it was too late. The Abominations at the giant crossbows released the steel pikes into the air toward the incoming Dragon Knights and their Dragons. The steel pikes pierced the tough scales of many of the Dragons, bringing them and their Dragon Knights to the ground. Some were wounded and many others died from the steep fall. Antillus, his Dragon, and a few other Dragon Knights and Dragons survived the initial shower of steel pikes and were turning to rejoin the other Dragon Knights led by Zidane and Tufar. From within the ranks of the Shadow Army were hidden archers poised with their bow and shadow empowered arrows ready. These arrows were released into the air toward Antillus and the surviving Dragons and Dragon Knights. The arrows cut throw the air, piercing holes into the wings of the Dragons restricting their flight. Those whose wings were pierced fell to the ground. Antillus and his Dragon were brought down by a steel pike and several arrows. They crashed to the ground with a tremendous impact that quaked the ground. Antillus's Dragon was severely injured and Antillus could not lift up his right arm. He held his spear in his left hand and held his right arm close to his body. His Dragon was on his belly and could barely turn his head. Many Shadow Demons surrounded them with their arms fashioned like blades. Antillus's Dragon conjured small orbs of flame and spat them at the oncoming Shadow Demons. Antillus fought off many of the Demons with his spear, jabbing them in the neck and head, and tossing them over his shoulder, but there were too many for him and his Dragon to fight off. Soon, he and his Dragon were swallowed by the sea of Shadow Demons.

Zidane, Stratos, Maia, and Tufar, along with the other Dragons and Dragon Knights, witnessed the fall of their General. Anger swelled within each of them, wanting to avenge their fallen comrades. Tufar led the other Dragons down toward the field. The attention of the Shadow Demons fell upon the incoming Dragons. The archers shot their shadow tipped arrows into the sky at them. Tufar and the other Dragons narrowly evaded the arrows. Tufar gathered fire in his mouth and blew a fireball at a giant crossbow obliterating it. The other Dragons did the same and destroyed the remaining giant crossbows.

"Tufar, we need to watch out for the archers below!" Zidane shouted to Tufar. At that moment, a second shower of arrows was released from within the Shadow Army scattering the formation of the Dragons. Several came close to piercing Zidane and Maia, but Zidane deflected them with his Dragon Blades and Maia used the power of the Necklace to place a barrier of energy around her. Several arrows passed them and pierced the shoulder of Stratos sending him backwards off Tufar's back. Zidane turned to reach out his hand in an attempt to catch Stratos, but Stratos was just out of his reach. Stratos plummeted to the ground.

"Bracelet of Mentu, grant me durability!" Stratos shouted as he continued to fall from the sky. The Bracelet glowed brightly and an aura radiated from the Bracelet to surround his body. Stratos crashed to the ground creating a small crater in the ground kicking up a thick cloud of dirt.

His vision was blurred, his sense of hearing was muddy, and his body did not move even when he tried. He struggled to get his vision cleared and fought to get to his feet. He slowly planted his hands into the ground and pushed himself up to one knee. His vision cleared as he heard an oncoming wave of Shadow Orc and Demons charging toward him. His helmet had fallen off when he crashed to the ground. He picked it up and secured it to his head. There was a shadow tipped arrow in his shoulder that he struggled to pull out. He winced in pain as he ripped it out. Stratos fought to get to both of his feet and to grip the Dragon Blades that were stuck in the ground from the fall. He faced the oncoming wave of Shadow Troops firmly planting his feet into the ground. As the Shadow Troops drew closer to Stratos, he sensed a sharp spike of energy close to him. A whirling crescent shaped beam of energy cut passed him and into the ranks of the Shadow Orcs and Demons. Many of the Shadow Orcs and Demons were cut down by the surge of energy and disrupted their battle formation. Stratos peered over his shoulder and saw the remaining of the Krystal Kingdom Army fighting their way through a crowd of Shadow Orcs. They were led by Aero, Damien, Aldar, and Craven in his beast form. Aero slashed his way to Stratos's side and gazed upon him.

"Zidane?" Aero asked in astonishment to the resemblance.

"No, I am Stratos, the Bearer of the Black Dragon Essence," Stratos responded with his eyes fixed upon the next wave of Shadow soldiers.

"But how is that possible? I believed there was only one Bearer of the Dragon Essence," Aero said confused.

"Yes, there is... in this universe, but there is no time to explain at the moment. We need to survive this battle," Stratos said with his eyes becoming flushed with shadow energy.

"Agreed," Aero began to focus his energy into the steel of his sword. Craven, Damien, and Aldar joined Stratos and Aero along with the Vampire, Lycan and Elf soldiers of the Krystal Kingdom.

"For Rhydin!" Aero shouted raising his sword to the sky.

Stratos and Aero then led the charge into the Army of the Shadow. Stratos rushed to the front of the Krystal Kingdom Army charge with both Dragon Blades in hand and his eyes fixed on the frontlines of the Shadow Army. The troops of the Shadow Army stopped in their march and set their spears and swords waiting for the oncoming soldiers. Shadow energy fumed from the eyes of Stratos and soon his body was enveloped with a dark aura, "Night Shade!" a dark sheet of energy hid not only himself but also the soldiers of the Krystal Kingdom. This fog of shadow extended toward the lines of Shadow Orcs and Demons. There was an eerie hush among the ranks of the Shadow soldiers who faced the cloud of shadows. They did not know when or where the Krystal Kingdom troops would attack or if they were going to attack at all. They became confused and frantic. The eyes of the Shadow Orcs and Demons became wide and anxious searching the shroud of shadows for the soldiers of the Krystal Kingdom Army. A chilling howl was heard from within the cloud of shadows followed by several more. The Shadow Orcs and Demons dropped to defensive positions, bracing themselves. The Lycans burst out from the shroud of shadow with intense ferocity, leaping out toward the Shadow Orcs and Demons with their claws and fangs ready to tear through the soldiers of the Shadow Army. Craven led the surge of Lycans out from the shadows. He tore into the necks of several Orcs and Demons with his claws and fangs. Aero and Stratos were next to burst from the cloud of shadows leading Damien, Aldar, and the rest of their army into the weakened lines of the Shadow Army. Aero, Stratos, Craven, Damien, Aldar, and the rest of the Krystal Army continued to fight valiantly through the sea of shadows making their way toward the edge of the forest.

In the sky, Zidane, Maia, and Tufar led the Dragons and Dragon Knights over the sea of Shadow Orcs and Demons. Maia released arrow after arrow into the army of Shadow troops, piercing their heads and necks. Zidane used his Dragon Blades to deflect the arrows and shadow empowered spikes being fired from the ranks of the Shadow Army.

"This army seems endless," Maia continued to release arrow after arrow.

"The Shadow Realm did seem endless when we were there," Zidane moved his head to the side narrowly avoiding an arrow from below.

"You must defeat the Shadow Lord to be rid of this Shadow Army," Tufar growled then released a fireball from his mouth into the Shadow Army scattering many troops.

"Where will I find the Shadow Lord?" Zidane crossed his blades in front of his body deflecting several arrows.

"He is here. The Shadow Lord will want to be here to witness what he thinks will be the final battle to take over Rhydin," Tufar maneuvered to one side avoiding a barrage of shadow empowered spikes.

"How should I defeat the Shadow Lord?" Zidane asked.

"You must somehow use light against him. And once that happens, you must use your most powerful attack," Tufar responded.

"Tufar, I-I cannot," Zidane stammered.

"You must, Young Dragon. It is the only way," Tufar's voice turned stern.

"The last time I used it I nearly killed myself," the fire of his Essence burned from deep within that night. It was with rage and vengeance that this fire burned wild and brightly. That night, Zidane channeled this fury into his Dragon Blades and unleashed the Inferno

Rage to scorch the flesh and soul of Brakus. There was no other power that matched it that Zidane had ever felt.

"The last time you used the Inferno Rage, it was purely out of anger and vengeance. You must concentrate and control the fire within you, Young Dragon. If you do not, it will consume and destroy you from the inside out," Tufar responded dodging a myriad of arrows.

"I do not know if I can, Tufar," Zidane's eyes were lowered and gave a doubtful shake of his head.

"Zidane, you have to. We are all counting on you and have faith in you and your abilities," Maia encouraged releasing an arrow at an Orc below. Zidane inhaled a deep breath and closed his eyes. He concentrated on the energy level he had over a decade ago when he first summoned the Inferno Rage. It was true rage what he felt then. How could he control the raging wildfire within him?

"I know you doubt yourself, Young Dragon," Tufar eyed the unsure Ruler, "But you cannot let your doubt cloud your mind or pull you back. You must rise above all and summon the fire within you," Zidane closed his eyes and focused on the pulsing fire within his heart.

LOOKING TO THE STARS

I N THE UNDERGROUND CHAMBER OF the Western Palace, the elders,
women, and children of the Krystal Kingdom waited anxiously for
the battle above them to cease. The chamber was cramped with the
survivors of the Vampire Coven, the villagers who fled from other
provinces of Rhydin, and those who lived close to the Palace. The
chamber was dimly lit. The walls and floor were made of smooth
stone making it uncomfortable for most to sit on for a long period
of time such as this. From in that underground chamber, they heard
the war cries, they felt the rumbling of battle, they even heard the
clashing of steel against steel. Melina sat with M' Kara and Troy, with
guards around them, nervously waiting for the return of her husband.
Everyone in the chamber was quiet, afraid of making a sound. Each
of them became increasingly anxious with each quake of the ceiling
and ground. A knock was heard at the door which startled everyone
in the chamber. One of the guards looked to Melina and she signaled
for him to answer it. Melina, M' Kara, and Troy rose to their feet
to see who was at the door at this time. Once the guard opened the
door, Melina, Troy, and M' Kara saw that Carline and Tritan had
survived their kidnapping ordeal in the Shadow Realm. Troy and M'
Kara were the first to embrace them and welcome them back home.
Melina hugged them both tightly and kissed them on the forehead.

To Melina, M' Kara, Troy, Carline, Tritan and the others who
took refuge in the underground chamber an eternity passed as they
waited for this battle to end. They all sat quietly huddled together.
Anxiety continued to fill their hearts with each and every explosion

heard and every rumble felt. Troy, M' Kara, and the Twins sat in a circle being very quiet. M' Kara was reading through the Ancient Spell Book even with the lights being very dim while Troy sat and fiddled with a shuriken between his fingers and the Twins sat on the stone floor looking at the expressions on the faces of those who were in the chamber with them.

"We cannot just sit here...," Carline started to say in a soft tone. "...and hope our family is safe," Tritan finished.

"What should we do then?" M' Kara looked up from the spells book.

"We do not know," the Twins responded in unison.

"Maybe we can get out of here and watch the battle from the east wall," Troy whispered.

"But how are we going to get out of here?" the Twins leaned in closer to their cousin.

"The guards won't let us out," M' Kara added.

"Is there an illusion spell in that book?" Troy asked as he looked over M' Kara's shoulder.

"I think so," M' Kara flipped through the pages.

In the meantime, Melina was speaking with a guard not far from where Troy, M' Kara, Carline, and Tritan were sitting. She periodically checked over her shoulder to see what they were up to. She was somewhat cautious of letting any of them out of her sight, fearing that they might wander off again. As she turned her attention back to the guard, a door closing shut was heard and the guard turned to find no one there. Melina checked on the children and found they were still sitting in a circle in silence.

Quietly and quickly, the Twins, Troy and M' Kara made their way down the maze of halls. They trotted up the stairs toward the doors to the east wall.

"Did it get darker?" M' Kara looked to the sky when they opened the door and felt the cooler than normal air.

"I-I do not know," Troy gave a shrug of his shoulders.

"The shadows...," Carline started to say "...are here," Tritan finished. They then looked over the edge of the wall and saw the carnage of the battlefield. They saw the sea of Shadow troops, the scattered troops of the Krystal Kingdom Army and the Dragons and Dragon Knights flying over their heads.

"Does anyone see my father?" Troy asked as he frantically scanned the battlefield.

"No. And I don't see my father," worry was in M' Kara's eyes as she too looked for her father.

"It is hard to see in this darkness," the Twins said. They continued to survey the battle searching for their family.

"I see Craven and the Lycans there," M' Kara pointed in their direction.

"Yes, and my father and Uncle Zidane are down with them," Troy's voice raised with excitement.

"That is not...," Tritan started to say. "...our father," Carline finished.

"Who is it then? He looks like your father," M' Kara looked to the Twins.

"His name is Stratos," Tritan said.

"He helped our father and mother save us," Carline added.

On the battlefield, Craven, Aero, Stratos, and the rest of the Krystal Kingdom Army continued to fight their way through the sea of shadow. Stratos demonstrated tremendous ability, equal to Zidane. He stomped on the earth creating ripples to throw off the balance of the Orcs, Demons, and Abominations who stood in their path. Shadow energy seeped from the Dragon Blades as Stratos slashed and hacked his way through the troops of the Shadow Army. Aero was fighting alongside Stratos. He found a renewed strength while fighting alongside him. To him, it was as if Aero was fighting alongside his brother. The scars and fatigue that were afflicted upon his body did not affect him. Energy coursed through his body and seeped through the steel of his sword as he slashed at the necks of the Shadow Orcs, Demons, and Abominations. Not far behind them, Craven, Damien, and Aldar were finishing off the Shadow troops that may have been wounded by the attacks of Aero and Stratos. The Krystal Kingdom Army fought as one. Not one soldier was killed during this final surge through the sea of Shadow troops. The Shadow Army was being pushed back onto their heels as this last push of the Krystal Kingdom Army continued to surge through their ranks.

"Fall back! Draw them into the woods!" the Orc leader shouted. An Abomination sounded the retreat and the Shadow Army began to fall back into the woods.

"They are retreating," Maia looked to the battlefield from Tufar's back.

"It may be a trap," Zidane's voice conveyed his weariness of this retreat.

"Maia, search for Stratos's mind and warn him of a possible trap," Tufar growled as he and the other Dragons circled above. Maia placed her fore and middle fingers on the Necklace of Isis and concentrated its energy in to her mind.

"*Stratos, be careful. They may be luring you into a trap,*" Maia said within Stratos's mind. Stratos immediately slid to a halt and searched the tree lines for any sign of an ambush.

"Why have you stopped?" Aero looked from the woods to Stratos.

"Maia warned me of a possible ambush," Stratos responded as he continued to search the tree lines.

"I do see something there," Aero pointed his sword toward the spot. At the very edge of the woods, there were many shadowy figures marching toward the clearing.

"They cannot still have reinforcements," Aldar groaned at the sight of more Shadow troops.

"We do not know if we can fight through another army," it sounded as if the fight was driven out of Damien from the way he spoke.

"We do not have the strength or the numbers," Craven's ears flattened against his head.

"Numbers or strength do not win a war," Aero's voice interrupted the cloud of doubts hovering over his comrades.

"Strategy will decide the outcome," Stratos added as he looked over his shoulder to those that fought alongside him.

The Orc Leader was amidst the Shadow Troops as they made their retreat toward the woods. Suddenly the Shadow troops stopped in their retreat short of the woods. The Orc Leader pushed his way to the front, "What is going on up here?! Why'd you stop?!" he barked. An Abomination pointed at the shadowy figures standing at the edge of the woods. The shroud of shadows made it difficult for them to clearly see who was there.

"Reinforcements," an Abomination hissed.

"I don't think so," the Orc Leader sniffed the air. One of the figures stepped out of the shadows and into the clearing. The figure wore a dark cloak and had a long broad sword strapped to one hip.

"Who is that?" a Demon hissed.

"It can't be," an Abomination shook his head with wide eyes.

"The Vampire Prince," the Orc Leader said through its clenched teeth. Kulla continued to walk toward the Shadow Army with the Scepter of Osiris in hand.

"You will go no further!" Kulla's voice boomed.

"How are you going to stop us!?" the Orc Leader 's tone was arrogant. Clearly, Kulla was at a disadvantage in his eyes. Kulla raised the Scepter of Osiris into the air signaling for the Army of the Undead to emerge from the shadows of the tree line. The Shadow troops took many steps backwards at the sight of this new army.

"Just so that you know, we disposed of the Abomination contingent at the Ruins of Keshnar. With ease I must say," Kulla said with a growing grin on his face. The Shadow troops grew angrier, gripping their weapons tighter and bearing their teeth.

"I do not advise charging at us. The outcome will not be in your favor," Kulla warned them. An Abomination could not hold his composure and charged straight for Kulla with its war club ready to swing at Kulla. Kulla stood his ground and grinned.

"That was a grave mistake," Kulla calmly said. As the Abomination drew closer to Kulla, its leg was cut from under him, a spear pierced through its torso, and then it was decapitated. Three of the soldiers of the Undead Army attacked the Abomination with uncanny speed and precision. The three Undead Soldiers who brought down the Shadow empowered Abomination stood side by side glaring at the Shadow Army as if challenging them to charge. Kulla, along with the rest of the Undead Army, joined the three soldiers. The Shadow Army took several steps backwards, but was trapped between the Krystal Kingdom Army led by Aero and Stratos, and now the Undead Army led by Kulla. Half of the Shadow Army faced in the direction of the Undead Army and the others faced the Krystal Kingdom Army. Above them the Dragons and Dragon Knights continued to circle above them.

"Zidane, is that…?" Maia leaned forward to look at the new army that appeared from the woods.

"Yes, it is Kulla and with a new army with him," Zidane also leaned his head to focus his vision.

"That would be the Undead Army. They pledged their lives to be in the service of Osiris," Tufar explained.

Kulla took several more steps toward the Shadow Army along with the Undead Army. The troops of the Shadow Army facing the Army of the Undead backed away from them except for the Orc Leader.

"What are we afraid of?! They do not compare to us in strength!" the Orc Leader roared.

"You will be afraid," Kulla's eyes slowly glowed white. He took the Scepter of Osiris and held it in front of him. He released it allowing it to hover above the ground in front of him.

"Ancient Spirits, I ask that you grant me your power!" Kulla said with his arms outstretched. The wind began to blow and swirl about Kulla. The head of the Scepter glowed and throbbed with pure energy. The glow from the Scepter grew and began to give light to the shadows all around.

"What's happening?!" an Orc raised his arm to shield his eyes from the Scepter's light.

"Fury of Osiris!" Kulla shouted in a resonating voice as he released a barrage of energy orbs from the Scepter of Osiris. They streaked from the Scepter and homed in on the Shadow troops in front of the Army of the Undead. The orbs sunk into many of the troops of the Shadow Army and soon after began to expand from within the Shadow soldiers until they exploded into ash.

On the eastern wall of the Western Palace, M' Kara, Carline, Tritan and Troy continued to watch the battle ensue. They were even more anxious as they watched their family and friends fight off the Shadow horde. The flash of many lights attracted their attention. Their eyes fell upon the origin of the bright lights.

"M' Kara isn't that..." Carline started to ask."...your father?" Tritan finished.

"Yes, it is," M' Kara said with a growing excitement. A smile came across her face seeing her father return and was safe for the moment.

"I still have not seen the Shadow Lord on the battlefield," Troy was seemingly disappointed.

"Maybe he is scared seeing how our army is beating them," M' Kara said proudly.

"It seems too easy," Troy gave a shake of his head.

"Don't jinx it," the Twins scolded in unison.

"Will our army be able to fight off the Shadow Lord himself if he shows up?" M' Kara turned her worried eyes to her friends.

"We hope so," the Twins sighed.

"I know so. Uncle Zidane, Aunt Maia, Lord Kulla, and my father are the best on that battlefield," Troy tightened his fists as they rested on the wall.

In the sky above the battle, Zidane, Maia, and Tufar along with the Dragons and Dragon Knights continued to circle above.

"It appears that the Shadow Army is surrounded," Zidane said.

"Kulla arrived at the correct time. What are you and I to do now?" Maia gripped her bow more tightly in anticipation of their next action.

"Tufar, lead the rest of the Dragons and Dragon Knights to the Northern Mountains. I am sure Arteus will need aid fighting the Winged Demons," Zidane turned his eyes to the north.

"I will, Young Dragon. Remember to concentrate and control the wildfire within you. If you do not, then you will be consumed," Tufar turned his head to look to the Dragon Essence Bearer.

"I understand," Zidane gave a deep breath, then looked from the Bracelet of Ra to Maia who gave a reassuring smile to him.

"Are you ready?" Maia asked.

"I am. Are you?" Maia gave a nod to him then gripped her bow in hand and drew her short sword. Zidane readied both of the Dragon Blades.

"Go Maia and Young Dragon. May the Heavens protect you," Zidane leapt off of Tufar's back and was closely followed by Maia. Zidane's cape allowed him to glide through the sky toward the ground. Maia used the power of the Necklace to guide herself safely to the ground. Zidane's eyes were focused on the soldiers of the Shadow Army who dwindled in numbers more rapidly since Kulla and the Army of the Undead arrived in great numbers. Zidane and Maia landed in the middle of the Shadow horde and immediately, the Orcs, Abominations, and Shadow Demons attacked them. Zidane and Maia stood back to back facing them. The steel of Zidane's Dragon Blades flared red as the intense heat fumed from them. Maia used her bow to block each of the attacks thrown by the Shadow soldiers who attacked her, then slashed and stabbed at their necks with her short sword. Zidane spun around, ducked under, and leapt over slashes and bludgeoning onslaughts from the Orcs and Abominations around them. Seeing several Orcs charge at him, Zidane sheathed his Dragon Blades and then stomped on the ground to rouse a small wall of earth in front of the Orcs. With a movement of his hands, he pushed the wall of earth into the charging gang of Orcs, knocking them backwards. A slash of a Demons arm disarmed Maia of her short sword. She spun away from a blade slash and in mid-spin she drew an arrow from her quiver. With a snap of her wrist, she threw the arrow into the forehead of the Demon. Several more Demons shifted their arms to blades and readied themselves to attack Maia. Maia concentrated to use the power of the Necklace. With a motion of her hand she used that power to push the Demons away from her. Zidane and Maia found themselves back to back once again.

"Where are the others?!" Maia exclaimed releasing an arrow into the neck of an Orc.

"We are in the middle of the Shadow Army. It may take them some time to get to us," Zidane released an orb of lightning from his palms into a small group of Shadow Demons and then quickly drew both of his Dragon Blades. Maia stabbed an oncoming Demon with an arrow, quickly withdrew the arrow from the Demon's head, and then released it into an Orc's throat. Lightning crackled and coursed throughout Zidane's arms and the steel of the Dragon Blades. Zidane stabbed the points of the blades into the ground and allowed the pent up lightning to surge from his body into the ground. The lightning streaked across the ground underneath the feet of the oncoming Demons sending them into uncontrollable convulsions. The ground shook under the feet of Maia and Zidane as they saw an Abomination charge at them with a massive war club in hand. It readied to swing its club at Zidane, but Maia used the power of the Necklace to stop the Abomination in its attack. This allowed Zidane to use a powerful gust of wind to launch himself into the air and slash the Abomination's neck. Maia smiled, but then turned to find that another Abomination crept behind her. It was ready to attack but a figure leapt into the air behind it and stabbed its blade into the Abomination's skull. Stratos landed on his feet in front of Maia, "Are you and Zidane alright?" his breaths were heavy and sweat dripped down his brow.

"What took you so long?" Maia teased as Aero, Aldar, Damien and Craven fought their way to Stratos's side.

"Our apologies, we were a bit occupied," Aero grinned. Zidane got back to them.

"Still alive?" Stratos looked to his fellow Dragon Essence Bearer.

"You expected anything else?" Zidane quirked an eyebrow at him. Zidane, Maia, Aero, Stratos, Craven, Aldar, and Damien all stood side by side along with the rest of the Krystal Kingdom Army behind them.

On the other side of the battlefield, Kulla was fighting his way through the Shadow Horde with the Army of the Undead close behind him. He used the power of the Scepter to ward of the Demons and Orcs that attacked him. He summoned the strength and power of souls of past warriors and heroes. When he did, the image of their souls hovered above his body and mimicked his every movement. Some of these warriors wielded war hammers, some spears, and others swords. All of these souls came from different eras and were of different races, and Kulla summoned their power at will.

The fighting tactics of the soldiers of the Undead Army were quick and precise. One of the soldiers weakened an enemy and moved on. Another soldier came in behind the first to finish off the enemy by either slashing at its neck or stabbing it in the head. A Shadow Demon crept in to the peripheral vision of Kulla catching him off guard. The Demon morphed its arm into claws and slashed at Kulla's face. Kulla staggered backwards from the force of the blow. Kulla slowly looked up from the ground. There were three slash marks across his face. To the surprise of the Demon, the slash marks rapidly began to heal.

"That was a mistake," Kulla said through his vampire fangs. Kulla hissed and leapt to the air. Kulla slashed at the head of the Demon on his way down to the ground, cleaving it in two. Kulla rose to his feet with his eyes flushed white bearing his vampire fangs.

The troops of the Shadow Army grew even wearier as they saw the numbers of their army dwindle. They saw they were being surrounded by the Vampire Prince and the Army of the Undead, and on the other side they were cut off by the Elf Rulers of Rhydin. The Orcs and Abominations in the Shadow Army huddled back to back and soon realized the Shadow Demons that remained were not among them.

"Where did they go?!" the Orc Leader looked all about his Orc and Abomination kin.

"There!" an Abomination hissed pointing its club at the ground. The Demons sank to the ground and began to slither their way passed the soldiers of their enemies.

"Cowards!" the Orc Leader yelled at them. An Orc tried to mimic the escape of the Shadow Demons, but was not able to.

"Why can't we do that?" the Orc growled as he desperately tried again and again.

"The Shadow Lord did not tell us we can't do that," the Orc Leader tightened the grip on his great sword.

"Do you surrender?!" Zidane yelled to them with his eyes flaring red. The Orc Leader clenched his teeth tightly. His body shook with the anger he felt toward the Shadow Lord. The Orc Leader then finally dropped his sword and lowered its head in defeat.

"What are you doing?!" an Abomination hissed.

"Our numbers are small and the Demons have abandoned us. We have lost this battle," the Orc Leader growled. The rest of the Orcs and Abominations finally dropped their weapons and lowered their heads in shame. The soldiers of the Krystal Kingdom Army rejoiced at the surrender of the Shadow Army. They held their weapons to the sky and shouted. All rejoiced except for Stratos and Zidane.

"What is wrong?" Maia walked to Zidane's side.

"Something is not right," Zidane calmly said.

"What do you mean?" Aero asked.

"The Shadow Lord has not appeared. The only troops there are the Orcs and Abominations he empowered with the Shadow. Even though these troops have surrendered, the Shadow Lord can summon an entire army of Shadow Demons," Stratos said grimly. Zidane, Maia, Aero, and Stratos looked to the sky and it continued to grow darker. The ominous sheet of shadow in the sky continued to cover the land.

"The shadows have not stopped," distress was in Maia's voice.

"That is because the Shadow Lord has not been defeated," Stratos growled with frustration.

"We need to find him," despite all of the fighting, Aero seemed to be ready to charge off and find the Shadow Lord himself.

"I think he has found us," Zidane pointed a Dragon Blade to the edge of the woods.

Above the ground in the woods, hovered a blanket of pure shadow. It hung thick and heavy. It darkened the woods all around it. None could see beyond this shroud; not even the eyes of an Elf could pierce these shadows. It crept closer to the edge of the woods and in front of this creeping blanket of shadow was a dark figure that hovered above the ground. The figure was in the shape of a man, but was covered in the darkest of shadows. Unlike any man, this figure did not take steps, but glided across the ground like the shadows of trees as the sun moved across the sky. An aura of shadow energy surrounded and fumed from his dark body. He had no definite face except for his eyes were yellow and lidless.

"Kulla! Behind you!" Maia shouted at the top of her lungs. Kulla turned to find the Shadow Lord creeping behind him and the Army of the Undead. Several of the Undead Soldiers crouched into an attack stance.

"Your Undead Soldiers cannot harm me," the Shadow Lord gave an arrogant laugh. Two of the Undead Soldiers charged side by side at the Shadow Lord with the points of their spears aimed at his neck. The Shadow Lord extended his arms at the charging Undead Soldiers. His arms stretched with shadow energy and wrapped themselves around the Undead Soldiers. Like a python squeezing its prey, the Shadow Lord squeezed and crushed the two Undead Soldiers and tossed the remains aside. Three more Undead Soldiers charged at the Shadow Lord, but were quickly dealt with. The Shadow Lord released shadow darts from his fingers at two of them. The third quickly dodged the darts and leapt to the air with his scimitar raised above his head. The Shadow Lord shaped his arm into a shield blocking the Undead Soldiers attack and threw him in to a tree.

"What evil is this?!" Kulla exclaimed as he turned his attention from the Orcs and Abominations to the Shadow Lord who disposed of several Undead Soldiers with ease.

"Kulla, fall back to us!" Zidane shouted.

"Fall back!" Kulla shouted to the Undead Soldiers to abandon their positions in surrounding the Shadow empowered Orcs and Abominations. Kulla did not take his eyes off of the Shadow Lord who continued to creep out of the woods.

"Zidane!" the Shadow Lord called out to him pointing directly at him. Kulla, Maia, Aero, Stratos, Craven, Aldar, and Damien looked at Zidane whose eyes did not waver.

"You and your Kingdom will fall at my feet for what you have done to me!" the Shadow Lord shouted with shadows fuming from his body.

"What is he ranting about?" Aero looked from the seemingly crazed Shadow Lord to his brother.

"Do you know him, Zidane?" Kulla asked.

"I-I do not know," Zidane's body was tensed, but the grip on the Dragon Blades was loose. What could he have done to this being?

"You cannot have your spirit shaken by him. We need you now more than ever. You must fight like the Dragon that you are," Stratos bumped Zidane's shoulder with his clenched fist to bring him back to focus and out of his hesitation.

"Vengeance will be mine!" the Shadow Lord raised his arms to the sky. Out from the thick fog of shadows that trailed behind the Shadow Lord rose many more Shadow Demons.

"How are we to deal with this?" Maia asked drawing an arrow from her quiver.

"Together. With the power of the Ancient Relics," Zidane responded while looking down at the Bracelet of Ra. Kulla, Maia, and Stratos nodded and readied themselves.

"What are we to do," Aero asked with Craven, Aldar, and Damien behind him. Zidane looked from Aero to the Elf, Vampire, Lycan, and the Undead Soldiers who endured this long battle.

"Fight for Rhydin. Rid Rhydin of this Shadow. Send them back to the Shadow Realm," Zidane said with a growing intensity. His grip on the Dragon Blades tightened with confidence. The steel of the blades flared and sparked with fire. Zidane eyes fumed with fire. All of the Krystal Kingdom's troops readied for one last stand.

"Maia, are you ready?" Zidane looked to the one who had his love.

"I am," Maia responded sensing what she was to do.

"Aero, Aldar, Damien, and Craven, you will lead the rest of the troops into the Shadow Army," Zidane looked to them.

"Understood, Brother," Aero said. Craven, Aldar, and Damien nodded their heads and all took deep breaths.

"Stratos, Kulla, and Maia, we fall in behind and then face the Shadow Lord," Zidane turned his eyes to the maniac who dared to invade their home.

On the other side of the field, the Orc Leader, the Orcs, and the Abominations who remained fell back to within the ranks of the Shadow Army near the Shadow Lord. The Orc Leader took his place next to the Shadow Lord and was with his great sword in hand.

"What do you want us to do?" the Orc Leader grunted.

"You have done your part. You've weakened the Krystal Kingdom significantly for my Shadow Demons. Your services are no longer required," the Shadow Lord hissed as he plunged his hand into the Orc Leader's chest. The Shadow Lord began to drain the life force from the Orc Leader and grew stronger with each passing moment. Another Orc roared and stabbed his broad sword into the arm of the Shadow Lord. The Shadow Lord threw the Orc Leader into a nearby tree and swatted at the attacking Orc sending him several feet backwards.

"I gave you your Shadow abilities, and now I will be taking them back!" the Shadow Lord shouted holding out his hands toward the Orcs and Abominations draining them of their shadow endowments. The Shadow Lord grew stronger as he absorbed the shadow energy from the Orcs and Abominations. They slowly changed back to their normal states drained of their energy and strength. They fell to their knees and then on their faces and backs.

"What should we do with them?" a Demon hissed.

"Leave them, they are of no significance. They can do nothing," the Shadow Lord's words were ice.

On the side of the Krystal Kingdom Army, before they began their last charge, they all witnessed what the Shadow Lord did to the Orcs and Abominations. Their eyes widened and jaws dropped.

"Why did the Shadow Lord do that?" Maia's ears flattened against her head.

"The Orcs, Abominations, and others he assimilated were expendable to him. They were used to weaken us so that he can use the Demons to finish us off," Zidane surmised with unwavering focus.

"Less troops for us to worry about," Stratos grinned.

"Stratos is right," Aero nodded.

"I know, but it just seems wrong to me," all looked to Zidane confused as to why he said that. Over ten years ago, the Orcs' sole purpose was to wipe out all those who were in the Krystal Kingdom. Now Zidane feels sympathy for the creatures they battled against in that Great War. The Shadow Lord signaled for the Shadow Demons to begin their charge.

"Maia, now!" Zidane shouted. Maia used the power of the Necklace to place a barrier around her body. She then sprinted, with bow and an arrow in hand, toward the charging Shadow Demons. Her panther ears were pinned back, her tail was tucked close to her body, her strides were wide, and her eyes were focused on her target.

"She is a fool," the Shadow Lord laughed. The charging Demons formed spears of shadow energy and hurled them at Maia. The barrier surrounding Maia's body deflected and negated the power of the spears. Maia took the arrow and aimed it at the middle of the Shadow horde. She gathered energy from the Necklace into the head of the arrow. She slid to a halt with the arrow continuing to gather energy in its head.

"Arrow of Isis!" she shouted as she released the arrow into the horde of charging Shadow Demons. The arrow roared through the air and disintegrated all in its wake. There was a gap in the middle of the Shadow Horde where Aero, Damien, Aldar, Craven, the Undead Soldiers, and the rest of the Krystal Kingdom soldiers charged into, passing Maia. Aero was the first to slash and stab at the Demons heads and necks. Aero and the others cut down the middle of the army and widened the gap.

"Charge!" Zidane shouted with his eyes flaring with fire. Zidane, Stratos and Kulla began their charging, joining with Maia, into the heart of the Shadow Army. The Krystal Kingdom Army and the Undead Soldiers of Osiris did not allow any of the Shadow Demons to pass them in attempts to get at either Zidane, Maia, Kulla, or Stratos. A Demon leapt into the air and formed one of its arms into a blade. It was ready to slash at Kulla, but Aero met it in the air cutting it down. Other Demons broke through the Krystal Kingdom lines and attempted to stop Zidane, Maia, Kulla, and Stratos from reaching the Shadow Lord. They were only met with streaks of pure energy unleashed from Aero's sword. Others were intercepted by Craven and the other Lycans. More Demons leapt over the lines and charged directly at Zidane, Maia, Kulla and Stratos. Several Demons hurled a myriad of shadow pikes at them. Zidane and Stratos quickly sheathed their Dragon Blades and slid to a halt side by side. With a motion of both of their hands they roused the earth, creating a wall to deflect the shadow pikes. Maia then leapt on to their shoulders and over the wall of dense earth and rock. She took aim with three arrows and charged the arrows with energy from the Necklace.

"Tri-Shot!" Maia shouted releasing the three energy charged arrows at the charging Shadow Demons. The arrows exploded at the feet of the Demons sending them in every direction. Kulla was next over the wall of earth. He summoned the soul of a warrior who wielded a massive war hammer. The soul was broad and muscle bound. It wore a thick, heavy beard and wore a helmet with horns jutting out from either side. Kulla raised the Scepter and the warrior raised its war hammer above his head mimicking Kulla's movements. Kulla brought down the Scepter to the ground and the soul of the warrior brought down its war hammer down upon a grouping of Demons. The force of the blow created a deep crater in the ground with the remains of the Demons at the bottom. More Demons charged at Kulla, with blades for arms, ready to strike. Kulla swung the Scepter across his body and the hammer of the warrior crashed into the chests of the Demons, sending them into the air. Zidane and Stratos were the last to jump over the wall of earth. With motions of their hands, they created powerful gusts of wind to blow away any and all Shadow Demons that came close to attacking them or Maia and Kulla.

"Maia, fire an arrow!" Zidane said as he began to gather streaks of lightning in his fingertips. Maia nodded and released an arrow at an oncoming Demon. In mid-flight, Zidane released the streak of lightning into the arrow. The streak of lightning charged the arrow and when it pierced the neck of the Demon, its body convulsed until it moved no more.

The Shadow Lord huffed with impatience the closer Zidane and the others drew to him. He stood with his arms folded in front of his chest and his eyes glowing yellow with anger and frustration.

"What are we to do, my Lord? They are getting through to us," a Demon hissed.

"Fuse yourselves together and form a larger Demon," the Shadow Lord replied coldly. At his order, the Shadow Demons paired with one another then began to meld into each other. The resulting creature was far larger than any one Demon. The fusion of two Demons formed a nine foot tall, broadly built behemoth. There were several of these Shadow Behemoths that formed.

"Now go, and rid me of those infidels!" the Shadow Lord shouted. The Shadow Behemoths took slow and labored steps. The ground shook with each footstep. Zidane, Kulla, Maia, and Stratos felt the earth shake beneath their feet and paused in their attacks.

"I thought we were rid of the Abominations," Kulla's mouth was agape in awe of the tremendous creatures.

"Those are not Abominations, Kulla," Zidane said with his eyes widening.

"What are they?" Maia slid to a halt.

"They are Shadow Behemoths. They are a fusion of two Shadow Demons creating a larger and stronger Demon," Stratos responded with his eyes fixed upon them.

"How are we to deal with them?" Zidane looked to his once rival.

"The same way we dealt with the smaller ones. Except their necks are a bit higher and are a bit more difficult to take down," Stratos responded.

"They look slow," Kulla observed.

"They are. Use that to our advantage. We are much faster and more agile than they are," Stratos said. Zidane, Maia, and Kulla nodded and prepared their attack on the Shadow Behemoths. Two of the Behemoths threw their arms into the ground causing it to crack and fume explosive shadow energy. Like the hazard field in the shadow realm, there were pockets where the energy built up and was ready to explode at any moment. In their charge at the Behemoths, they avoided the geyser-like explosions of shadow energy. Zidane and Stratos moved the earth beneath their feet to launch themselves into the air, avoiding the explosions. Maia used the power of the Necklace to contain the explosions. Kulla summoned a soul who bore a massive shield to protect himself from the shadow energy.

"Get them!" the Shadow Lord's eyes flashed with rage and frustration. Zidane and Stratos halted and motioned for the earth to rise around the feet and lower legs of two of the Shadow Behemoths to trap them and not allowing them to take another step. Maia slid in front of the trapped Behemoths, releasing arrow after arrow into their necks. The Behemoths reeled back, but were not vanquished. Kulla charged toward them and aimed the head of the Scepter at them, "Soul Spark!". The head of the Scepter glowed and throbbed. Orbs of soul energy sparked and streaked toward the chests of the Behemoths. Both of the Behemoths convulsed then fell to the ground. Zidane and Stratos leapt over the convulsing bodies and charged toward the others. Two of the Behemoths stretched their arms at the Dragon Essence Bearers. Zidane and Stratos used gusts of wind to launch them into the air above the outstretched arms of the Behemoths. They both drew their Dragon Blades and summoned streaks of lightning into the steel. Both stabbed the necks of the Behemoths causing their bodies to convulse and then drop. Only three Behemoths stood between Zidane, Stratos, Maia and Kulla, and the Shadow Lord. Zidane sheathed his blades and ran slightly ahead of the others. He leapt to the air and gathered flames into one of his clenched fists. As he landed, he threw his fist to the ground. His fist created a wall of intense flames that surged across the ground toward the Behemoths. One of the Behemoths barely side-stepped the wall, but the other two were caught and soon engulfed.

"Shrouded Lightning!" Stratos released streaks of shadow laced lightning at one of the flame engulfed Behemoths. The Behemoth dropped to the ground with flames scorching it and black lightning coursing through its body. Kulla slid to a halt and thrust the Scepter to the ground.

"Soul Surge!" Kulla shouted as the Scepter hit the ground. The head of the Scepter glowed with energy. This energy surged down the Scepter and into the ground. The energy from the Scepter streaked across the ground and exploded at the feet of the other flame engulfed Behemoth.

The last Behemoth morphed its arm into a blade and stretched it to attack Maia. Maia leapt backwards avoiding the blade. She then ran up the Behemoths arm with unwavering balance. She launched herself off of the Behemoth's shoulder and spun to face the back of the Behemoth's head. While spinning, she drew an arrow and shot it into the back of the Behemoth's head. The Behemoth dropped to the ground. With all of the Shadow Behemoths vanquished, there was nothing in the way of Zidane, Stratos, Maia, and Kulla and the Shadow Lord.

"You think you four can defeat the Lord of the Shadows?!" The Shadow Lord exclaimed fuming with shadow energy.

"We know we can," Zidane responded drawing both Dragon Blades.

"Zidane, I will kill your friends, and then savor killing you," the Shadow Lord pointed directly at the target of his ire.

"You will not have that chance!" Maia shouted aiming an arrow at the Shadow Lord.

"Ah, the Little Kitten has become a Tiger. Maybe I will kill the others and save you for myself," the Shadow Lord said with an evil laugh. Zidane's eyes fumed with fire and dark smoke billowed from his flared nostrils at the comment the Shadow Lord made about his wife. With his jaw clenched, Zidane fused the hilts of the Dragon Blades. A flare of fire flashed from the joining of the two hilts and a surge of fire coursed through the steel of the blades. In a fit of anger, Zidane charged at the Shadow Lord.

"No, Zidane!" Stratos shouted trying to stop the angered Zidane.

"Yes, come to me," the Shadow Lord hissed watching Zidane charge in rage. The Shadow Lord formed his two arms in to two massive maces. As Zidane drew closer, the Shadow Lord swung one arm at Zidane. With his superior agility, Zidane slid on his knees under the swinging mace, quickly got to his feet, but was hit by the other arm and slid across the ground. Stratos, Kulla, and Maia began their attack on the Shadow Lord after watching Zidane narrowly escape an attack that could have ended his life. The Shadow Lord noticed Zidane's companions charge and from the shadow energy surrounding his body he formed two more arms. These arms grew from his sides and he soon formed them into maces as well. Two of the arms attacked Kulla and Maia. Kulla summoned the warrior with the massive shield to block the attack from the giant mace. Maia created a barrier using the Necklace to deflect the bludgeoning blow. Stratos ran past them and leapt at the Shadow Lord with Dragon

Blades ready to strike. The Shadow Lord swung his arm to knock him out of the air.

"Mentu, grant me durability!" Stratos shouted crossing his arms in front of him bracing for the blow. The mace crashed into the chest of Stratos sending him backwards into a tree, cracking it. Zidane got to his feet to join Maia and Kulla. The onslaught of the Shadow Lord's bludgeoning arms continued. Maia continued to use the Necklace to deflect the attacks, but was weakening with each blow that made contact with the barrier. Kulla was being forced backwards with each blow as he still was using the power of the shield bearing warrior. Zidane detached the hilts of the blades and sheathed them. He roused the earth to create dense walls blocking the Shadow Lord's blows. The Shadow Lord used two arms to crash through the walls of earth created by Zidane causing him to be knocked backwards. Stratos regained his composure and sheathed his blades. He focused his energy and stomped on the ground creating a ripple of earth to surge toward the Shadow Lord. The Shadow Lord was thrown off balance not allowing him to continue with his onslaught upon Zidane, Maia, or Kulla. Zidane quickly seized the opportunity and gathered fire around both of his fists. Charging at the Shadow Lord, Zidane threw punches releasing shots of flames. The Shadow Lord could not dodge all of the flares of flames. His arms were set ablaze and he struggled to put out the flames.

"Soul Surge!" Kulla shouted as he thrust the Scepter into the ground releasing a surge of soul energy across the ground.

"Tri-Shot!" Maia shouted releasing three energy charged arrows.

"Shrouded Lightning!" Stratos shouted releasing streaks of dark lightning at the Shadow Lord. All of these attacks crashed upon the Shadow Lord causing a deafening explosion. A dark cloud of smoke and dirt hung in the air. Zidane, Stratos, Maia, and Kulla were poised in defensive stances waiting to see what happened to the Shadow Lord. Several moments passed and the cloud of dirt and smoke still lingered.

"Can you see anything?" Maia aimed an arrow at the cloud.

"I see nothing," Zidane responded drawing both of his Dragon Blades and inched forward toward the cloud.

"Be careful, Zidane," Stratos said with his eyes fixed upon the cloud.

"We do not know if the Shadow Lord is still there," Kulla said with the Scepter and broad sword ready. In an instant, the Shadow Lord's mace shaped arm shot out from the cloud of smoke and dirt attacking Zidane. Zidane narrowly side-stepped the arm coming within inches of his face. Soon thereafter, the other three arms shot at Kulla, Stratos, and Maia from the cloud of smoke and dirt. Maia and Stratos dodged the attacking arms, but Kulla was hit in the chest and sent several feet backwards. He lied on the ground holding his ribs.

"He will be fine. Concentrate on the Shadow Lord!" Stratos shouted to Maia when he caught a glimpse of her looking back to Kulla. Stratos slashed his blades lashing gusts of wind at the Shadow Lord. Maia saw the Shadow Lord blown backwards from the gusts of wind and released a barrage of arrows at him. The Shadows around the Shadow Lord's body absorbed the arrows to the shock of Maia. The Shadow Lord turned all four of the arms he possessed into blades and began to violently slash at his enemies. Zidane and Stratos fused their swords at the hilts and blocked each of the fierce attacks. Maia was a few feet behind Zidane and Stratos as they blocked the Shadow Lord's slashes. She released arrow after arrow over the shoulders of Zidane and Stratos. Each of the arrows pierced the torso and shoulders of the Shadow Lord, but had to effect on him. All three were then pushed back by a pulse of shadow energy that emitted from the Shadow Lord's body.

"Our attacks have no effect on them," Zidane's breaths were heavy.

"How are we to harm him with that happening?" Maia groaned slowly getting to her feet.

"We have to continue to wear him down. We will eventually find an opening," Stratos winced.

"The only thing that comes close to harming him that we have right now is your fire conjuring, Zidane," Kulla clutched at his ribs.

"You cannot harm me! I am invincible! My vengeance upon you Zidane is at hand!" the Shadow Lord shouted creeping closer to them.

"Power of the Red Dragon, Zidane," Stratos reminded him. Zidane sheathed both of his blades and focused his energy.

"We will give you cover," despite the pain radiating throughout his body, Kulla stood by his comrades ready to fight. Maia nodded and readied her bow. Zidane rose to his feet and gathered fire around both of his fists. His eyes flared red with fire. Dark smoke billowed from his nostrils and hung heavy in the air.

"Go now!" Zidane's voice was the signal for Stratos to charge at the Shadow Lord. He sheathed both of his blades. The Bracelet of Mentu glowed brightly granting Stratos tremendous speed. The Shadow Lord formed two of his arms back into maces and stretched them to attack the charging Stratos. Each of the Shadow Lord's attacks were quickly dodged by Stratos. As he drew closer to the Shadow Lord, he caught one of the attacking arms and held it. He firmly planted his feet in to the ground. The Shadow Lord attacked with another arm, but that arm too was caught by Stratos.

"Mentu, grant me strength!" Stratos's muscles seemed to grow in mass as the Bracelet glowed and gave Stratos uncanny strength. The Shadow Lord attempted to pull away from Stratos, but Stratos stomped on the earth and roused it to enclose his feet and keep him rooted to the ground. The Shadow Lord grew frustrated. Zidane took the opportunity and made his charge, with flame engulfed fists, at the Shadow Lord while Stratos had him in his grip. The Shadow Lord attacked Zidane with his free arms that he morphed into blades.

"Tri-Shot!" Maia released three energy charged arrows at one of the arms of the Shadow Lord, causing it to recoil.

"Soul Spark!" Kulla released a spark of soul energy from the Scepter at the other attacking arm causing it to drop to the ground lifeless. Zidane's focus became more intense as he drew close to the

Shadow Lord. He leapt to the air and threw punches and kicks at the Shadow Lord. Intense flares of fire lashed out from the punches and kicks. The flares exploded upon the torso and shoulders of the Shadow Lord causing him to reel back and winch in pain. Zidane landed in front of the Shadow Lord.

"Invading Rhydin was a fatal mistake," Zidane said with his eyes flashing red and dark smoke continuing to billow from his flared nostrils. He gathered immense flames around his clenched fist. The Shadow Lord's yellow eyes widened as Zidane was about to throw an attack at him. As Zidane was throwing the punch at the Shadow Lord's chest, the flames around his fist formed into the head of a roaring Dragon.

"Dragon Fist!" Zidane shouted as he threw the thunderous punch. The Shadow Lord was thrown backwards from the immense force of the blow. The arms Stratos held in his grip were torn from the sides of the Shadow Lord and fell to the ground. The arms sank into the ground and dissipated. The Shadow Lord lied a good distance away from them with his chest scorched from the thunderous attack. Zidane's eyes faded back to their natural hue and the flames around his fist died. Dark smoke no longer billowed from his nostrils. He stood there with his eyes fixed on the body of the Shadow Lord breathing heavily. Stratos, Kulla, and Maia joined at Zidane's side.

"Is it over?" Maia was reluctant to lower her bow.

"I hope and pray it is," Kulla responded holding his ribs. Stratos looked back and saw Aero, Craven, Aldar, Damien and the rest of the Krystal Kingdom Army and the Undead Army finishing the rest of the Shadow Demon horde. Zidane looked back to the army as well and saw Aero raise his sword to him in victory. Zidane gave a smile of relief. The feeling of relief was short lived as Zidane's ears twitched. He quickly turned around to find the Shadow Lord rising up from the ground.

"Be on your guard!" Zidane shouted drawing his blades. Stratos, Kulla, and Maia turned also to find the Shadow Lord facing them and rapidly healing from the scorch wound on his chest. Shadow energy fumed from his body and his eyes flashed yellow with anger.

"When will this end?" Stratos growled through his teeth.

"End?!" the Shadow Lord exclaimed, "It will only end when Rhydin is engulfed in shadow and Zidane is dead!"

At that moment, the Shadow Lord thrust his hands into the ground. Shadow energy poured from his body into the ground and surged toward Zidane, Stratos, Maia, and Kulla. The ground erupted with a series of explosions.

"Mentu, grant me durability!" as the Bracelet glowed, Stratos crouched down and crossed his forearms in front of him. Maia placed a barrier around her body using the power of the Necklace of Isis. Kulla summoned the soul of the shield bearing warrior. With a motion of his hands, Zidane roused a wall of earth. All were in attempts to block the volatile explosions of shadow energy. An explosion erupted in front of the four throwing them into the air. Aero, Craven, Aldar, Damien, and the troops from the Krystal Kingdom and the Army of the Undead were thrown back from the aftershock of the powerful explosion.

Tritan, Carline, Troy, and M' Kara saw the explosion from the eastern wall. They saw the members of their family sent into the sky by the fatal explosion. Their bodies tensed as they saw their limp bodies hit the ground with dull thuds. M' Kara bit her lip watching to see if her father would get up. Tears began to well in the eyes of Carline and Tritan when they saw their parents' bodies go limp in the air during the explosion.

"We have to do to something," Troy said through his clenched teeth.

"But what can we do?" the Twins asked.

"We know the Shadow Lord doesn't like the light from the North Star," M' Kara looked up to the shadow shrouded sky. They then heard what sounded like a neigh from a horse. All looked down to the courtyard to find Sundancer looking up to them. Carline, Tritan, Troy, and M' Kara looked to one another, then made their way to the courtyard. M' Kara and Carline mounted Sundancer while Troy and Tritan went to the eastern gate. Both pulled on the lever to open the doors. As Sundancer rode through the eastern gate, Troy and Tritan leapt onto his back and the five of them rode on toward the battlefield in hopes to help their family.

To Zidane, it seemed like he was unconscious for an eternity, but he was only out for several moments. His vision was blurred as he opened his eyes and the rest of his senses were muddled. The muscles in his body felt as though they were paralyzed. He struggled to turn over from his back, but his body would not allow him. His strength was been drained from the explosion. With his senses not being focused, his ears did not twitch as the Shadow Lord loomed over him. He heard the maniacal laugh of the Shadow Lord. Zidane tried to crawl away from him but was closely stalked. Each time Zidane attempted to get to his feet, he was pummeled down by a clubbing blow. Zidane shouted in pain as the Shadow Lord gave the bludgeoning blows, and with each blow came an evil laugh. Zidane looked around only to see Maia, Kulla, Stratos, Aero, and the combined army of the Krystal Kingdom and the Undead Soldiers on the ground almost lifeless.

"You are beaten, Zidane! You have failed your subjects! There is no one to help you! The Sun cannot even give power to the Bracelet of Ra you wear!" the Shadow Lord hissed as he hoisted Zidane off of his feet by his throat. Zidane's vision began to clear up and most of his strength returned as he desperately focused his energy while the Shadow Lord was ranting.

"The Sun… may not be… shining… but it is…still there!" he forced from his lips whilst in the Shadow Lord's grip. "Solar Flare!" Zidane summoned what power he could from the Bracelet of Ra. A blinding light emitted from the bracelet obstructing the Shadow Lord's vision. The Shadow Lord yelled in pain, dropping Zidane to the ground. Zidane's strength waned as he summoned the power of the bracelet. He struggled to get back to his feet so that he could attempt to rouse Kulla, Stratos, Maia, Aero, and the others. He knelt over Maia and placed his hand on her forehead. Her eyes fluttered open and she slowly raised her head from the ground.

"Are you alright?" he was still trying to catch his breath.

"I believe so," her voice was weakened. At that moment, Zidane was blind-sided by the Shadow Lord. He formed one of his arms into a war hammer and swung it into the ribs of Zidane sending him spinning several feet away from Maia. Zidane attempted to recover quickly and get to his feet but was hit again with another bludgeoning blow. The Shadow Lord formed the other arm into a blade and raised it to the air to bring down upon Zidane. In mid-swing, two arrows pierced the Shadow Lord's arm. He looked back to find that Maia was recovering and was getting to her feet. The Shadow Lord whipped around and was ready to strike at her, but a surge of energy hit him knocking him away from his path toward Maia. He found that Aero conjured a streak of energy from his sword. The Shadow Lord's anger grew. He held out his hands to unleash an onslaught upon the two, but a sudden surge of energy temporally paralyzed one of his arms. Kulla used the power of the Scepter to summon a 'Soul Spark' and released it at the Shadow Lord preventing him to attack. The Shadow Lord was struck from behind by an orb of shadow energy unleashed by Stratos. Immense rage built within the Shadow Lord as he saw his enemies surround him. Zidane joined them with Dragon Blades drawn.

"It is finished, Shadow Lord! You cannot defeat us all!" Zidane shouted.

"You are wrong, Zidane! The merger is nearly complete! Rhydin will be plunged into an eternal shadow and I will kill you!" the Shadow Lord shouted with a laugh. An aura of shadows emitted from the Shadow Lord's body and it grew as he concentrated his energy. The Shadow Lord unleashed this pent-up energy. This wake of energy knocked everyone several feet backwards, creating trenches in the ground as they slid. Zidane looked up to find the Shadow Lord looming over him once again. The Shadow Lord grabbed Zidane by the throat and lifted him off of his feet.

"You will suffer a slow and painful death Zidane for what you did to me! You will suffer the same fate you friend Rosey did!" the Shadow Lord said as he thrust his hand into Zidane's neck and began to pump shadow poison into Zidane's veins. After a few moments, a great sword was thrown into the arm of the Shadow Lord. The Shadow Lord dropped Zidane and turned to find the Orc Leader was the one who threw his weapon. Behind the Orc Leader were the remains of the Orc and Abomination troops that survived the initial attack of the Western Palace.

"You fools! Do you not realize what you have done?!" the Shadow Lord exclaimed.

"This is revenge for trying to kill us," the Orc Leader growled.

"I have no time to deal with you!" the Shadow Lord shouted. He raised his hands to the air and summoned a small contingent of Shadow Demons from a cloud of shadow to face the surviving Orcs and Abominations. The Orcs and Abominations growled and clenched their fists around their weapons as they prepared to charge upon the Shadow Demons.

"Take their heads and you take their life," the Orc Leader growled. An Abomination gave a thunderous roar and the surviving Orc troops recklessly charged at the Shadow Demons. They crashed upon them like the tremendous waves of the ocean crashing on the rocks of the shore. The Shadow Lord turned to find a ball of fire being thrown at his head by Zidane. The ball of fire only grazed the Shadow Lord's face as he leaned his head to one side to dodge it. Zidane was doubled over in pain as he felt the effects of the shadow poison ravaging at his body. The others were still knocked out by the last attack by the Shadow Lord.

"You feel the poison coursing through your body, don't you Zidane? You feel it ravaging your insides and eating away at you, don't you, Red Dragon?" the Shadow Lord hissed his taunt at Zidane, stalking him while his prey struggled to keep his balance and composure.

Zidane's body felt feverish and he began to sweat profusely. His eyes began to dull, and his vision blurred. He heard the Shadow Lord's voice and evil laugh, but he could not pinpoint where it was coming from. His sense of hearing was being affected by the poison. The Shadow Lord gave several bludgeoning blows to his chest and head. The last blow knocked his helmet off. Zidane was thrown to the ground from that blow. The world around Zidane felt like it was spinning. He felt incredibly dizzy. The Shadow Lord crept upon Zidane and once again hoisted him by his neck, thrusting his arm into Zidane again, poisoning him.

Tritan, Carline, M' Kara, and Troy made it to the battlefield on the back of Sundancer. They saw the bodies of Elves, Vampires, Lycans, Orcs, and Abominations litter the grounds of a bloody battle that lasted for hours. They drew within two hundred yards of where Zidane and the others were battling the Shadow Lord himself. They dismounted and crouched close to the ground to watch.

"Oh no, Lord Zidane is in trouble," M' Kara nervously bit at her inner cheek.

"How can we help him?" Troy pounded his fist to the ground.

"Summon the power...," Carline said. "...of the North Star," Tritan finished.

"How are we supposed to do that?" Troy's ears perked at the seemingly wild plot.

"The Three Wise Kings asked the Star to lead them to the newborn child, maybe we can ask it to give us strength," M' Kara was able to follow the Twins' line of thought.

"Who is to do it though?" Troy asked as they all looked to each other.

"We will do it. We *are* called the Gemini Twins," the Twins' lips lifted into a grin.

"Is there a special chant you're supposed to say?" M' Kara asked.

"I think we..." Tritan said. "...make it up...," Carline added.

"And focus our energy," they both said in unison.

"Alright," M' Kara and Troy said as they backed away from the Twins. Tritan and Carline stood to face each other. They held each other's hands as they closed their eyes and inhaled numerous deep breaths, focusing their energy.

"Focus our energy," Tritan calmly said.

"Feel each other's energy," Carline said.

"We are one," they opened their eyes to reveal how brightly they glowed white. Around their bodies, a white aura of energy rose. Their energy circulated between the two of them, making them twice as strong. Troy and M' Kara were surprised to see the Twins demonstrate this ability. The Twins looked into the sky at the North Star that dimly shone through the canopy of shadow. They both inhaled deep breaths.

"In the Darkest of Nights, you've shone Bright," Carline lowered her head with closed eyes.

"In the Deepest of shadows, you gave us Light," Tritan took a firmer hold of his twin's hands as the power within them swelled to nothing they had ever demonstrated before.

"Now North Star, give us your Might!" their voices resonated beyond what one would think an adolescent was capable of. An aura of energy slowly grew from within the Twins as they chanted. Troy and M' Kara looked up to the sky and noticed constellations in the sky beginning to dimly glow. Orion, Aquarius, Libra, Draco, Delphinius, Ursa Major, and lastly Gemini all glowed brightly in the sky above the cloud of shadow.

"It's happening," M' Kara's eyes brightened with excitement. Troy gave a smile as well, but also kept an eye on what was going on with the battle. As the moments passed, the constellations shone more and more brightly in the sky. With the Twins seemingly reaching the peak of their combined energy, the constellations passed on their energies to the North Star, connecting with it and with one another to create a web of light in the sky. The light throbbed and grew with the purest of lights in the sky above. The North Star absorbed the light from the surrounding constellations. When the North Star finished absorbing the light from the other constellations, it shot the light down to the

Twins, passing it on to them. The Twins absorbed this great light. They then faced the battlefield where the Shadow Lord was,

"Light of the North Star!" with a sweeping motion of their hands, they unleashed a tremendous wave of the purest light that spanned the entire land. It surged in all directions; to the north, east, south, and west of them it swept. The shroud of shadow that hovered over the land began to shatter like glass and fade as the wave of pure light surged throughout Rhydin.

The Shadow Lord had Zidane in his grip and was injecting more of the shadow poison in to his body. All of a sudden, he began to feel weaker by each passing moment. The grip he had on his adversary's neck weakened, and the poison did not flow from his body. Zidane looked to find a wave of pure light slowly gather in a concentrated spot. He saw the power of the North Star rain down in a column of light.

The bright, warm light from the North Star woke Maia from her unconscious state. Although she was still hurt and not quite able to move her body at will just yet, she was able to focus her eyes to see the purest of lights. She managed to slowly turn her head to see Zidane in the Shadow Lord's grip. Shadow poison had been forced into his veins. "No," her voice was weak, and ragged. She reached out to him, "Fight," she forced from her lips. She strained to move, but her body was too weak. Summoning the power of the Necklace of Isis to do anything was out of the question for her now as well. With tears in her eyes, she inhaled a deep breath, "Fight, Zidane! Fight!".

Zidane's ears perked up when he heard Maia's cry to fight. Her voice reached into his heart and delved into his soul. It reignited the fire in his very Essence. Zidane fought the poison even more now seeing the strength of the Shadow Lord waning. He clenched his jaw and closed his eyes. An aura of fire began to emit from his body. His muscles tensed as the flames flowed throughout.

"No! No! This cannot happen!" the Shadow Lord exclaimed as he saw the mysterious wave of light approach him and saw Zidane's body throb with the energy of his inner wildfire. Dark smoke billowed from his nostrils as Zidane fought more and more against the Shadow Lord. Then finally, with a dragon-like roar, a raging inferno shot from his mouth and his eyes were flashing angrily. Zidane broke free of the Shadow Lord's grip and burned the shadow poison that was ravaging his body. An eruption of flames and intense heat burst from Zidane's body throwing the Shadow Lord backwards to the ground. With flames surrounding his fists, his eyes glowing violently red, and dark smoke billowing from his nostrils Zidane stalked the Shadow Lord with Dragon Blades in hand and the Light from the North Star behind him. As the Light from the North Star surged across the land and touched Stratos, Maia, Kulla, Aero, the troops of the Krystal Kingdom and the Undead Army they rose with new life in their eyes and renewed strengths in their bodies. The Shadow Lord laid on the ground squirming as the Light from the North Star drew nearer to him. As the wave of Light surged through him, he let out a scream that would shake the hearts of the bravest. His muscles tensed and convulsed. He clawed at the ground desperately trying to get away from the Light. The Shadow from his body began to melt away from his skin and collect on the ground around him. The Shadow seemed to have its own life and began to collect itself and attempted to slink away from the Light. Zidane watched the Shadow creep away from the body it possessed as the Light was passing. Stratos, Maia, Kulla, and Aero were a few feet behind Zidane and looked upon the body.

"Who is it?" Aero gripped his sword tighter.

"I do not know," Zidane's eyes flared red. The man who was possessed by the Shadow began to stir and groan. The man slowly stood with his back to Zidane and the others. The man was not tall, but was of a medium build with dark hair. He was wearing a sleeveless loose-fitting tunic, pants that were torn at the knees, and boots with worn down soles.

"Who are you?" Zidane demanded.

"Why Zidane, you still do not recognize me? After all, you were the one who banished me to the Shadow Realm," the man turned to face Zidane and met eye to eye with him. Zidane's eyes returned to their natural color in shock of the true identity of the Shadow Lord.

"Anaius," Zidane's breath was taken from him learning the identity of the one who caused so much pain.

"Yes, Zidane. It is I, Anaius. A former pupil of Chen Shun, and one of the best students, but not *the* best student," Anaius growled through his teeth.

"Why have you done this?" Aero asked.

"Vengeance and power! Vengeance upon Zidane for banishing me to the Shadow Realm. And I want the power to rule Rhydin. For over a decade, I was in that dark realm not knowing if I was going to live or die. I had no food or water," he spat, "I learned the way of the Shadow while I was there and learned I could manipulate it and use it," a crazed look came about his eyes when he spoke of the Shadows, "With this new found power, I planned to overthrow the Shadow Lord so I could come back to Rhydin and take Zidane's life!" Anaius shouted to Zidane.

"You do not want to do this, Anaius. The Shadows will consume you and corrupt you beyond repair," Stratos shouted.

"Oh, but I don't want to be repaired. I have learned to love the Shadows!" Anaius gave a chilling, maniacal laugh. Zidane and the others noticed the Shadows that possessed Anaius was creeping back to rejoin him. Zidane and Stratos quickly sheathed their blades and with motions of their hands they used the earth to throw Anaius out of the Shadow's reach. The Shadows seemed to grow angrier and began to bubble and fume. Soon it swelled and took on a form that was similar to that of Anaius when he was possessed.

"What do we do now?" Kulla asked as all dropped to defensive stances.

"Aero, take the Krystal Army and the Undead Army of Osiris to fall back to the walls of the Palace," Zidane looked over his shoulder to his brother.

"And what will you do?" Aero asked. He received his answer

when Zidane's eyes flared red with fire. Aero nodded and led Craven, Aldar, Damien and the rest of the Army back toward the Palace.

"What are we to do?" Maia's eyes did not waver from the entity of Shadow.

"Hit it with everything we have using the Ancient Relics," Zidane said through his clenched teeth. Maia nodded and drew an arrow from her quiver. Kulla sheathed his sword and readied the Scepter of Osiris. Zidane and Stratos drew their Dragon Blades. All of their eyes were fixed upon the Shadows that continued to grow in front of them. The Shadow let out a tremendous roar and slammed its arms into the ground. Shadow energy surged across the ground in a wave toward Zidane, Maia, Kulla, and Stratos. *Focus your energy. Control the Wildfire,'* Tufar's voice echoed in Zidane's mind.

"Don't let it consume you," Maia's voice was hushed, yet it was loud enough for Zidane's elf ears to catch. All were focusing their energy, utilizing the powers of the Relics they bore.

"Fury of Osiris!" Kulla shouted as he released a barrage of soul energy orbs from the head of the Scepter that hovered above the ground in front of him. The barrage of orbs slowed the wave of shadow energy.

"Arrow of Isis!" Maia released an energy throbbing arrow into the wave. It clashed with the wave and assisted the power of Osiris is slowing down the shadow wave. The clashing of the power of Isis and Osiris with the shadow wave was at a standstill. Stratos fused the hilts of his blades and focused the energy from the Bracelet of Mentu. He began to spin the blade in front of him and the energy from the bracelet surged into the steel of the fused Dragon Blades.

"Mentu's Rampage!" Stratos released the building energy of the bracelet. The cyclone of energy, along with the power of Osiris and Isis, began to slowly push back the shadow wave. The Shadow grew furious and struggled to use more power so that it didn't become overwhelmed by the power of the Relics. Zidane's body radiated and fumed with fire. An aura of flames surrounded his body the more he focused upon it. An uncontrollable rage did not fill his heart. It was a rage that was focused and channeled. As Zidane raised the Dragon Blades above his head, the aura of flames surged throughout the steel and radiated from the blades. A cyclone of fire swirled around the blades. Zidane then felt the power of the Bracelet of Ra begin to build energy as the fire from his heart surged through his body and into the Dragon Blades. The Bracelet of Ra glowed vibrantly and added its own power to the whirling flames. *'Do not let it consume you,'* Tufar's voice again resonated within Zidane's mind. The power of the Bracelet of Ra and the cyclone of fire began to fuse, creating an inferno of fire. Zidane felt this great power and was in complete control of it.

"Ra's Inferno Rage!" Zidane slashed the Dragon Blades to the ground releasing the great inferno of fire and pure energy of the Sun. The inferno joined with the powers of Isis, Osiris, and Mentu pushing back the wave of shadow. The Shadow hissed and roared struggling to push back the powers of the Relics. Anaius rose to his feet and saw the Shadow struggling against the unleashed furies of the Ancient Relics.

"No! You cannot destroy it!" Anaius ran toward the Shadow as if attempting to rescue it from its fate. Anaius leapt into the Shadow, attempting to fuse with it once more. The powers of the Ancient Relics overcame the Shadow and overtook it with a thunderous explosion. The tremendous force of the explosion knocked Zidane, Maia, Kulla, and Stratos several feet into the air backwards. The explosion was felt even in the underground chambers of the Western Palace. Melina, the guards, the villagers, and the Vampire Coven all held their breaths and huddled together fearing what happened above their heads. Aero, Caven, Damien, and Aldar looked back to see the cloud of smoke and dirt hang heavily in the air after the explosion.

"Should we go back and see if they are alright?" Aldar looked from Aero back to the plume of smoke and dirt.

"Aldar and Craven come with me. Damien, you lead the rest of the Army into the walls of the Palace," Damien nodded to Aero and did as he was ordered. Aero, Craven, and Aldar quickly made their way back to the battlefield to check on Zidane, Maia, Kulla, and Stratos.

As Aero, Aldar, and Craven reached the area where Zidane and the others were fighting the Shadow, they saw devastation. An immense trench formed in the ground resulting from the clash of the powers between the Ancient Relics and the power of the Shadow. There were scattered embers of fire within the trench and mounds of ash and soot. There was no trace of the Shadow or Anaius within the trench or the crater where the explosion erupted.

"Lord Aero, there they are," Aldar pointed to where the Ancient Relic wielders laid. Aero, Craven, and Aldar rushed to their sides.

"They're alive," Craven said shifting back into his human form. Kulla was the first to stir and rise to a sitting position. He struggled to clear his vision. Maia was the next to rise. She rubbed her head trying to remedy the throbbing pain she felt. Stratos and Zidane were the last to stir. Their bodies ached from the fight with the Shadow Lord. Even with the protection of the armor, their bodies felt wrecked.

"How does everyone feel?" Aero looked to his family and comrades.

"Wonderful," Kulla answered with a sarcastic tone. All rose to their feet, but Zidane was slow rising to his feet. He held his ribs and moved gingerly.

"It is a good thing I am wearing the Wildfire Dragon Armor. My body would be feeling worst after that battle," Zidane said as he was being helped by Aero and Maia.

"The Shadow Lord is gone for good," Stratos said with relief.

"What about them?" Maia pointed her bow to the Orcs and Abominations who remained. The Orcs and Abominations walked toward Zidane, and the others after their fight with the Shadow Demons. Just over half that engaged with the Shadow Demons survived. The Orc Leader was leading the group toward Zidane with his great sword in hand.

"Yes, what are we to do with them? We have been hunting them for the past decade," Kulla's hand reactively touched the hilt of his sword. All had their hands on their weapons ready for a fight.

"Wait," Zidane sheathed his swords.

"Why?" Aero was ready to lunge at the Orcs and Abominations.

"If they wanted to fight they would be charging at us," Zidane said. All looked to each other and then to the former soldiers of Sekmet who approached. Zidane slowly walked toward the Orc Leader with their eyes meeting and not wavering. They drew within several feet of one another and stared at each other. Stratos, Maia, Kulla, Aero, Craven, and Aldar stood close behind Zidane with their hands ready to draw their weapons. The surviving Orcs and Abominations stood behind the Orc Leader with their muscles tensed and fists clenched. The Orc Leader took a few steps toward Zidane and raised his weapon. Zidane quickly dropped into a defensive stance, but found the Orc Leader dropped his great sword to the ground and knelt to his knees, bowing his head. The rest of the Orcs and Abominations followed the actions of the Orc Leader and knelt before Zidane. A look of confusion came across the Zidane's face.

"Do with us what you will. We are prepared for whatever punishment," the Orc Leader stated with his head still bowed. Zidane clenched his jaw and drew both Dragon Blades walking toward the Orc Leader. He clenched his fists around the hilts of the blades and looked upon the Orc Leader and the rest of the Orcs and Abominations. Zidane raised the Dragon Blades into the air as if to stab them into the Orc Leader's neck. He then plunged the blades downward. The swords did not drive through the neck of the Orc Leader, but into the ground next to him. The Orc Leader saw the blades stuck in the ground to either side of him and looked up to Zidane. He found Zidane offering his hand to him. The Orc Leader looked at Zidane's hand and then into Zidane's silver eyes that did not bear any hatred toward the Orc Leader.

"You do not want to kill us?" the Orc Leader asked still kneeling.

"You saved my life from the grips of the Shadow Lord. I have a different consequence for you," the Orc Leader took Zidane's wrist into his large hand and rose to his feet.

"What are you going to do with us?" the Orc Leader growled.

"You and the rest of your comrades will be banished to the Southwestern Province of Rhydin where you will build and prosper," Zidane said with a growing grin on his face. Stratos, Maia, Kulla, Aero, Aldar, and Craven all looked to each other as if asking what Zidane was doing.

"How can you be good to us? Our people have been at war with you for over a thousand years," the Orc Leader said letting go of Zidane's wrist.

"That war was not your doing. You were used as tools to eradicate the Elf race," Zidane responded.

"What do you mean?" the Orc Leader growled as if not liking the notion of being used.

"Your people were not so different from Elves at one point in the past. I believe the Elves and your people are close cousins. That all changed when Sekmet came into power in the Southwestern Province and had your entire race under his power. I do not know how it came to be that you and your kin were put under his iron will, but that is something that we can discover at a later time. All I know is that your minds were altered making you believe that the Elf race thought we were better than you in every way. Sekmet fueled your anger and used you to attack the Elf Kingdom," Zidane spoke as if he himself witnessed what happened generations ago.

"How do you know this?" the Orc Leader asked with skepticism in his voice.

"I have the memories of two beings. One of which lived during the time the Orc first became soldiers in Sekmet's army," Zidane said.

"You say we are to grow. How are we to grow when there are no females among us?" the Orc Leader looked back to his kin as if searching for any females among them.

"Sekmet banished your females and some males into the Southwestern Mountains that lie not far from Sekmet's old Fortress.

You will find them there," Zidane responded. The Orc Leader looked from Zidane to the other Orcs and Abominations that stood behind him.

"Will there be anything else?" although he were a larger being, he seemed smaller than Zidane due to his humility in front of the Dragon Lord.

"You will build your civilization under the banner of the Krystal Kingdom," Zidane said after a few moments of thought.

"Are you sure you want this, Zidane?" Aero whispered in his ear.

"I want this to be a unified and peaceful land, not divided. I also do not want to eradicate a race who was corrupted by an evil power and did not know the actual truth," Zidane turned his eyes to Aero.

"He is right, Aero. If Zidane's memories are correct, they can go back to the way they were over a thousand years ago," Maia said.

"I trust your judgment, Brother," Aero sighed, conceding to Zidane's decision.

"Are we on one accord?" Zidane reached his hand out to the Orc Leader.

"We are, Lord Zidane," the Orc Leader took Zidane's wrist in his hand.

"You will leave immediately to build your society. If you need any help, do not hesitate to ask anyone, Lord... um... what should I call you?" Zidane asked. The Orc Leader thought for a moment as if searching for something in his mind.

"I....I don't have a name," the Orc Leader shook his head.

"Well, we cannot have the ruler of the Southwestern Province without a name," Zidane said with a slight grin. Zidane then turned to the others for any suggestions.

"How does Torr sound?" Stratos proposed. Zidane gave a smile and turned back to the Orc Leader, "Yes, how does Torr sound?".

"Thank you, Lord Zidane," Torr said with a slight bow of his head.

"You are welcome, Lord Torr," Zidane smiled.

On the way back to the Western Palace, Zidane, Stratos, Maia,

Kulla, Aero, Craven, and Aldar noticed a gathering of the soldiers from the Krystal Kingdom and the Undead Army. They were circled around something, but they could not tell what. They pushed their way through the crowd and at the center they saw Troy holding Carline and M' Kara holding Tritan, along with Sundancer behind them looking down upon the Twins. Both Carline and Tritan's bodies were limp. Zidane and Maia rushed to their children and held them close.

"What happened?" Aero looked to the officers within the ranks of the Army.

"Carline and Tritan used the power of the North Star," Troy responded in a quiet voice.

"How were they able to do that?" Kulla asked with a puzzled look on his face.

"They focused their energies and chanted," M' Kara simply answered.

"Will they be alright?" Stratos asked looking down on the Twins.

"They are just exhausted," Zidane placed his hand over Carline's forehead.

"That surge of power was too much for someone their age," Maia was holding Tritan close to her.

"The best remedy for them now is a sufficient amount of rest," Zidane lifted Carline into his arms and Maia picked up Tritan into her arms.

"Zidane, I will lead the Soldiers of Osiris back to Egypt and check on Rosey," Kulla said.

"Very well. Take Sundancer with you. He will make the trek up the mountain easier," Kulla nodded and took Sundancer's reins into his hands and then swung himself onto Sundancer's back.

"Papa, can I come too?" M' Kara asked. Kulla nodded and held out his hand to her. She took it and was hoisted onto Sundancer's back in front of him. Kulla and M' Kara led the Soldiers of Osiris toward the woods and disappeared into the tree line.

"Lord Zidane, I and the other Lycans must get back to our camps.

We have left many of the women and children in caves nearby," Craven said.

"Your services were greatly appreciated, Craven. Thank you," Zidane said as he bowed his head. Craven shifted into his wolf form, as did the other Lycans, and let out a bellowing howl toward the moon before running to the southern end of the woods. In the meantime, Zidane and Maia carried Tritan and Carline in their arms back to the Palace along with Aero, Troy, and Damien at their sides with the surviving Elf and Vampire soldiers of the Krystal Kingdom.

HEALING

F OR A FULL FOUR DAYS they slept peacefully. The surge of power from the Constellations and the North Star proved too much for their young bodies to handle. Many in the palace watched over them during the days and nights they were sleeping, including Melina, Aero, and Kulla, along with M' Kara. The Twins awoke in their room to a familiar face tending to them. Their vision was blurred as they opened their eyes. At first they only saw flowing, scarlet hair. As their vision cleared they saw kind, gentle green eyes looking down on both of them.

"Rosey?" the Twins said seeing the familiar smile.

"Aye children, I'm here," Rosey said.

"The antidote...," Carline said. "...worked," Tritan finished.

"That it did. I have both of you to thank. Otherwise, who knows what would've happened to me," Rosey smiled at the children she helped raise.

"You are welcome," the Twins said.

"You should get your rest still. Go to sleep, young ones," both of the Twins yawned and turned on their sides and fell back to sleep. Rosey ran her fingers through their dreadlocks before leaving their room. She saw Maia walking out of her bedchamber wearing a long flowing satin nightgown with a slit that ran up the one leg.

"How are they?" Maia clutched her hands close to her chest with anxious eyes.

"They woke up. They are doing fine. They just need their rest," Rosey's tone was reassuring to Maia's ears.

"Do you not need rest after what you have been through?" her amber eyes searched for any fatigue in the Shadow Shinobi's eyes.

"I cannot sit still for a moment. It's my nature," Rosey responded with a shrug of her shoulders.

"Promise me you will not exert yourself," Maia placed her hand on Rosey's shoulder.

"I promise, Little Kitty," Rosey smiled then hugged the woman who had become such a good friend over the years.

"We both have brave children," Maia said with a sigh.

"That we do, Little Kitty," Rosey looked toward M' Kara's room.

"Where have Zidane and Stratos been?" Maia asked.

"They have been in the dojo sparrin' and meditatin'," Rosey responded.

In the dojo of the palace, Zidane and Stratos were training with each other for the past four days. Night and day they sparred, meditated, and practiced various exercises honing their abilities. They were preparing themselves to go back to Stratos's world and universe to free it from whatever dark power ruled it in Stratos's absence.

"How are we to free my world, Zidane? There are only three of us that will be going," Stratos asked with doubt in the back of his mind.

"Once we find your brother and sister, where ever they may be, they will be able to help us. If they are anything like Aero and my sister Paige, they will be relentless in overthrowing the dark power. I can assure you that we will free your Rhydin," Stratos nodded at Zidane's words then rose to his feet. Zidane rose to his feet as well and dropped into a firm defensive stance. Stratos went into an attack stance and they both resumed in their training.

In the following weeks, the Krystal Kingdom started its healing process from the onslaught of the Shadows. The Krystal Kingdom mourned the losses of a great Vampire ruler, Zell; a brave Elf Captain, Demus; and a noble Dragon Knight, Antillus, and his Dragon. The Rulers from the various Provinces and tribes gathered at the point where the Eastern, Western, Woodland Realm and where the Southeastern Provinces met and shared in the remembrance of great leaders of the Krystal Kingdom. Soon after, the Vampire Coven crowned the heir to the throne, Kulla. His wife Rosey, although she was human, was crowned the Queen of the Vampire Coven and M' Kara was named heir to the throne. Zidane, Maia, Aero, Carline, Tritan and Troy were among many of those who attended the coronation.

The Orcs and Abominations traveled to the Southwestern Province of Rhydin, led by Torr. They discovered the female Orcs in the Southwestern Mountains. There were only a handful of males that were living among them. Torr did what Zidane said. He led the Orcs and Abominations with sound judgment. They abandoned their murderous and pillaging ways. They built a small village within the Southwestern Mountains that were beyond the ruins of Sekmet's Fortress, expanding upon the huts that were already there. A large wooden gate was built around the huts and watchtowers were established at the corners of the walls. They now hunted and gathered for food. They would frequently have visitors from the Vampire Coven, led by Kulla, and the Lycans, led by Craven, to help with the building of the Orc village. It was during one of these visits that Kulla renamed the Abominations who were a cross-breed of Orcs and Ogres. From then, they were known as Uruks. The Orcs and Uruks were given crystals much like the other races of the Krystal Kingdom. The Orcs and Uruks of the Krystal Kingdom now wore crystals the color of a bottomless abyss, the onyx crystal.

In the Western Palace, Maia was standing on the balcony looking out toward the sunset. She felt the last bit of sunrays kiss her bronze skin before it set for the night. She leaned forward with her hands against the banister. Her tail did not sway as it usually did when she was content. Her head was lowered and tears welled in her eyes.

"They will be alright, you know," Zidane was leaning against the frame of the balcony doorway.

"I cannot help it. This is the first time they will be away from home," she walked over to Zidane and wrapped her arms around his waist and placed her head on his chest.

"They have survived in the Shadow Realm for a number of weeks. I believe they can survive being on Earth with Master Shun," Zidane said with a smile and held her close to him.

"I know. It is my motherly instincts getting the best of me," Maia forced a smile.

"They are ready and Stratos is waiting as well," Rosey said from the doorway of the bedchamber. Maia took a deep breath and exhaled it slowly.

"Are you ready?" Zidane looked into the glistening amber eyes of his wife. She wiped away the last bit of her tears and nodded her head. Zidane and Maia took their hooded long coats from the rack beside the bed. Maia took her bow and quiver of arrows that sat on the bed and Zidane strapped the Dragon Blades to his waist and strapped the Horn of Summoning Dragons to his belt. Rosey walked with them to the Twins' bedchamber. Tritan and Carline sat next to each other on the edge of one their beds. They packed two bags for their journey to Earth. One bag contained clothes they would need and in the other were books from their studies at the schoolhouse.

"Are you both ready?" Maia's voice cracked trying to stifle a sob from surfacing. The Twins looked up from the stone floor. "We are ready," they both responded with a solemn tone in their voice.

"Let us go then," Zidane walked in and took the bags with their books and studies. The Twins got off the bed and took their bags of clothing. Zidane, Maia, Carline, Tritan, and Rosey walked down the series of halls to the door leading to the courtyard. Kulla, Aero, Melina, Stratos, Troy, and M' Kara waited at the door for them to arrive. M' Kara and Troy gave a hug to both Carline and Tritan. Aero and Melina brought both close to them for a farewell hug. Aero fought back the tears he felt welling in his eyes while Melina wiped away the ones that fell from her eyes.

"We will miss you Uncle Aero and Aunt Melina," the Twins said in between sobs.

"I will miss you both as well," Aero hugged them tighter.

"We are extremely proud of you both and love you very much," Melina added.

"You will look after the Krystal Kingdom while we are gone," Zidane looked to Aero.

"How long will you be gone?" Aero asked.

"We do not know for certain," Maia responded.

"As long as it takes to free my world," Stratos added.

"Be safe you three," Rosey said. Zidane, Maia, and Stratos nodded.

"Be careful on Earth," Troy said to the Twins with a single tear rolling down his cheek.

"We will," the Twins nodded.

"And don't forget about us," M' Kara sobbed uncontrollably.

"We won't," the Twins said as they shared in a hug with M' Kara and Troy before they all left the foyer and went outside to the courtyard. Zidane took the Horn of Summoning Dragon from his belt, inhaled a deep breath, and blew into the horn. The deep bellowing sound of the horn echoed and resonated throughout the western hills. All eyes were to the sky as the moments passed. A thunderous roar was heard from above. Tufar emerged from the thick clouds and circled the palace before landing in the courtyard.

"Greetings, Young Dragon," Tufar said in a low voice.

"Hello, Tufar," Zidane said with a bow of respect. Kulla, Aero, Stratos, Melina, Maia, Tritan, Carline, Troy, and M' Kara all bowed in reverence to the Great Red Dragon.

"Is everyone ready?" Tufar asked. Tritan and Carline nodded their heads and slung their bags over their shoulders. They were the first to climb onto Tufar's back. Zidane turned and clasped wrists with Kulla, then with Aero.

"Be safe, Brother," Aero said.

"I will," Zidane responded. Maia went to hug Troy and M' Kara goodbye. Troy fought back the tears welling in his eyes while M' Kara could not contain her tears. Aero looked upon Stratos and into his eyes.

"Take care of them," Aero said in a calm voice.

"You have my word," Stratos clasped wrists with Aero. Zidane,

Maia, and Stratos then climbed onto the back of Tufar behind the Twins. They waved goodbye to Aero, Kulla, Melina, Rosey, Troy, and M' Kara. All five returned the wave as Tufar stretched out his wings and flapped them, kicking up clouds of dirt, lifting them into the air. Tufar turned to the east toward the Keshnarian Ruins.

Once at the Ruins, Zidane, Maia, Stratos, and the Twins leapt down to the ground. The Twins carried their bags on their backs and gazed upon the Ruins with curious eyes. Zidane, Maia, and Stratos wore their long coats with the hoods pulled back. Their weapons were strapped to their hips under their cloaks, and they carried satchels with other provisions they required for this trip to the alternate universe. They ventured into the Temple where the Gate of Caelum stood. The room was very dim. Zidane searched for torches in the wide room. There was one at each corner of the room and a couple along each wall. Zidane closed his eyes and held his hands out with the palms facing up. He inhaled deep breaths and conjured several small balls of flames in his hands. They slightly hovered above his palms and circled each other. As Zidane exhaled, he released the fireballs at the torches. The features of the Gate became clearer to the Twins. They stood in awe of its craftsmanship. As they approached the Gate, they saw the pedestal that stood in front of it. Zidane approached the pedestal and took out a parchment from his satchel.

"This will take us to Earth?" the Twins asked.

"Yes, it will," Maia ran her fingers through their hair.

"How long will….," Tritan began to ask. "...we be on Earth?" Carline finished the thought.

"As long as it takes you to master your craft," Zidane responded looking back over his shoulder at them fighting back a tear. He turned his head to the pedestal where the dials were to set the Gate of Caelum for Earth. Zidane touched the symbols on the pedestal to open the Gate for the Twins to go to Earth and meet with Chen Shun on the other side. The corresponding symbols on the Gate itself glowed as Zidane touched the symbols setting its destination. As the last symbol was set, a burst of light emitted from the Gate as it opened. The Twins gazed upon the light of the Gate and then back to Zidane and Maia who stood next to them. Zidane and Maia hugged both of their children. Tears streamed down all of their cheeks as they embraced each other tightly. Stratos stood beside Tufar and watched the family embrace each other for the last time before the children embarked on their own journey while Zidane and Maia left for another perilous mission. Tritan and Carline then turned to Stratos and approached him. Both then opened their arms to Stratos as if asking for a hug. Stratos hesitated for a moment then looked at Zidane and Maia. Both nodded their heads and Stratos leaned forward to hug them both.

"Thank you for helping...," Tritan started to say. "...to save us," Carline finished.

"You are both welcome," Stratos said with a smile on his face. After releasing their embrace on Stratos, the Twins turned to Tufar. They folded their hands in front of them and bowed in respects to the Great Red Dragon. Tufar returned the bow and smiled. Carline and Tritan walked toward the Gate with their bags slung over one shoulder. As they drew within a few feet of the Gate's opening they looked back to their parents, Stratos, and Tufar. Tears streamed from their eyes as they got one more final glimpse of their family before they stepped through the Gate. As they turned their heads back to face the Gate, they held each other's hand and took the few steps to walk through. As the Twins stepped through, the light dissipated and the Gate was closed. Maia buried her face in Zidane's chest and let the tears stream down her cheeks. Zidane held her closely to comfort her. A single tear rolled down the cheek of Stratos.

"Why do you shed a tear, Young Dragon?" Tufar leaned his head toward Stratos.

"Those would have been my children if I did not stray from the path that I was to travel," Stratos said fighting back more tears.

"Now is not the time for regrets, it is the time for redemption. You will travel to your universe, you will meet with the Black Dragon, and with the Red Dragon and Maia at your side, along with the Black

Dragon, you will take back your world and cleanse it of the darkness," Tufar said as if speaking directly to the Black Dragon Essence within Stratos.

"Thank you for believing in me, Tufar," Stratos looked up to the Red Dragon.

"Are you ready to take back your world?" Zidane asked as he and Maia approached Stratos and Tufar. Stratos looked from Zidane and Maia up to Tufar.

"I am," Stratos said purposefully.

A faint blue light gathered from all the energies of Rhydin, illuminating the Gate of Caelum chamber and grew more in intensity and size. The blue illumination burst into a bright light and from this explosion of light, the transparent face of Mesnara appeared.

"Greetings Zidane, Maia, Stratos and the Great Red Dragon, Tufar," she said in a voice that echoed in the chambers. All bowed their heads in respects to the Spirit of Rhydin.

"We thank you for your help in getting our children back," Maia stepped toward her.

"You are welcome Maia and Zidane. And do not worry, Tritan and Carline are in good hands with Master Chen Shun. I will watch over them as they train," Mesnara said with a smile. Maia and Zidane returned the smile.

"Stratos, I do have something that may belong to you," Mesnara turned her wise eyes to him.

"What is that?" Stratos asked as he stepped forward. Mesanra's eyes glowed vibrantly and two beams of light shot from them. A faint blue light hovered in front of Stratos and the mask that covered half of his face materialized. As he took the mask, the light dissipated. He held the mask in his hand and looked upon it. He then strapped it to his face.

"Stratos, you have been given a second chance. You now have the opportunity to redeem yourself by liberating your world from the terror that has struck it. You will need to be at your very best to free your world. You will only have the aid of Zidane and Maia, but if you do this correctly, you will have a full army at your disposal. Are you ready Stratos, Bearer of the Black Dragon Essence?" Mesnara's eyes looked deeply in to Stratos's.

"I am ready, Mesnara. The Bearer of the Black Dragon Essence will strike fear into the hearts of those who enslaved my world," Stratos said strongly with his eyes glowing with intense shadow energy.

"Good. Zidane and Maia, you may need some help in traveling across the land," Mesanara said. She pursed her lips together and let out a light whistle. Hooves were heard trotting down the stone corridor and light sparks were seen with each trot.

"Sundancer?" Zidane looked in disbelief. Sundancer trotted to Zidane and Maia's side. Maia ran her fingers through his mane and then wrapped her arms around his thick neck.

"Sundancer was essential in the survival of not only the Twins, but also Troy and M' Kara. Sundancer will be of great use to you both in your journey with Stratos," Mesnara said.

"Thank you, Mesnara," Maia said with her hand still in Sundancer's mane.

"In addition, Lord Zidane, I must give you something that will help you in the fight," Mesnara said as her eyes glowed blue. With two beams of bright light emitting from her eyes, Mesnara summoned the Wildfire Dragon Armor in front of Zidane. The eyes of Zidane, Maia, and Stratos widened as the Wildfire Dragon Armor hovered above the ground.

"I am to take this with me? I cannot carry or wear this armor everywhere I go," Zidane paced about the armor.

"You will not have to. With the power of the Heavens, I will link the powers of this Armor with the Bracelet of Ra," Zidane looked at the Bracelet of Ra that was secured to his wrist and then to the armor."Hold the Bracelet toward the armor," Zidane did so, then Mesnara breathed a glowing mist that allowed for the Wildfire Dragon Armor to be absorbed into the Bracelet. With a sudden jolt of bright light the absorption was complete.

"How am I to summon my armor?" Zidane asked as he looked once again to the Bracelet.

"You must utter these words to summon it. 'Flames of the Wildfire, empower me'. The power of the armor will engulf you. You will then be adorned in your armor. And when you want to remove the armor, you simply utter 'Wildfire, be at ease', the armor will then be at rest," Mesnara instructed.

"I understand. Thank you, Mesnara," Zidane gave a nod and then looked back to the Bracelet.

"What about me? I have no horse or armor," Stratos asked.

"Among the wild horses, you will find Sundancer's counterpart. The armor you must earn from the Black Dragon on your world, Stratos," Mesnara said.

"Tufar cannot come with us?" Maia looked back to Tufar.

"No, I cannot make this journey with you. My place is in this world. If I were to travel with you, there will be an imbalance in the parallel universes. Besides, the Black Dragon in Stratos's world will be there to offer his help and wisdom as I have in this world," Tufar reassured the trio.

"Thank you for all that you have done," Stratos looked up to him.

"You are welcome, Young Dragon," Tufar smiled.

"Are you ready?" Mesnara asked.

"We are," Zidane, Maia, and Stratos responded in unison. Mesnara turned to face the Gate of Caelum. She herself began to glow brightly as she focused her power. A beam of light emitted from her toward the Gate itself. The symbols on the Gate glowed and with a burst of blinding light the Gate opened. Zidane and Maia climbed onto Sundancer's back while Stratos commanded the wind to lift him into the air. Zidane and Maia looked over to Stratos whose eyes grew intense as he stared into the Gate's opening.

"Go forth, and fear no darkness!" Tufar roared. Stratos flew through the air on the wind currents he commanded, closely followed by Zidane and Maia on the back of Sundancer. They journeyed to save an enslaved world.

<u>**Chronicles of Rhydin Series**</u>
Book 1: Chronicles of Rhydin: Legend of the Red Dragon
Book 2: Chronicles of Rhydin: Stars and Shadows
Book 3: Chronicles of Rhydin: Uprising
Book 4: Chronicles of Rhydin: Legend of the Dragon Heart
Book 5: To Be Announced
Book 6: ???

I want to take this opportunity to thank a few people who contributed their time and resources to this book. First, I want to thank Godmother Christine Bass, and childhood friend, author and editor, Jeree Jakee Boyd, for lending their eyes and time to this manuscript. I would also like to thank my parents, Aaron Sr. and Linda, for investing in this title. And lastly, I would like to thank Tyron Allen (TJ) once again for lending his talents in designing the cover art for this book.

Printed in the United States
By Bookmasters